GODS & ANGELS

Ophelia Wolf

ISBN 979-8-9878368-0-4

Cover art by Md Imtiaz Jony and Ophelia Wolf with special
thanks to Karolina Esqueda Rocha
Author photograph by Tatiana Daubek
Book design by Jesse Pinho

To Ace,
for always making me feel like anything is possible.

Acknowledgments

First and foremost, I would like to thank Brace Negron. Not only did you patiently listen to the first draft of every single chapter, giving me detailed notes and feedback, and proofread the entire book, but you also inspired one of the main characters in it. Maybe even more importantly, I'd like to thank you for the many, many hours we spent driving through the Catskills discussing and figuring out the world of this story. Your constant support inspired me and carried me through this journey.

Secondly, I need to thank Jesse Pinho for his many hours of work on the design and formatting of this book. I couldn't have done it without your expert eye, but, most importantly, your enthusiasm kept me going through those difficult last months.

Moreover, I'd like to thank Kaley Smith. You were my first loyal reader. Thank you for reading chapter after chapter, giving me notes and encouraging me to continue. Knowing that someone enjoyed the read gave me the courage to continue writing.

Ben Grimes, thank you for proofreading and getting me excited about this project again after I'd let it sit for months.

Karolina Esqueda Rocha, thank you for helping me sketch

out the book cover.

Md Imtiaz Jony, thank you for your beautiful work on the final cover and for the multiple revisions.

Thank you to Lila Jenova Dupuy for getting me back into reading fantasy in the midst of a pandemic. You got my wheels spinning again, and lent me the very books that ended up inspiring Gods and Angels.

And finally, thank you to the members of my launch team: everybody I mentioned above, as well as Sandra Johnson. The speed at which you read this novel moved me more than I can say.

For an accompanying soundtrack to this read,
follow the *Gods & Angels* Spotify playlist,
courtesy of Brace Negron:

playlist.godsandangels.com

GODS & ANGELS

Prologue

I

Lyla had never known for sure if she was a total hack, or if there was any legitimacy to her line of work.

And she could live with that.

Maybe she was swindling gullible people out of their hard-earned money, but she also gave them hope. Besides, the bills didn't pay themselves, and she'd learned at an early age that most people in this world were only out for themselves.

In her case, it was her and Max. It had been her and Max for as long as she could remember. She had his back, he had hers. And nothing ever got in the way of that. Even as they saw each other less and less due to Max's job, Lyla still would have walked through fire for him.

As a high school dropout, college had been out of the question. Lyla had tried odd jobs but had never lasted longer than a couple of weeks. "Attitude problems", "disregard for authority", and "complete lack of discipline" were often referenced when she'd resign or get fired from one of her many attempts at stability.

But she was already used to those words; they'd been flung

at her in most of the nine foster homes and half dozen schools she'd attended.

One desperate day, she'd set up a stand on the Venice Beach Boardwalk with a sign: "Tarot readings - $25". She hadn't thought anything would come of it, but she'd gone home that day with five hundred dollars in her pocket.

Eight years later, Lyla and Max were living in New York City where she read fortunes out of a basement in Chelsea.

She had other friends, and occasionally dated other boys and girls, but even at twenty-five the nightmares kept her from expanding her life far beyond her safe space... and that safe space was Max.

There are just some things you never get over. That boy had held her hand through most of those things, so no matter how much life tried to lure her into opening up to other people, it was Max's bed she always seemed to wind up in, in the end.

Not that he complained. Every time Lyla broke things off with him, he'd gracefully let her go. Every time she returned, he'd welcome her with open arms. He never asked questions about other lovers and never demanded more than she could give.

Lyla worried sometimes that she might be hurting him, but he didn't show any signs of jealousy. And truly if anyone knew his poker face it was her. It's possible he was just as confused as her. They'd started saying "I love you" to each other – and meaning it – long before hormones had twisted those words. And when it came to Max, she couldn't quite distinguish brotherly affection from sexual attraction.

Perhaps it was because she lacked the ability to appreciate romance, which so many of her friends claimed to be the magical ingredient missing between her and Max. As far as she was concerned, romance was the concoction of lies someone would

4

make you swallow before you realized who they truly were. And who they truly were was almost always a disappointment.

Max was, on the other hand, constant. Max was always there. Max would never betray her.

And, as fate would have it, Max was even worse than Lyla at holding down a job. When they'd first outgrown the system, it hadn't taken long for them to land on the streets, with no one willing to help, or even caring if they lived or died.

So, no, it did not bother her that she might be a fraud. Her business had kept them both alive and safely off the streets.

She did readings, rituals, and healings for people from every walk of life. Sometimes she figured that she was just very good at reading people, but other times... she could swear she felt strange energies swirling in and around her, as if she herself could will certain things to be. Occasionally, it almost appeared as if she could change people's thoughts and influence their actions. But then she would remember that her childhood would have been very different had she had the ability to make people do – or not do – certain things, and immediately retreat into the world of reason in which telepathy is a fantasy.

Today was one of those days.

First, there had been the young man who'd wanted to know if his runaway dog was still alive. She'd almost replied it was highly unlikely he'd survived New York City traffic, but she'd held back and had instead told him the dog had made it out of town to greener pastures. Maybe he'd realize at some point that it had been a euphemism not unlike "He retired to the farm in the sky"...

Then, there'd been the gaggle of teenage tourists who'd wanted to know which boys they should ask out. With them, she hadn't even pretended. She'd charged them for the hour, served them some very Irish coffee, had asked to see pictures of said pimply boys, and proceeded to advise them about which seemed to be the least insecure and douchey to her.

And then, the old lady had shown up again. For the seventh day in a row. She was ancient, wore mismatched clothes, and dyed her hair pink. And every single time, she would ask the most absurd questions about her love life, whether she should audition for Broadway, and proceed to ask Lyla about her own life, friends, and childhood.

Of course, Lyla never shared any personal details. Instead, she had a prefabricated fantastical background story that she would use any time people got too personal. And the old lady seemed more than happy to listen to her fables. In fact, she'd often lose interest in her own future, content to query Lyla about her fantasy life instead.

Said fantasy was, by no stretch of the imagination, peaceful. Lyla knew all too well that drama and tragedy made for good stories. But so did love and forgiveness, a happy ending in which heroes and heroines found wisdom and kindness. She knew all about drama and tragedy. Happy endings? Not so much. Forgiveness? None of her abusers had ever asked for it.

So instead, she based her tales on the books she'd read at an age at which she'd still believed that someday, someone would come and tell her that she was now safe and that they'd protect her from the world and from its monsters.

It got a little tedious, finding things to make up about her past. But the old lady always stayed for four hours and paid an additional thirty percent tip. Lyla didn't want to take advantage of her, but she seemed sharp enough to know what she was doing and would not take "no" for an answer. So, Lyla served her tea and spoke to her, offering any company and kindness she could, figuring that maybe that was exactly what the old lady was really paying for.

All in all, it had been a rather ordinary day, so the last thing she expected was to arrive home and find Max sitting on the bathroom floor, bruised and bloody.

2

M ax was leaning against the bathtub. He had a split lip, a swollen eye, cuts, bruises peppered his face and body, and he was clutching his side as if he might have fractured ribs.

"Max, what the hell?" Lyla blurted out, stumbling into the room.

"Couldn't find the first aid kit..." he replied, his voice raw, as if he'd screamed himself hoarse.

"It's in the kitchen. It's always been in the kitchen. Can you stand?"

"I walked all the way home. I'm sure I can make it to the kitchen." He winked at her with his usual bravado.

A few minutes later, they were sitting at the small kitchen table where Lyla expertly set his broken nose, administered butterfly stitches, and ordered him to apply ice to his eye and lip. Max, shirtless, kept twitching every time she got close to his ribs.

"You fractured one of those. You should be in the hospital," she admonished him.

"Oh, come on, it's nothing we haven't dealt with before," he deflected.

When they'd lived in the same foster home, he'd taken beatings for her more than once. Then too, he'd put on a brave face and claimed that it really wasn't as bad as it looked. She was reminded now of that fiercely protective little boy. How he'd always made sure to dry his tears before sneaking into her bed, where he'd hold her all night, as if he himself didn't need any saving.

"Fine. But you better promise to stay in bed and rest while this heals," she said.

"As long as you play nurse to my patient, I have no reason to go anywhere," he answered, suggestively.

"Don't push your luck, you perv. Now, are you going to tell me what happened to you?" she answered.

"Nothing. Just got mugged and beat up."

She raised an eyebrow. Since he'd been big enough to fight back, Max had never just taken a beating. But his knuckles looked like he hadn't defended himself. That didn't track. Yet, he stared straight at her, daring her to challenge his story. It was rare for Max to lie to her, rare enough that she didn't push him. Instead, she got up and helped him to his room.

By the time she'd gotten pillows and blankets from her own bed, he was lying in his, stripped to his underwear. She crawled in next to him and wrapped her arm around his torso as carefully as possible.

She was furious that someone had hurt him this badly. And she was scared. If anything ever happened to him, she didn't know if she'd ever function again. But he didn't need to deal with her feelings right now. So, she held back the tears that were making their way up her throat, and started caressing his chest instead. Max was strong. He'd been hitting heavy bags since he'd been old enough to convince a trainer to let him mop the floors in exchange for classes, giving him the lean but powerful muscles of a martial artist. But he still had the look of someone whose growth had been stunted by malnutrition. That had never bothered her though. He was a survivor, and every scarred inch of his body could attest to that.

A few minutes later, she was sufficiently distracted from her upset that she started using her mouth instead. Ever so carefully, she got up and hovered on all four above him, slowly kissing a line down his torso.

"Aren't you seeing that hipster guy these days?" he interrupted.

She looked up at him and said, "I'm breaking up with him. The beard just gets weird down there. That guy is hairy in all the wrong places." Casually, she continued licking a trail down his body.

"In that case...", he said, suggestively lifting his hips up toward her.

She licked up his length through his boxer briefs and briefly checked his face for a reaction. Then, she abruptly moved back to her side of the bed, keeping a safe distance from him.

"Not tonight, buddy. You have fractured ribs."

"Aw, they'd heal so much faster with a little help", he answered, giving her his best innocent puppy dog eyes.

"Nice try," she told him. "But this is your punishment for getting your ass beat and scaring the shit out of me."

He turned toward her and kissed her cheek. She knew what he meant to say – *Thank you for caring*. Instead, he grabbed her hand, squeezed it tight, and said, "Good night, beautiful," as he closed his eyes.

He was asleep in minutes.

3

L yla wasn't quite as withholding the next morning. Though she still worried about his ribs, it didn't stop her from pleasuring him and demanding he return the favor. Glowingly sated, she proceeded to set him up with food, water, and entertainment, and ordered him to stay in bed and rest up while she went to work.

Something had changed when she'd seen his bloodied-up face. Though they'd experienced plenty of danger and violence before, it worried her that he hadn't been honest about what had happened to him. He'd been elusive about his life and his work in recent months, trying for the first time not to pull her into whatever it was he was involved in. And, the more he distanced himself, the more she felt a deep need to know.

She met with her three girlfriends over lunch, Tania, Julia, and Daisy, and they teased her mercilessly about having yet again hooked up with Max. They claimed that he wasn't hiding anything but finally adding a little mystery to their relationship, and that this would be when she fell for him at last. Lyla brushed off their theories but couldn't deny that she enjoyed feeling like "one of the girls". Most days, she was on the outskirts of their friend group, a little too dark, a little too edgy, never really caring about romance, parties, and the latest fashion trends. But today, she was one of them: worrying only about what it was that was going through a boy's head, and how he'd made her feel that morning.

Maybe there was hope for her after all. Maybe she could move on and live a more regular life. Maybe someday, she'd even meet someone who'd make her want to leave the past in the past.

She was still deep in thought about these recent developments when the old lady arrived at the shop for her regular afternoon visit. Something was different about her today. If Lyla didn't know any better, she'd have said that she seemed younger, bursting with energy somehow.

The woman sat down at Lyla's little round table, her jewelry clinking around as she did, and demanded she read her palm. It wasn't on her list of skills, but the woman nearly begged her, and she didn't want to turn down her most loyal customer. So, she carefully reached out and took the wrinkled old hand in both of hers.

She rarely had any physical contact with her clients, but sometimes it had eased the process. She at least figured it might help her feel what it was the crone needed.

But as soon as she grabbed her hand, it wasn't that of a crone at all. Instead, a large, youthful, male hand rested between her palms. Stunned, Lyla withdrew her own as if she'd been stung. She looked up and saw the old woman smiling that same benign smile at her. And when she looked back down, the hand on the table was small and wrinkled again.

"Don't fear, child," the woman's low voice said. "I've dealt in magic myself. What you just saw was a vision. Take my hand and see if you can observe anything else."

That, she had not expected. This woman claimed to be a psychic, and that the spiritual was real. It might have been a little too much for Lyla, who was mostly a skeptic herself, but something in the lady's voice enticed her to try again.

Seduced into another attempt, she took the withered old hand between hers and closed her eyes.

Nothing happened at first, but then she sensed the slightest pressure from the woman's fingertips pressing up into her palm, and images started flashing in front of her closed eyelids.

She saw a clearing in the woods, too green to have seen human impact; she saw thousands of black feathers dropping from the sky; and then she saw what seemed like a colossal, man-made... statue? Two mountainously tall triangles of stone shot up from the ground, and at the top, between the two peaks, a hundred feet high, floated what looked like a slowly spinning wheel.

None of it made sense, and, as Lyla tried to understand what she'd just seen, the hand was pulled back from hers, and the old lady cleared her throat.

"I forgot that I am hosting tea today, I must run," she said as she dropped a wad of cash on the table between them.

Bewildered, Lyla didn't reply. In a daze, she picked up the cash, closed her shop early, and walked home. It was rare for her to doubt her own skepticism, but this had been yet another instance which would be hard to deny and forget. She couldn't explain what she'd seen, how she'd experienced those images with such clarity, or how they related to the old woman. All she knew was that she had seen them, and they were now branded into her brain like no memory ever could be.

Still ruminating on this strange encounter, she arrived home and found Max, freshly showered, standing in the kitchen, a towel wrapped around his hips. The sight temporarily dissipated all her questions about the fabric of reality.

But Max stopped her from going to her knees right then and there, finally admitting that his ribs felt wrong and that he needed to lay off any "strenuous activity" for a while.

Instead, she kissed a birthmark on the side of his neck, and they carefully cuddled up to each other. They watched several movies in a row, before finally falling asleep, peacefully, her head on his shoulder, his arm loosely wrapped around her.

4

The next morning, Lyla brought Max breakfast in bed, making good on her promise to nurse him back to health.

"Would you skip town with me, if I asked you to?" he blurted out between two bites of bacon.

Lyla's head snapped up. Something about the tone of his voice rang wrong in her ears. There was an urgency that made her stomach twist.

"What are you asking, Max?"

She set aside her eggs and looked at him seriously.

He ran his tongue over his split lip for a moment before answering.

"Look, I didn't get mugged..." he started.

"I know."

"I quit my job. And the people I was working for... they aren't very good people..."

Now, he had her positively alarmed. She could tell he was largely understating just how dangerous these people were. But under his cool façade, he was more scared than she'd ever seen him.

"Max, do you owe them anything? Do you know things you shouldn't know? What are we talking about here?" she asked.

"I need to get out of town," he said.

"Say no more. I'll pack for both of us. We'll head to the cabin in an hour. Disappear for a while," she replied, jumping up and beginning to rifle through his drawers.

She was perched on a chair, pulling a duffel bag out of the top shelf of his closet when he stopped her: "Wait. Ly. I don't want you to just run with me because that's what we do."

"Why else would I run with you?" she replied, slowly getting off the chair, and looking at him, baffled. "It is what we do. Max, you're in danger. And I love you. I'll come with you and make sure you're ok." Then she got back into action and kept thinking out loud, "We have enough cash saved up, and the cabin is stocked. We can disappear for quite a while before we'll need to think about making ends meet..." she trailed off, as she saw him sit up, mindful of his healing ribs, deep concern etched into his expression.

"Ly, stop. I love you too. But I'm not letting you follow me out of sisterly love. We're not kids anymore. This has to stop." He looked so determined, it scared her.

"What's that supposed to mean?"

"I'm in real trouble this time. And I'm not dragging you down with me just so that I can have company. I'm tired of playing brother and sister with you. You're my best friend, yes. But I also love you." He took a deep breath, and continued, looking her straight in the eyes. "*Love you*, love you. I don't want you to come with me unless you feel the same way."

She stood in the middle of his room, a pair of socks in one hand, and his duffel bag in the other, feeling small, lost, and clumsy. Though he'd seen every inch of her yesterday morning, and many times before that, the oversized t-shirt she was wearing suddenly felt too short. She opened her mouth only to realize she had no idea what to say.

"It's ok," he said, interrupting the awkward silence. "You don't have to say anything. I can pack my own stuff. But I won't leave until tonight. Take the day to think about it. If you decide you'd like to come with me, not as my sister and friend, but as my girl, I'll be at the storage unit at six."

All she managed to say was "Okay." She stared at him for a moment, feeling like a deer in headlights. Then she slowly turned and walked out of the room.

5

Shell-shocked, Lyla put on some clothes, brushed her teeth, and ran out of the apartment as fast as she could.

As if on autopilot, she took the A train and found herself on Rockaway Beach before realizing where she was going. It was warm for an autumn day, but New Yorkers didn't go to the beach after Labor Day, so she found the solitude she needed.

It still struck her as strange that the sun rose over the ocean here. She was so used to California's beaches where the sun set over a horizon of endless water. California, which Max now proposed to return to. Academically, she knew that it was the most beautiful place she'd ever seen. She knew that they'd be safe at the remote cabin out there. No one knew of it. And they'd made sure they could survive there for weeks if need be.

And yet, that desert and those beaches held too many painful memories for her. She'd embraced New York, with its blizzards, endless winters, and unbearably humid summers. She welcomed all of it because it meant that she'd made it out. Unlike in her nightmares, in which she'd find herself back in the dry desert heat, back in a life she had no control over, her heart twisting in agony, telling her she'd die if she didn't escape.

She had that dream at least once a month. And every time, she'd crawl into Max's bed, seeking the comfort of his body, the realization that they were adults now and that he'd never let anyone hurt her again.

Max...

Max was in love with her. Max wanted to change their relationship. Max wanted her to be more than what she'd been to him all these years. Something she wasn't sure she could be.

She did not feel the same way.

Or did she?

She began walking up and down the beach, remembering the first time she'd met him. Both her parents had just died in a car accident, and she'd been placed in her first foster home. She was five years old and scared. Max, who'd been abandoned at birth and had never known any other kind of life, had struck her as the most stubborn and hardened boy she'd ever met. He'd looked her up and down, assessing her - for what, she couldn't tell. There had been nothing warm or considerate in the way he'd looked at her all through dinner. He'd seemed to calculate how she'd play into the home's dynamic.

Many years later, she'd understood what he'd been thinking. He had realized that there was now someone smaller, more fragile, and more scared in the house. He'd decided on the spot that she was his responsibility, and with that decision his life had suddenly gotten a whole lot harder than it already had been.

As for the foster parents, it hadn't taken long for her to understand that the smiles and polite conversation had mostly been for the benefit of the social worker who'd brought her over, and, after a rather depressing dinner, she'd gone to sleep in her new bed feeling more alone than she could ever have imagined possible.

She remembered feeling as if her chest would cave in, the knowledge rooting itself deep into her mind that the world would never be all right again. Just as she'd started crying, trying to muffle the sounds of her sobs with her pillow, she'd heard a rustling from the other side of the room and seen the little boy drag his blankets over to her to create a makeshift bed next to hers on the floor. He hadn't spoken a word all night - she couldn't even remember his name - but when he'd reached out to take her hand, she'd stopped crying and felt a little less alone.

Was Max her security blanket?

No. That wasn't fair. She'd paid back the favor many times over and, with time, their relationship had grown far past the needs of two abandoned children.

A few years later, they'd both run away and wound up in separate homes. But their alliance, their friendship, and the love between them had only kept growing. He protected her whenever he could, and she took care of him in whatever ways she could think of.

She still remembered the first time she'd realized that Max was not related to her. It was his eleventh birthday and she'd given him a stolen skateboard so he could play with the other boys in his school. He'd hugged her, kissed her on the cheek and pulled back with the most dazzling smile. And suddenly her body had given her signals she'd only felt a handful of times before – and never with Max: that boy was cute, and, no matter how they'd met, he was not her brother.

A couple of months later, he'd asked if he could practice kissing with her, so he'd "have better game with the girls in school." She'd never been kissed at the time, and she remembered feeling shy and excited, and her brain going blank as butterflies exploded in her stomach. She further remembered wondering if there was always that much saliva involved and how people dealt with that...

But she'd also been acutely aware of the fact that she was practice for his real girlfriends. Girls who didn't have nightmares. Girls who had parents, homes, allowances, and didn't feel awkward or lost. Girls who weren't freaks like her.

Looking back, she realized that she'd never met any of those girls, that they probably had never existed, and that "kissing practice" had been a pretext. But she also remembered the rejection she'd felt at the time. It hurt to admit, but she'd probably closed herself off to the idea of romance with Max on that day. It had hurt too much to want someone she thought she could never have.

So, she'd started seeing girls herself, and boys, always keeping a safe distance, making sure she never felt that kind of pain again.

And yet, she always wound up in Max's bed.

Nothing had really changed.

Nothing had changed.

She was in love with Max. Had always been in love with Max. But she'd been too messed up to realize it all those years.

She looked at the time. She had just about enough time to make it to the storage unit. She hadn't packed, but all she needed was in her purse.

Excited and carrying a complete certainty like she'd never felt before, she started walking back to the subway. On the train, she pulled out her phone and texted Max:

"Wait for me. I'm coming."

6

It was the longest subway ride of her life. She'd changed everything by texting him those five words. How was she to approach him?

Hi Max. Sorry it took me the better part of two decades to figure this out. Wanna be my boyfriend? I guess we already live together anyhow!

God, they did already live together. And now they were running off to a remote cabin together. Her idea of long-term had been two months at best so far. She never got serious enough to buy someone a present. But she lived with Max. She celebrated every holiday with him. They knew everything about each other. As for sex, they'd done just about every depraved thing she could think of.

That thought gave her the shivers. It had been a while since one of their "sex benders" as they called them, but she knew every inch of his body, every muscle, every groove... *Easy, girl, you'll be driving for four days straight before you'll get the luxury of a shower and a bed*, she told herself.

She was so hot and bothered by the time she made it to the

storage unit, it took her a moment to realize that he wasn't there. The attendant hadn't seen anybody, and when she checked her phone, she saw that her message had been delivered, but not read.

That meant that she could surprise him with her news. He was late and she was physically unable to stand still and wait for his arrival. Instead, she sprinted to their building and raced up the stairs, not bothering with the elevator. Her heart beat a million miles an hour as she imagined telling him that she wanted to take this step with him, that she was ready to be happy.

It stopped beating when she made it to their apartment: the door had been broken in.

And with that, the euphoric feeling evaporated, and her legs turned to jelly. In that moment she knew something terrible had happened. She could barely stand, but she fought through the rushing in her ears, the darkness in her vision. She quietly pushed open the door and snuck down the corridor. She was tempted to shout Max's name in the childish hope that he'd answer that everything was ok. But she knew better.

Everything was not ok.

She'd been here before. In the moment where one wants to beg the universe for a do over – but it's too late.

Max's bedroom was a bloodbath. His face barely recognizable, his body broken like a cheap doll, he lay on the mattress she'd left him on, face up, eyes wide open. All of his fingers had been cut from his hands, and there were large incisions all along his body, as if it had been carved into with a giant pair of scissors. But those gashes hadn't killed him: a large chunk of his throat had been ripped out and he'd bled to death.

The pool of blood he lay in, was almost dry.

He'd been dead for hours, his phone resting next to him. Reflexively, she pushed the button on his display and read, "*One*

New Message – From: Princess Lyla"

He'd died not knowing how she felt.

Lyla broke.

As she draped herself over Max's body, too empty to cry or feel anything beyond the horror of having lost the one thing that mattered in the entire world, she saw something move in the corner of her vision. She didn't want to bother turning around. She just wanted to give up and die.

But then it spoke.

"My orders were to bring you in alive, but you... you just smell too delicious not to eat... you smell like the kind of food I like to play with first."

As a psychic, she'd often spoken of energies and battles with demons and monsters, but she'd mostly assumed those were metaphors, images humans came up with to make the world a little more magical, and to make sense of why life hurt so damned much.

When she looked up and turned to the corner of the room, Lyla knew: they had never been metaphors.

7

The thing crouching in the corner of Max's room was significantly scarier than anything her imagination could have come up with. Enveloped in a shiny black carapace, it sat on two legs and four arms that ended in pincers. It regarded her with its oversized yellow eyes, the pupils of which were rectangularly shaped like those of a goat. But that's not what disturbed her most about the creature. It was the intelligent, assessing look in its eyes that gave her a profound feeling of wrongness. That was as best as she could describe it. That thing, whatever it was, did not belong in this world. Everything about it screamed *alien*. And what made it worse was that it had spoken. She stared at it, unable to comprehend how something so grotesque looking could speak in a human voice.

And yet, she wasn't afraid. She had nothing left to lose. Let the monsters drag her away, kill her, eat her...

Max had died not knowing how she felt.

Her last word to him had been "Okay". And then she'd run out of the apartment like a coward. He'd offered his heart up on a platter. And she'd left him to be sliced to pieces by a monster.

The thing kept staring calmly at her, as if it had all the time in the world. No doubt it would pounce on her the second she tried to run. She knew all too well that predators couldn't help attacking scared prey. But she was too weary to run anyhow.

As it kept staring, she noticed two things: its legs ended in hooves– and it was chewing on a piece of meat. Blood dripped down its chin and a flap of skin hung from its mouth, a flap of skin with a birth mark shaped like the one on the side of Max's neck.

At that sight, she lost it. She jumped off the bed, fury burning through her every muscle. The thing cocked its head to the side, as if unsure what she was doing. Then, faster than Lyla could register, it lowered itself to the ground and tucked its head, ready to pounce on her, a low growl emanating from its throat.

She would die. She had no weapon. Hell, she didn't even know what the thing was. But none of that mattered. At least she'd die with Max. She sure couldn't face living after what had happened to him. Maybe it would be less of a betrayal if she expired right by him, killed by the monster that had torn the life from him too.

But her body had other plans than to simply roll over and die. An instinct rising from the depths of her being, she straightened her spine and looked the thing straight in its ugly goat eyes.

And then, she screamed.

A primal scream that had no beginning and no end. A scream like she'd never uttered before. In it were all her pain, her rage, her disappointment at the world. As she screamed, she saw it all: the last time her parents had tucked her into bed, and how the safe and loving world she'd known had been torn from her; every time she'd been abused in a foster home, beaten, molested and worse; every time she'd been powerless to help Max while he suffered the same; she saw her eighteenth birthday, a send-off into a world that hadn't given two shits about her; she saw herself on that day of her first tarot reading, how she'd stood on a cliff edge, ready to jump, and the only thing holding her back had been that Max needed her to live; she saw every hurt, every disappointment, every betrayal; she saw a world that had never cared about her, a brutal world that had crushed her one agonizing piece at a time.

Lyla screamed and screamed. And through it all she saw Max, the little boy who'd never batted an eyelash at putting himself in harm's way for her, who'd given her something to live for, who'd never had anything but kindness in his heart, and who'd been repaid by the world with harshness and violence. Instead of appreciating his goodness, it had crushed him under its ruthless thumb, giving him nothing but pain. And he'd smiled through it all. He'd smiled that careless, beautiful smile that dared the world to dish out more hurt. Right up until this monstrous creature had slashed him to death.

Some part of her brain vaguely registered that the thing flinched and cowered back under her assault. But she knew it didn't matter. Her angry scream burned with her love for Max; with her desire to see something good in this grey world. But love didn't conquer anyone. It never had. Love was no more than a futile distraction from the fact that this place was hell. It had kept her going all these years, but deep inside she'd known that, in the end, it wouldn't matter how much she and Max loved each other.

Maybe she'd always known that they'd come to a bloody end. It was poetic after all.

And then, she ran out of breath. Lyla fell to her knees, barely able to hold herself up. Panting, her head spinning, she looked up to see the creature click its four pincers, as if it could barely contain its excitement.

"My turn," it growled, its angry eyes glowing, drool dripping off its large teeth.

She tried to lift her arms to ward it off, but her body wouldn't respond. Her vision went dark, and she slumped to the side, just as she realized that there was a third being in the room.

She heard a voice, but she couldn't make out any words. All she knew was that it soothed her; it sounded like going home.

Home.

Maybe that's what the blissful darkness was.

Part One

1

Lyla didn't open her eyes when she woke up. She had no idea how long she'd been unconscious, but judging by the pounding in her head, it had been a long time since she'd had any food or water. Her everything hurt, but nothing more than her heart. Oblivion had been kind. She couldn't remember dreaming, but for a while there she'd been in a place where Max hadn't died. The moment she'd awoken though, it had all come rushing back: Max's declaration; the slightly defeated look in his eyes as he'd told her to take the day to think about it; and the pool of blood he'd died in. A wave of grief like no other crashed over her. She turned on her side, desperate to go back to sleep lest reality suffocate her to death.

But the voices wouldn't grant her that peace. Two men were speaking near her in hushed tones. Her brain was too foggy to make out what they were talking about. Nor did she care to. What were they doing in her apartment? Somehow, she'd survived the monster who'd killed Max. Maybe it had lost interest after she'd passed out?

Desperate to cling on to something, her brain got back into

gear. She'd have to bury Max. God knew she didn't want to; she wanted to keep whatever she could of him. But he deserved better. She'd have to call the police; they'd open a murder investigation, and let the case go cold soon after. She'd seen it happen before. They wouldn't care to find out what happened to someone like Max. They'd ask a few questions and they'd cut him open to pretend they wanted to find his killer. The thought of it made her gag. She didn't want to give them his body. At the same time, she felt a completely irrational sense of relief that they'd clean all the blood off him, and that she wouldn't have to do it. Did that make her a horrible person?

And then there'd be the funeral. Who would attend Max's funeral? Would it just be her when they put his broken body into the ground? She doubted she'd have the strength to give Max the farewell he deserved. Though she knew that wasn't even the worst of it. The worst was that the world would continue spinning like nothing had happened. The worst was that the sun would keep on rising and shining every morning, mocking her pain. Just like those stupid voices that wouldn't stop murmuring.

"Get out!" she tried to shout. It came out a whisper.

"She's awake," said one of the voices, approaching her bed.

"Get out, get out, get out..." she kept repeating, slowly getting her protesting body into a sitting position and opening her eyes.

She was not at home.

Instead, she was lying in a bed in what seemed like a hospital ward. Except that it didn't have the look, smell, or feel of a hospital. This place felt warm and cozy somehow. A window took up an entire wall, giving her a view of green plains and a blue sky. The light in the room was warm and the walls were covered in wall hangings and tapestries in soothing colors. The bedspreads weren't hospital white but all colors of the rainbow instead. And the place was strewn with mismatched furniture, couches, and slouchy chairs. In a strange way, it reminded her of her psychic shop with its candles and incense.

One of the men stood at the foot of her bed. He was short, with tan skin and piercing blue eyes. The other man had similarly odd coloring - light brown skin, with green-golden, almond-shaped eyes and shoulder length black hair. He approached her and she realized how huge, muscular, and absolutely terrifying he looked.

"Who are you?" she croaked.

Ignoring her question, he shoved a glass of water into her face and said, "Drink."

His face and tone were chillingly cold. She shrank as far away from him as possible, but her body barely cooperated. In reaction, he merely sighed, as if annoyed by her behavior. "I'm the guy who saved you from the demon. Now, drink!"

"That voice I heard, that was you," she realized. "What the hell were you doing in my apartment? Who are you? And where the fuck am I?" She hoped that she sounded somewhat fierce, but she was so thirsty the words were barely audible.

As if he read her mind, he cocked an eyebrow at the glass in his hand. She reached for it and drank. Something about this terrifying mountain of muscle had reawakened her survival instinct. She had no idea where she was or what these people wanted, but she better find out fast and get back to Max's body in one piece. She owed him that much.

He waited until she'd drained the glass, before taking it back. Then, with the same impassive expression he said, "You'll need at least three days to tank back up. You blew almost all your magic in that one attack. That was incredibly reckless," he chided and turned to go.

"Magic? What the hell are you talking about?" she answered.

He stopped, then slowly turned around. She thought he'd been scowling before, but apparently that had just been his face.

"Your energy, your will, your power. You threw the whole of it at the demon without..." he trailed off and took a step toward her. He looked furious, but added, rather gently, "You have no idea what I'm talking about, do you?"

She just stared at him. What he'd said sounded insane. But so were goat-eyed, hoofed, pincered, talking monsters crouching in bedroom corners. So had been that scream of hers.

He turned away toward the other man, who still stood patiently at the foot of her bed.

"Somebody could have warned me about this," he said, reproachfully. "I can't believe I'm going to have to train a fledgling. As if I had nothing better to do!"

He walked to the door, then turned around to the other man again and said "If you know what's good for you, you'll give him a heads up. Hermes is going to be pissed!" Then he turned in Lyla's direction. For a moment, he seemed to hesitate. Then he shook his head and said, "Rest. You're going to need it." After a moment, he added, "And if I were you, I'd be a little more cautious about invoking Hell in this place. Invoke god and heaven all you like. They are fictions. Hell, not so much."

2

" That was Azrael," the other man said with a smile. "Don't take it personally. He's been grouchy ever since he realized he was named after the angel of death." He gave her an appraising look. "My name is Jerahmeel, but you can call me Jeremy. You must have a lot of questions. May I sit with you and answer them?" he asked, cocking his head toward the comfortable armchair next to her bed.

"Doesn't seem like I have much of a choice," she replied.

He didn't move. Instead, he answered, "You should always have a choice. You're too weak right now to make it out of this bed alone, much less back home. But if that's what you want after your questions have been answered, we'll bring you back. And if you don't want to get any answers right at this moment, I won't make you listen to me either. I would however urge you to consider the fact that you were attacked in your own home, and that the danger has most certainly not passed."

She vividly remembered those rectangularly pupiled eyes. "That thing— it said it had orders to bring me in alive. Bring me where? To whom?"

"To its master," the man replied, in that same soothing voice. "I wish I could tell you that it was an easy danger to eliminate. But I'm afraid there was a lot more to why the demon was sent after you than–"

"If it was sent after me," she interrupted, "then Max was just collateral damage..." The full blow of what had happened hit her like a truck. Somehow, she'd assumed that Max had been beat up by the same person - or creature - that had returned to finish the job, and that she'd simply been in the wrong place at the wrong time. But it was the opposite. Max would have lived had it not been for her.

Sensing her pain, Jeremy gently said, "I'm sorry about your friend."

"He wasn't just a friend," she answered, unable to stop the tears.

He looked at her sadly. "Then I'm even sorrier."

Jeremy waited patiently while she fought to control her sobs. It had been a long time since she'd cried in front of a stranger, but once she allowed her tears to flow freely, she feared their supply was infinite. When she could finally breathe well enough to speak, she asked the only question that was left: "Why?"

"May I?" the man asked, pointing to the chair. She nodded. He sat, slowly, composing his face, as if wondering where to start.

"The short of it is: because you're Hermes' child. Your parents never had a chance to tell you, but you were adopted. I know that's the kind of news one should break carefully, but there's nothing left to it but to tell you the full truth. You were taken away from your birth parents and hidden – first with your adoptive parents and then in the system. And now that you're a grown woman, the monsters that took you want to use you for your power."

"What power?" she asked.

"Your father is one of the mightiest entities in this world," Jeremy explained. He hesitated and then dove in headfirst. "What Azrael said about god? Anything religion has come up with is complete fiction. However, a long, long time ago, beings came here that fit the bible's description of angels, though they were probably more alien than angels. They waged a battle here. Some of them had been sent to conquer the earth. They became what we, here, call "Fallen angels". Others followed to protect humanity. But they weren't supposed to, so they were punished for their offense – they fell too. Their punishment was that they'd never be allowed to return to their home dimension; they were cursed to forever guard humans. There were ten of them. And humans, being who they are, thought them Gods. They started creating myths and legends around them. So, the Ten adopted the names that they'd been given by their charges. Hence: Hermes."

"Wait," Lyla interrupted, her tears finally drying up. "There were twelve Olympians, plus Hades. Also, they were rapey, bloodthirsty sons of bitches."

"In the stories, yes. Stories that have nothing to do with reality. Stories that humans made up in order to justify their own backward behavior. As for the number, Zeus, Hera and Dionysos are fiction. The other ten are the guardians of this planet. Eight now – Poseidon and Aphrodite are gone," he added with a sigh. "I know it's a lot to take in, but you don't really have time for a gentler introduction. The ten Gods bred with humans to keep the species going. Their offspring are called angels. But after generations, the bloodlines get too diluted, so over the centuries, they've... refreshed it, so to speak. As Hermes did with your birth mother."

Jeremy stopped, gauging her reaction. When she didn't say

anything, he continued, "Each one of the Ten has a specialty, and their descendants' purpose is to uphold said specialty. I, myself, am from Aphrodite's bloodline - a priest of Aphrodite's, as we call ourselves. We are healers. All of us carry our ancestors' magic in our blood, but we hone it differently. Hermes' priests are guardians. Their job is to get souls onto the right path... sometimes through suggestion, sometimes by force. That is your legacy." He paused, then, with a smile, he added, "I believe this is where you tell me that I must be out of my mind."

"I don't know what to believe. I did see that monster. And I've felt things I couldn't explain. But angels? Gods?"

At that, he stood up, turned his back to her, and a giant pair of white wings sprouted from it. She was staring at him, as he slowly turned around, a grin on his face. Each wing was five feet long and feathered in a white purer than fresh snow.

Jeremy sat down, throwing his legs over one arm of the chair and draping his wings over the other. "You have them too, though the look on your face tells me you've never seen them," he smirked. "As opposed to the Gods, we can call them up at will. Azrael and I agreed to keep our wings to ourselves so you wouldn't freak out waking up to a couple of angels."

She looked at him, baffled. Here was a man - "priest," he'd called himself - with ginormous wings, casually draped across an armchair. Of all her questions, she wasn't sure why this one mattered, but she asked, "Which bloodline does Azrael belong to?"

Jeremy hesitated for a second before answering, "Hermes."

"He said he'd be training me..." She remembered how he'd called her a "fledgling", as if it was the worst insult he could think of.

"Hermes has been looking for you for a long time, but the Fallen used magic to hide you. We found you very recently and have been keeping an eye on you. Your father wasn't sure how to pull you out of your life, so instead he kept tabs on you. That's how Azrael knew to be there when the demon attacked you. Hermes wants you to train, and he's asked him to mentor you. That is, if you agree of course."

"What kind of training are we talking about?" she asked.

"I believe it's meant to be threefold. Angel history. Hermes priesthood training. And regular combat skills."

She looked down at her hands. The word "combat" had reminded her of Max. Max who'd trained her in self-defense. Max who was irrevocably gone. "I'm tired," she whispered.

Jeremy stood up, folded his wings back into his back and said, "I could help you sleep if you'd like..."

She was too weary to ask what he meant, so she simply looked at him through her tears and nodded. Approaching her slowly, Jeremy reached out and touched her forehead.

Before she knew it, she was asleep.

3

When Lyla opened her eyes again, she realized it had all been real. None of this was a dream. She was in this ward because demons were after her. Monsters existed and Max was dead.

Jeremy was nowhere in view. Thank god for some privacy. Ever so slowly, she climbed out of bed and made it to the door behind which she assumed she'd find the bathroom. Much like everything else in this place, it was too welcoming for her current state of mind.

When she came back, Jeremy rushed toward her. "You shouldn't be out of bed on your own. What were you thinking?"

"Max," she replied, sluggishly, "I have to go back for Max."

"Sweetheart, Max is dead," Jeremy said, concern in his voice.

"I know. I know. But I can't leave him like that." She brushed him off, annoyed.

"It's been taken care of," he replied. When she stared at him, he added, "We couldn't leave his body for the authorities to find. He has been cremated and all evidence of what happened has been destroyed."

She couldn't believe it. Max had been erased. His body, the body she'd been caressing what seemed like just hours ago was no more. She'd never see him again, never touch him again. Feeling sick, she rushed back to the bathroom, and dry heaved into the toilet, realizing it might have been days since she ate. She'd been deprived even of the satisfaction of vomiting up whatever food was supposed to give her nutrition. She continued nonetheless, coughing, feeling her tears well up and stream down her face. And then a hand pulled back her hair and another gently stroked up and down her back.

She didn't know why she felt so comfortable crying in front of this stranger, when nobody other than Max had seen her cry in twenty years, but, before she knew it, she was leaning into him, sobbing, unstoppable tears streaming down her face, as Jeremy gently rocked her back and forth. In some inexplicable way, he felt like the eye of the storm. Though she never trusted strangers, he was the rock to hold on to while her life fell apart around her.

And hold on, she did.

No.

She had no choice but to hold on to his presence. He was an irresistible force, she couldn't say "no" to.

When she could breathe again, she looked at him and asked, "What do I do now?"

Jeremy who'd sat down across from her and hugged her tightly, pulled back. He looked at her seriously for a moment, never breaking the contact between them. Then he slowly brushed the hair out of her face and said, "The way I see it, you have two choices. You can pretend you never heard the truth about your heritage and return to reading strangers' tarot cards, living a careful life in the shadows, hoping the demons won't find you again. Or you can stay here and become the person you were always meant to be." He looked at her and added, "No matter what you choose, life as you knew it is over." Then he leaned in and, ever so gently, used his thumb to wipe the tears off her face. "What would Max want you to do?"

She didn't know how this stranger knew that those seven words were the best way to manipulate her. And yet, as she looked deep into his blue eyes, she didn't see any manipulation. All she saw was a profound sincerity.

What would Max want her to do? He'd want her to be safe. But more than that, he'd want her to fight. He'd want her to show the metaphorical finger to the things that were trying to keep her down. As she thought of Max, she could almost see him, looking at her with his reddish-brown eyes, smiling and saying, *Fight on, beautiful girl. Fight on!*

She didn't think she was as strong as Max had always believed her to be, but in that moment, she looked up at Jeremy and said, "Option Two. I choose the red pill."

He smiled and sat back, letting go of her for the first time. "Good. I was hoping you'd stay. Now let's get you back to bed."

He carried her out of the bathroom and tucked her into her hospital bed with more gentleness than she'd known even from her parents when they'd been alive. When he turned away, she asked, "You said history would be part of my training. Are there any books I could read to pass the time?"

Jeremy turned around, a boyish grin on his face. "I'm so glad you asked," he said. He walked out of the ward and returned a few minutes later with a stack of books.

She picked up the first one on the pile. It was large and leather-bound, but not particularly old. She opened it to its first page and read "*Gods and Angels – A History, by Zaphkiel III*". Did the angels not have last names? On the bottom of the left page, she read that this was the fifth edition of this book, published only a few years ago.

Jeremy came to her bedside one last time, offering her a plate of eggs and toast. She wanted to refuse, but he looked at her insistently until she picked up the fork.

And then, she began reading:

For the sake of clearer definitions, we shall henceforth use the words "Fallen", "God", "angel", "lost" and "demon" as follows:

We shall call the aliens that came to earth to conquer it (Lucifer, Azazel, Ramiel and so on), "the Fallen".

We shall call the ten aliens who followed them to protect humanity (Poseidon, Apollo, Aphrodite and so on), "the Gods". They are also known as "The Ten".

The Gods' progeny are known as "angels", whereas the Fallen gave birth to a variety of creatures. Their first attempt at creating a legacy on earth are known as "the lost", or "the lost children". It is unknown how many attempts followed. We know of some of the Fallen's abandoned experiments: vampires, werewolves, and more. Ultimately, they succeeded in creating a following when they birthed the "demon" race.

Little is known about the Gods' and Fallen's home, and even less is known as to why the Fallen were sent to destroy humanity. What we do know is that they thought and acted as a hive mind of sorts, which begs the question as to how the Gods broke off from the hive and disobeyed orders. The most sensible explanation appears to be that some sort of schism had begun happening within the hive.

It is very rare for the Gods to speak of those days. It may be that they cannot remember, or that they aren't able to translate the thoughts and feelings of a hive into something that would make sense to us. Or maybe, it simply pains them to remember.

When the Fallen and the Gods first came to earth, they fell from grace. Where they had been parts of a whole, they suddenly discovered individuality. They lost the part of them that connected them to their planet and, instead, grew a very human characteristic: they began thinking of themselves as separate. They'd never needed names before, but as they came here and started to self-reflect in this new manner, they took over the names the humans gave them.

Each one of them had taken a little bit more of something from the hive's power. So, they were reborn as specialists. The humans that occasionally interacted with them saw those differences and created myths and legends around them. The Gods did not particularly care for those, though they did adopt the names their charges had given them.

And so, they became The Ten:

- *Aphrodite, the Healer*
- *Apollo, the Seer*
- *Ares, the Soldier*
- *Artemis, the Blesser*
- *Athena, the Scholar*
- *Demeter, the Witch*
- *Hades, the Guide*
- *Hephaestus, the Forger*
- *Hermes, the Guardian*
- *and Poseidon, the Challenger of Destiny herself*

After the Gods thwarted the Fallen's plans, they came to a stalemate. The Gods tried to return home. But they were no longer welcome. Not only had they disobeyed the hive, but their new condition was repugnant to their own kind. They were punished for their crime of disobedience by never being allowed back home lest they be executed on sight. And so, they became the eternal guardians of humanity instead, though their alienness did not allow them to interact with their charges much.

After having experienced themselves for so long as part of a bigger being, they were cruelly punished with abject loneliness and isolation.

We do not know whether the Fallen also attempted to return home, or whether they simply chose to stay on a planet into whose heart they could inspire fear and pain so easily.

Intrigued by the Gods' various specializations, Lyla skipped to a later chapter that explained their powers in more detail.

She was still fuzzy on how magic was used, but she found out that Apollo and his descendants had the gift of foresight; they had visions about the future and tried to make sense of them in order to help plan ahead in what seemed like an endless extension of this war between Gods and Fallen.

Ares and his priests were the Gods' military. Their magic came out in their superhuman strength and fighting capacity.

They were backed up by Artemis and her people, who appeared to stand back on the battlefield and buff the front-line soldiers with spells for strength, rage, and more.

As for the weapons used in such confrontations, they were crafted by Hephaestus' followers, out of materials and with protections and sigils on them that made them far superior to anything humans could dream of.

One of the Fallen's experiments had led to the existence of undead entities – zombies, ghosts, and others. Apparently, it was Hades' job to handle those, and to limit the damage they did in the world of the living.

Hermes and his descendants were also guides of a sort. They helped misguided souls, be they human or other. Hermes' priests tried to get them back on track and would only take them out of commission when absolutely necessary.

Had Azrael asked the demon if it wanted to repent before he'd killed it? No, that seemed like too big a word for the brute. Though it appeared that Hermes' children were the most multifaceted in how they combined both magic, a capacity for empathy, and regular fighting skills.

Athena's followers were scholars. With a capacity to process information much more effectively than anyone else on the planet, they recorded the angels' histories and all known information regarding the Fallen, including family trees. Being the academics of the magical world, they also studied emerging types of magic. It occurred to her that Zaphkiel III must have been a priest of Athena's.

Demeter's gift was that of natural witchcraft. Her descendants were experts on plants and potions who used the natural world and its elements in their magic - as opposed to everyone else whose power emanated in themselves alone.

Where Demeter could make healing potions, Aphrodite's descendants simply healed by the nature of who they were. They had a natural gift for profound empathy and truly unconditional love, which apparently gave them healing powers over others. Jeremy had mentioned that Aphrodite herself was dead. Lyla made a mental note to ask him about it.

And finally, there was Poseidon. He seemed the most powerful of all. Apparently, he'd had the power to undo events that had already been set into motion. She presumed he could have gone to 1933 Germany and simply erased Adolf Hitler. But his power had come at a great cost. First of all, he and his priests could only very rarely use it, so they had to make it count. And secondly, his descendants were long lived and powerful, but they were sterile. In other words, all of them were directly related to Poseidon himself, but now that their father had been killed, they were dying out.

4

Her study was interrupted by Azrael's arrival. This time he hadn't bothered to hide his wings, and Lyla noticed that they were larger than Jeremy's and covered in shining grey feathers. She hated to admit it, but they were beautiful. She gauged that it had been about a day since their first meeting, and she hadn't missed his grumpy presence. Without preamble, he walked up to her, dropped some clothes on her bedside table and said, "Get changed. You need another day to fully recover, but we'll start with some of your training today. I'll give you a tour of the compound and we'll talk about what you've been reading."

She looked up at him and wondered what would happen if she refused to follow the schedule he'd clearly determined for her. She was tempted to spite him, but her curiosity about her surroundings won out. She'd been stuck in bed for two days now and needed to hold on to any diversion possible so she wouldn't think about Max. So, she grabbed the clothes and crossed over to the bathroom without a word.

She'd perfected the art of distraction since her parent's

death. That first, original trauma had nearly killed her. Would have killed her, if it weren't for the little boy with the big heart and the beautiful grin. Later, she'd learned there was only one way to survive: keep moving. And she had. Every time she'd been abandoned by another family, every time new foster parents had turned out to be as vile as the last, every time she'd been used, abused... she'd simply kept moving. It had become her mantra. She knew it was denial, pure and simple. What was she moving toward? Max had always been her reason to stay alive. There no longer was a reason. So why not give up?

She didn't like the answer to that question, but she knew it to be true: as much as she was terrified of life without Max, she was even more scared of dying. Dying alongside him, killing herself after what she'd done to him, would have been the decent thing to do. But she was too much of a coward. He'd always been the stronger one between the two of them, the better one. While she was useless dead weight.

Bent over the bathroom sink, clutching its edges tight, unable to suck breath into her lungs, she kept repeating, *Keep moving, keep moving, keep moving*, in her head.

She couldn't breathe. She was dying. She'd get what she deserved. Was it what she deserved? Maybe she deserved to live and suffer. To miss Max every single day. To have her heart broken every morning when she realized he was gone. Maybe that was her punishment for being too weak to die.

Tears were streaming down her face now, and, still, no air would make it down her pipes. Slowly, she felt herself crumble to the floor. And then she heard the door open. She'd forgotten to lock it. Shit, someone was walking in on her panic attack.

She looked up and saw Jeremy step in, a horrified look on his face. For the first time since she'd met him, he seemed angry, disgusted. Who wouldn't be at the sight of her?

He crouched down next to her, seeming to deliberate something for a moment. Then he touched her temple and all the pain and terror seeped out of her, leaving her feeling light and free. Her airways opened up again and she gulped in a deep breath. Staring at him, she exclaimed, "You took my pain away... You shouldn't have done that!" irrationally angry that he'd deprived her of her burden.

"No, I shouldn't have," he answered seriously. "It's only temporary. It'll come back, and it'll be worse when it does. But I didn't think you'd want Azrael to see you like this."

"I don't care what Azrael thinks of me!" she lied. She wasn't sure why, but she did care. Maybe she just wanted to keep the last shreds of her dignity.

"You should. Your life is hard enough as it is," he replied, impassively.

Well, that was ominous.

"Fine. Thanks. Now that I feel nothing, may I have some privacy?" she asked, waving her clothes in his face.

"Of course," he replied. "Just one more thing." He waved a hand in front of her face. "A little glamour to cover up your tears," he added and left the room.

Lyla looked in the mirror and found her face looking fresh, any blotchy evidence of her meltdown erased. Jeremy had used magic to change her appearance, and she hadn't felt a thing. Between that and the brute waiting for her outside, she was thoroughly out of her depth. But her thoughts were also clear for the first time since Max's death. She knew what had happened, remembered every moment of it. But she had no emotional reaction to the memory whatsoever. Her mind felt eerily cold and calculated since Jeremy had touched her. And she figured there was nothing left to it than to get changed and go get some questions answered by the big guy.

She'd been grateful that she'd been left in the clothes she'd worn the day of the attack. Jeremy hadn't pushed for her to get changed, even though it was entirely irrational of her to be so possessive of her sweat and blood-stained shirt and pants. Now, she couldn't wait to get rid of them. What a silly thing to be attached to, Max's blood, the last evidence of his existence. She threw them in the trash and pulled on the pants and shirt Azrael had provided. They were made of an odd material, warm and yet so light that she could barely feel it on her skin. The shirt had two elongated openings in the back. Since angels could pull their wings in and out at will, she assumed they made them disappear to get dressed, and then made them reappear through the slits in the back of their clothes. How strange. She looked forward to using hers. It would be delightful to learn to use her power, if only so she could shred the monsters who'd gotten Max killed into tiny little pieces.

Lyla walked out of the bathroom with a smile on her face. She looked around and noticed for the first time how crowded the ward was. Her head had been too muddled up to realize it before, but there were injured angels lying in half the beds. Some of them were conscious and some passed out, but all of them looked human and had their wings tucked away. She also noticed that Jeremy was far from the only person tending to them; there were half a dozen additional healers rushing from bed to bed, working their magic on the unconscious angels and speaking to the ones who were awake. She'd been in such a haze she hadn't noticed any of the busyness of the place.

Tucking away the information, Lyla approached Azrael. His eyebrows drew together at the sight of her. She answered his quizzical look with a peppy, "Good to go!"

The large angel looked over at Jeremy, who ducked away guiltily. So, Azrael knew what Jeremy had done and didn't care for it. He shook his head and started out of the room.

She hadn't paid attention in the hospital ward, but now realized that the place was lit by torches hanging on the walls, each giving out more light than seemed possible.

Lyla followed him out as he proceeded to explain that they were on the ground floor of the compound, which they called the temple. It was where the priests of Hermes' lived and worked. The upper floors had individual cells, as the priests' sleeping quarters were called (hers was to be cell 316). The lower floor housed the hospital, the kitchens (which looked like a warmer version of her high school cafeteria), the gym (a massive room full of weights, heavy bags, and constructions she couldn't identify), and one of the largest libraries she'd ever seen. And then there was the courtyard. It was large and had several fighting rings surrounded by wooden and canvas dummies for striking practice. It also held an entire wall holding knives, swords, and all sorts of medieval looking weapons she'd never seen outside the movies. Looking up from the courtyard, she noticed that every window had a small balcony attached to it, for landing she supposed. Instead of elevator shafts, each staircase was also built around a large empty space in which angels could simply fly up to any floor.

As they walked around the compound, other angels respectfully nodded their heads to Azrael, but she couldn't help noting that there was an odd mixture of fear and contempt in their eyes.

On their way back to the library, he informed her that the highest floor housed offices, Hermes' quarters, and the war room. They were apparently off limits to her. Well then...

When they sat down at a table in the currently empty library, Azrael asked, "Any questions?"

"Yes," she answered. "Where are we?"

"On an island off the coast of Greenland. The temple is part of a town where Hermes' descendants live peacefully. We have priests of Aphrodite's working in the hospital, and priests of Athena's in the library, and others come in and out. But mostly this place is for Hermes' bloodline. There's an entire town outside the compound. A few Hephaestus angels have weaponry shops there too. Not all of us decide to follow the blood's calling. And not all of those who do, make the cut. This island is a safe place for any descendant of Hermes', so they don't have to hide out in the human world. Each God has a place like this somewhere in the world, tucked away under veils that hide it from humans."

So, the big brute was capable of stringing together more than two sentences.

"Wait, are you saying humans have no idea this island is here? How did we get here?" she asked. "We're a long way from Kansas..."

The joke went entirely over his head.

"Each God has a territory that is strictly under their protection," Azrael answered in his annoyingly dry voice. "There is enough magic around it that it creates a glamour of its own. Humans who get close just feel a strong urge to change direction. And the Gods themselves veil the entire place so the Fallen won't find us. As for how we got here... we traveled through a portal," he added.

"A what, now?"

"A portal. Only priests regularly venture into the human world. If we're on a mission of no urgency, we'll fly to our destination. If we need to make it somewhere instantly, we use a portal. Portal magic is unique to the Gods. The one in the war room can take any of us directly to anywhere we might need to go."

"A portal that takes you wherever you want to go? How?" she asked.

"I don't know. I don't make it a habit to second guess Hermes. But if you'd like to get your head bit off, you go right ahead," Azrael retorted.

"I'm terribly intimidated," she answered, faking a shiver. "I've never dealt with threatening authority figures before, you know?"

"Not like this, you haven't. And you wouldn't be joking around if Jeremy hadn't..." he trailed off, then sighed and shook his head.

"Yeah, I'd be shaking in my boots if I was wearing any," she deflected, and added, all business, "I have more questions."

Azrael looked furious, but he bit back whatever reply he wanted to give her and simply waited for her to go on.

"I gather that every bloodline has slightly different powers. What are yours? And what's the point of this whole place?" Lyla asked.

"The point," he started, clearly hanging on to the last threads of his patience, "is that without us humanity would be wiped out by monsters. They usually run in packs, but you were lucky to only face a single one. If I hadn't been there, it would have torn you apart before you knew what was happening."

In an oddly detached way, she realized that the mention of the monster that had annihilated Max and almost killed her too, didn't make her feel anything.

"We train in regular combat," Azrael continued, "but we also inherited raw power from Hermes. Our magic is not like that of most angels, which is geared toward creation. Demeter's power for instance lies in the making of magical potions and spells. Hephaestus is capable of crafting weapons to carry magic itself in them. Aphrodite's is the power of healing that which is broken. Hermes' magic can be destructive or creative. When we apply it in combat, it has an impact on the world, the power to change it so to speak. We aren't supposed to apply it to fate itself as Poseidon's priests can. Or to nature as Demeter's do. Ours is meant to be applied to beings that refuse to repent and change their ways. We can persuade lost souls or vanquish them in battles of will. As for how it expresses itself, that depends on the priest, but we use our wings to send our power into the world."

"...or we scream..." she started, remembering her instinctive reaction to the demon that had murdered Max.

Azrael hesitated. That was a first.

"Sonic attacks are rare. In fact, I couldn't find any record of a priest of Hermes' using one before," he said, slowly. "Maybe it was a fluke. We'll start your training with the use of your wings and graduate to more difficult things later."

"Well, it's not exactly like it did me much good against the demon, is it?" Lyla answered, laughing.

For a split second she could have sworn she saw ire in Azrael's eyes. Then he blinked and it was gone. "Of course, it did. You greatly injured the demon."

"What are you talking about? It looked at me as if it was about to eat me."

"It was about to eat you. But you blew off its legs and half its shell. It wouldn't have survived the attack," Azrael answered.

"I don't remember that..."

"As I told you that day, you threw all your power at that demon. It's a miracle you survived at all. You were probably too dazed to see straight. But I assure you that you mortally wounded the beast."

Lyla wished she had a cocky response to that, but she was baffled. The memory itself of fighting the monster – since apparently that's what she'd done – suddenly made her dizzy. Through the fog of her memory, she asked, "Why were you there?"

"After years of searching for you, Hermes finally found you a few weeks ago," he answered, carefully. "We'd been monitoring and following you, looking after your safety, while he came up with a plan to introduce you to our world."

"The old lady–"

Azrael nodded. "Jeremy in disguise." For the first time, he smiled at her. She hated it. His smile was sad and full of pity.

Looking at that smile, she was struck in the chest with a sudden burst of fury. They'd been poking around her life, guarding her maybe, but also intruding. She knew she should be grateful to Azrael for saving her life, but she felt irrationally angry that others had been speaking of her and making decisions that ultimately led to her having no choice as to how she'd live her life. As fast as the anger had risen in her, it subsided and gave way to a sudden wave of shame. That Azrael had seen her at her weakest, that he'd seen Max's body in pieces, was abhorrent to her.

She abruptly got up, deciding she'd had enough for one day. The big guy followed suit and took her back to the hospital without a word. As she got back into bed and turned away, she heard him whisper to Jeremy, "She's slowly coming off it. Well done." He sounded furious. Without waiting for an answer, he left the ward.

Before she had time to process her meeting with Azrael, Lyla felt Jeremy's gentle hand on her shoulder.

"Sweetheart, get up. Your father is here to meet you."

5

When Lyla sat up, she almost screamed. The thing approaching her from the door looked nothing like a Greek god or a biblical angel. Hermes was seven feet tall, with massive snow-white wings dragging on the floor behind him. His head, which looked bald at first glance, was covered in down, the same bronze color as his skin. His eyes were those of a raptor, yellow with massive black pupils, currently focused on her. They held the same intelligent, yet cold and uncaring look as those of a bird of prey. And the similarity didn't end there. She noticed that he had no ears; instead, there were two holes in his temples. And as if all that wasn't enough, his fingers were tipped in brutally sharp claws instead of nails.

He sat down at the edge of her bed without asking for permission and opened his mouth, revealing canines reminiscent of a saber-toothed tiger's. Lyla's body went into immediate survival mode. She felt her heart pound in her throat and her breathing accelerate, as she swallowed, looked at the being in front of her, and tried to say hello, the sounds getting stuck on the way out.

He regarded her for a while before explaining, "I've come

to assess your power," in the strangest voice she'd ever heard. She blinked, processing the experience, and realized it wasn't his voice. His voice was that of any bass. It was the fact that it echoed, every syllable resonating for a second longer than it should.

Lyla stared at him, unable to form words.

"Well," he asked, impatiently. "What can you do? How has your magic expressed itself?"

That echo was so unsettling, it took her a moment to answer. After a couple of failed attempts, she murmured, "It hasn't. I can't do anything."

"That's impossible." He seemed angry now. "Show me your wings," he ordered, in an imperial tone.

"I don't know how," she whispered, looking away.

She wanted to retreat, to shrink away from this inhuman presence, but there was nowhere to go. He cocked his head to the side, and suddenly looked very much like he was about to pounce. Then he flared his wings and pulled his hand into a fist, as if drawing something out of her.

Lyla felt an excruciating pain flare up in her back. She screamed and tears made their way down her cheeks as her back broke open. Bones crunched like in old school werewolf movies, as something started growing out of her. Two limbs she'd never known she had, emerged, alien, unfamiliar and weak from lack of use. As the pain kept lighting her back on fire, she looked to the side and saw a white wing grow toward the floor.

When the pain finally subsided, she was hunched over, breathing heavily. At her sides hung her new appendages. White feathered like everyone else's here, hers were covered in blood and hung limply at her sides.

"Now hold them up," Hermes said, coldly.

She tried to move these strange new limbs, but she couldn't

even lift them an inch. After a moment, she admitted, "I can't." Her father's fury crackled like electricity in the air, and she felt the eyes of everyone in the ward on her now. She knew she should be angry at the public humiliation, but she hurt too much to even think about it.

"Fold them back in, at least," Hermes ordered. She tried. In vain. She looked at him through her tears, then hung her head, wishing she could disappear.

Finally, he stood, a disgusted look on his face, and said, "A child of mine, who can't make basic use of her wings! What a disgrace." He turned on his heel and left, slamming the door behind him.

Without looking up, Lyla peeked around the ward, noticing heads turn away, pretending they hadn't avidly watched the scene. Shame washed over her. She hadn't had time to process the fact that she still had a living parent. She hadn't had time to imagine what it would be like to meet him, to wonder if she'd still childishly hope for someone to protect her and make her feel safe. But she certainly hadn't imagined this.

She'd had enough rejection in childhood to last a lifetime, and she'd set out into adulthood, determined never to feel that kind of pain again. She wanted to say that Hermes was nothing to her, that she didn't care what he thought of her. But she did. She cared that yet another parent had decided she was worthless. And had chosen to humiliate her in public.

To make it worse, this episode had washed away any remnants of Jeremy's magic. As if for the first time, she remembered her pain over Max's death, the horror of his mutilated body, her abject loneliness and terror at having to live without him.

Lyla doubled over, her vision going black, unable to breathe. Until she felt a familiar hand on her arm. It felt like sunlight after the darkest of nights, and she hung on to that lifeline for dear life. Slowly, Jeremy's presence grounded her enough to sit up and breathe. Never stopping the contact between them, he put his other hand on her cheek and wiped away her tears with his thumb.

"I'm so sorry," he said. "I had no idea he'd come today. If I'd known, I'd never have taken your feelings away like I did."

She vaguely heard him, but her grief was a rushing in her ears, an ocean she'd keep on drowning in until she finally could join the dead in oblivion. Jeremy forced her chin up, so she'd look him in the eyes.

"Look at me," he said. "My hands. I know they feel warm to you. Focus on them."

She did. It helped clear her head enough to at least remember where she was. The pain was too much, it would kill her, she was sure of it. "Can you help me sleep again?" she asked, ashamed of how helpless she sounded.

"I'm sorry, sweetheart, I can't." When he saw the despair in her eyes, he gently added, "I've already messed with your emotions once today. I shouldn't go into your brain again so soon. I'm so sorry."

People said they were sorry all the time, but being sorry meant that you felt sorrow. It was the most misused expression in the English language. When Jeremy said it though, there was genuine sorrow emanating from him. He gently ran his thumb back and forth on her cheekbone and said, "I'm not going to leave you alone though. I promise. First, let's get you into another bed, your sheets are soaked in blood."

Never letting go of her, he stood up, took her hands, and gently helped her stand. She nearly tumbled back as she did so. Her wings were so heavy they dragged her upper body back. Patiently, he helped her to the next empty bed, pulled back the covers and gently guided her down onto her belly. The back of her clothes was wet and sticky, but Jeremy didn't seem to think that was a priority. Always keeping at least one hand on her skin, he gently pulled the covers over her and sat down on a chair where she could see him. He held her hand in one of his and caressed her hair with the other.

"When you fall asleep, your wings will fold right back in. Close your eyes. I'll be right here. I'm not going anywhere. I promise."

She knew there were things she was meant to think about, to process. But his command made her forget all of them. She closed her eyes and simply felt the soothing caress of his hand, through her hair.

For just a moment, she allowed herself to imagine that those hands belonged to someone else. That she was at home, going to sleep with the one person that meant everything to her, that tomorrow she'd get up to argue over whether the eggs should be scrambled or fried, and that she'd end up frying them because he always let her win.

"Good night, Max," she heard herself say.

6

Jeremy's face was the first thing she saw when she opened her eyes the next day. He was asleep, crumpled in a chair, his head leaning against the wall behind him, still holding her hand. The window – this wasn't the hospital. Panicked, Lyla realized how small the room was. There was a single bed, a chair with a tiny desk, a small wardrobe, and barely enough room to stretch. And Jeremy sat between her and the exit. She'd trusted him these last few days, but that didn't mean she wanted to be alone in a small room with him.

Ever so slowly, Lyla withdrew her hand from his. As she slipped out from under the covers, he screwed up his face, muttering something under his breath. He looked pained. Was he having a nightmare? Sitting up, Lyla hesitated. She didn't want to be unkind to Jeremy by showing him her unease. He'd done nothing to deserve it. But old habits die hard. Biting her lip, she placed a foot onto the hardwood floor. It creaked as she shifted her weight onto it, and Jeremy's eyes snapped open.

Lyla froze, fighting the instinct to flee. Looking at his face, she noticed dark shadows under his deep blue eyes. Those hadn't been there when she'd first met him three days ago, had they?

Jeremy frowned at her defensive position, then, registering her unease, he lifted both hands and ever so slightly hunched his shoulders, making himself smaller.

"This is your cell, Lyla," he said in a tone she'd heard soothe skittish horses. "I carried you over here last night, because I didn't think you'd want to wake up with everyone else in the ward. But coming to in a strange room... I didn't think... My apologies."

Lyla forced herself to take a few deep breaths and to sit back down. She'd overreacted. Over the years, she'd learned to listen to her instincts about people. She'd noticed a pattern in her foster homes: she'd always been able to tell what kind of people she'd been saddled with long before they'd laid a hand on her. She'd honed those instincts, learning that danger was often quite predictable, if not always avoidable. Jeremy, however, didn't feel like that. He was one of the few people she'd ever met who felt entirely safe.

Consciously slowing her breathing, Lyla looked down at the floor and said, "I'm sorry."

"Don't apologize. It's my fault. I didn't know that you'd-" he cut himself off.

She looked away. *Please, don't finish that sentence.*

"I wasn't thinking," he finished. Getting up and purposely stepping away from her, he added, "Let me give you some privacy. Everything you need should be in the wardrobe or in the adjoining bathroom. I'll be back in half an hour with breakfast."

The silence that followed his exit rang in Lyla's ears. For the first time since her life had ended, she was alone. The thought almost crushed her.

She was all alone.

She got up and looked out the window. Angels trained in

the yard, not only in and around several fighting rings down on the ground, but also at various levels up in the air. The sight was spectacular enough to distract her for a moment. Angels, with large white wings swooped around, wrestling each other in midair, until one of them descended back to the crowd to find a new sparring partner. She looked up and saw a pair of angels, facing off on each other, about six feet apart. They were flaring and flapping their wings in each other's direction. And every time one of them did, the other ducked or weaved as if dodging a physical hit. When they were too slow to avoid the impact, they'd swing through the air, knocked back by a very real force. They must be throwing magic at each other, she realized with wonder. She couldn't see the power, only it's origin and impact points, but there was no doubt that it was real.

This strange world had replaced her own. She'd have given anything to get a do over, to tell Max she loved him, and to leave town with him on the morning he'd asked.

But something tied her to this place. She'd realized it the day before, when her head had been clear. And though all her pain and suffering had returned, she couldn't forget that moment of clarity: as Azrael had answered her questions, something had felt profoundly right, something had told her that she was anchored to this place, whether she wanted it or not. That she'd always been. That, one way or another, it had been unavoidable for her to wind up here.

She felt it again now, looking at the magnificent creatures soaring around the courtyard.

How could she feel a sense of purpose, when her heart was shattering into millions of pieces over and over again every day?

Maybe it was survival. *Keep moving.* At any cost. Actively pushing the pain to the back of her mind, she explored the bathroom and took her first bath in what felt like an eternity, wondering what the plumbing system was like, considering the rest of the temple looked so medieval. It wasn't luxurious by any stretch of the imagination, but it had all the necessities, and she'd seen much, much worse. When she toweled off, she dared a look at her back in the mirror. It felt bruised, but the only evidence of last night's encounter with her father were two straight, faded scars, running down the upper half of her back along the sides of her spine.

The wardrobe had all the necessary clothes for a priestess too: some of the same uniforms she'd spotted walking around yesterday – dark colored form fitting pants and tops that, while extremely light, felt as sturdy in her hands as the chainmail Max had once jokingly tried out at a Renaissance Faire – and a couple of what she assumed angels considered casual outfits: leggings and backless tops. Testing her theory, she grabbed some scissors in the bathroom and attempted to stab the training clothes. She couldn't cut through them. Next, she put them on and found out that they fit her to perfection.

As promised, Jeremy returned with breakfast. He sat down on the ground, his wings draped over the floor to his sides, making sure she had a straight path to the exit, while Lyla ate at the small table.

"How are you feeling today?" he asked.

"Sore. My wings... it hurt when they came out. You didn't bleed when you showed me yours," she queried.

"What you experienced last night – it's only like that the very first time. Normally, when angels are born, they scream, much like humans, and then their wings pop out for the first time, and they scream some more. It's never painful again after that. All I can think is that the Fallen put some sort of suppression spell on you, and that's why your wings never manifested in the first place. I'm sorry you had such a painful experience."

He paused, then added, "Our wings, they're a point of pride and joy. They're never supposed to be an object of pain, or shame. I know you have a lot to catch up on, but I hope you can grow to love them. They are at the very core of what we are." He regarded her thoughtfully. Not with pity as Azrael had, but with compassion, as if he was truly there with her in this moment, accepting everything she was.

She didn't want to talk about her encounter with Hermes. Sensing that, Jeremy began telling her about her schedule instead. Today was a late start, but she was to be in the courtyard at six every morning. She'd begin by training in combat with Azrael. After lunch, she was to study any of the history books provided for her in her room, or in the library. And late afternoons would be spent in a room off the gym, where Azrael would teach her about magic. She nodded. *Keep moving.*

Interrupting her attempt at avoidance, Jeremy probed, "Lyla, how are you feeling, emotionally? I know it's only been a few days and a lot is being thrown at you. You can't possibly be all right."

"I'm not," she answered truthfully. "But I have a lot of practice in survival. And the only way I'll survive is by staying busy. I got a brief reprieve yesterday, my head was clear for an hour, but afterward..."

"My timing was terrible. I used magic on you that we almost never apply to fellow angels. I knew your pain would come back tenfold, but when I saw you on the bathroom floor... Azrael was waiting, and I was at a loss..." he trailed off.

"I didn't care. For one hour, I didn't care about any of it. Oh god, I threw out the clothes with Max's blood..." A new wave of guilt and grief overcame her, preventing her from swallowing around her eggs. Jeremy immediately grabbed one of her hands, and the pain didn't so much go away as it became more bearable.

"I recovered them for you. They're in the bottom drawer of your wardrobe. I figured, you might want them back," he said, squeezing her hand and pulling away again.

She looked down at him, unable to express her gratitude that he'd saved the last bit of evidence of Max's ordeal. Instead, she asked, "I've only met Hermes and Azrael, but they're so... cold. Why are you so much more human than everything else in this place?"

At that, Jeremy snorted. "Aphrodite's priests are not allowed to take their vows until they've lived amongst humans for at least one year. We're the only ones who do it. Even though we wind up healing angels mostly, it's supposed to teach us both humility and the depth with which our charges feel. It's - what do humans call it? - an internship of sorts. I spent my year working in a hospital. In the end, I think what I mostly learned, is that we're all alike. We all hope and dream and love, and ultimately die. Aphrodite's priests are born with a natural capacity for empathy, but nothing will deepen it like witnessing the struggles of humans. Besides, I probably picked up a few idioms along the way that make me more accessible to you," he added with a smile.

"Some of us never return," he continued. "They love it so much in the human world, they become teachers. Over the millennia, some of them have even been worshipped as gurus by humanity. I'd be lying if I said I hadn't considered staying myself. But ultimately, I wasn't willing to forego the use of my wings. Besides, my mother died while I was away, and it made me realize that I was needed here in the angels' trenches."

The depth of his grief was unmistakable, but he cut her off before she could say anything. "Yes, I'm an orphan too. But I haven't been through nearly as much as you have. Not that I presume to know what you've endured, but if the Fallen were the ones orchestrating your life, I can't even imagine the things you've survived."

Lyla still couldn't grapple with the idea that the Fallen had been pulling the strings on her entire life. "Did they kill my parents?" she asked before she could stop herself. She wasn't sure she wanted to hear the answer.

"They must have. And then, I can only assume that they set you up in increasingly difficult situations." Now that she thought about it, it was true. Every home she'd been in had been worse than the last.

"But why? Forget the fact that they're after a power I seriously doubt I have. Why not just raise me themselves?" she asked.

Jeremy took a moment before he answered. "The Fallen aren't exactly known for patiently nurturing creatures from the ground up. The only experiment of theirs that stuck were the demons, the only creatures they were able to make as a done product. With you, they'd have had to slowly raise you. They chose cruelty instead. Pawned you off for the years in which you wouldn't be of any use to them and tried to break you in the meantime."

"Break me?" she asked.

"Most people don't make it out of a childhood like yours intact. They hoped that the cruelty you endured would chisel away at your humanity and make you easier to turn."

"In that case, they win. They did break me."

Jeremy sat up straight and looked at her with such intensity, it was unsettling. "No, they didn't. Lyla, listen to me very carefully. I know you're reeling in pain right now, but the very fact that you can feel what you're feeling, that you care, that you are still able to love with all your heart, means that they failed. They can hurt you. They can torture you. But your heart is yours.

They can never take that from you."

She could almost hear Max echoing Jeremy's words from the depths of her soul. *He's right. As long as you feel, as long as you care, you're still alive, beautiful girl.*

And yet...

"But I'm all alone now," she answered, knowing how pathetic she sounded.

"No, you're not," Jeremy replied, grabbing her again, and holding up their joined hands. "Does this feel like you're alone? I promise you that you'll find more support here than you realize. Even with Azrael. Believe me, his bark is a lot worse than his bite."

7

A couple of hours later, Lyla wanted to thoroughly disagree with Jeremy's assessment. As far as she could tell, Azrael was an arrogant, dismissive ass. Standing in a corner of the large courtyard, apart from the training angels, she'd been receiving basic instructions on how to throw a punch for thirty minutes now. He hadn't asked if she knew anything about hand-to-hand combat, so she hadn't said anything. Instead, she'd patiently listened, picturing Max's face if he could see her, while Azrael droned on and on about the position of her feet, how to make a proper fist, and which knuckles to punch with, so she wouldn't break her hand.

When he finally held up a pad for her to punch, patronizingly instructing her on jabbing twice with her left, and following with a cross from her right side, she wanted to answer, "Yes, Sir, and I promise to try to twist my dainty little woman fists too!"

Instead, she got into position in front of him, and, quicker than he could blink, punched the pad three times. Her jabs were sharp and precise, while she twisted into the cross with her entire body, giving her power Azrael clearly hadn't expected.

The pad was shaped like a medium sized racket and made of sturdy brown leather, with a painted black target dot and circles. He'd told her that there was a tiny bell on the inside, that would only ring if the target was hit in its very center.

When she punched it, it rang out clearly, three times in a row.

"Like that?" she asked, innocently.

"That wasn't your first punch," he growled, frowning.

"No, it wasn't," she answered, and dropped the smile.

"How long have you been training, and how much?" he asked, that frown of his growing by the second.

"Ten years. Five times a week," she replied, sweetly.

"What kind of fighting?" he went on asking.

She pretended to think about it and, proudly remembering the name Max had come up with, answered, "I believe it was called 'the school of whatever works'."

"You should have said something instead of letting me drone on."

He was fuming now.

"You didn't ask. You saw a tiny, little girl, and decided to make assumptions. Don't worry, it's not the first time a man has underestimated me," she answered with some bite in her voice now.

At that, he stepped right into her space, his wings flaring up behind him, and ducked his head, so they were face to face. He spoke in a quiet, threatening tone, and she could almost feel the power emanating from him. "Let's get a couple of things straight here. First of all, I am not a man, because I'm not human. Secondly, I didn't underestimate you because you're female; I underestimated you because you were raised by humans. I've been saddled with the responsibility of turning you into a proper angel. Believe me, this is going to be a lot easier on you if you follow a few simple rules. The first of which is: Never. Waste. My time. Again."

He waited inches from her face, staring into her eyes. He was so close she could feel his angry breath on her cheeks. She wouldn't back down though. He was trying to intimidate her, and she wouldn't give him that satisfaction. So, she stared right back, not giving him an inch.

Finally, he backed down. Climbing through the ropes that demarcated the nearest fighting ring, he casually threw at her, "Get in here. Let's see what you can do for real."

Two hours later, Lyla couldn't deny the fact that Azrael was a great trainer. He'd dropped the pads and they'd sparred in the ring, just a pair of angels amongst dozens. While so many around them had been training on dummies and pads, countless tiny bells jingling all over the courtyard, like a peculiar musical accompaniment, he hadn't gone easy on her.

Unless she kept her advantage, it didn't matter how much training she had. A guy Azrael's size could beat her so quickly that it was laughable. But Max had taught her to work to her advantage. Speed and well-placed power were all she had to play with. And Azrael had appreciated her knowledge and expertise but had constantly challenged her and kept her off-balance, so she'd keep on working hard.

By the time she'd bathed and met him in the cafeteria, she was in a somewhat kinder mood toward the big guy. They sat down opposite each other, surrounded by warrior angels like Azrael. But as she looked around, she noticed that half of them were women – or females, she guessed. She paused, and suddenly understood.

"You treat females as equals," she said, more to herself than to Azrael. "There's no gender distinction here."

He regarded her for a moment before he answered. "Magic

is a great equalizer. Our males are bigger than the females, but that doesn't mean they're more powerful. Besides, females are the stronger of the species. Not only do they have the power to give life, but they survive pregnancy and birth. Why on earth would we try to subdue them?" He paused, then added, "I've heard about how human men treat their women. It's barbaric."

He didn't expand on his views of misogyny, which didn't surprise her, seeing as he didn't seem to ever use one more word than was necessary. Looking around some more, she asked another question that had been on her mind all day: "Everybody here is similar looking and yet so unique. They - we - are all ethnically ambiguous..." Having grown up in such a race conscious society, it was strange being surrounded by people who looked like her: mixing traits from disparate regions of the world, most of them had tan skin, and none of them could be pinpointed to any ethnicity.

"According to the Ten," Azrael answered, "They used to be the same as humanity. A tribal species, warring over territories, mistreating each other based upon skin color. But they evolved past those prejudices, and wound-up breeding for genetic diversity. Until, they became one unified species, mostly bronze colored with all sorts of features and hair and eye colors. The Ten interbred with humans, but ultimately, we're their progeny, so we look similar to them."

Lyla scoffed, "I always regretted not asking my parents where we came from, because I looked so different from most people. But I guess it's because I'm an angel..."

"The sooner you come to terms with that, the better," he answered and dug into his food, putting a definitive end to the conversation.

But there was one more thing she'd noticed. "Everybody here has white wings... But yours are grey. How come?"

As soon as she'd said it, she regretted asking. Azrael savagely stabbed his meat and looked at her with so much unveiled anger it made her want to retreat.

"If you have to ask that, you clearly have a lot more reading to do," he said, stood up, and walked away, clearing off his tray without another look at her.

Lyla sat at the table, stunned. She thought they'd made progress. She knew he didn't like her and that he resented having to see to her education, but why was he so sensitive about the color of his feathers?

Baffled, she made her way back to her cell, so lost in thought, she almost tripped over Jeremy on the way.

"Hi," he said, standing up from where he'd been sitting outside her cell door. "What happened to you?"

"Azrael-" she began to answer.

"What did he do now?"

"I... I asked him why he has a different wing color from everyone else here, and he got all sensitive," she replied, making her way into the room.

"I see. May I come in?" Jeremy asked, waiting at her door for an invitation.

Lyla nodded and took a seat on her bed. The healer entered, dropping a book he'd brought onto the table and sat down on her one chair, his wings draped over its low back. Things were a lot less tense than earlier that morning. But then, as unusual as it was – when she didn't let fear rule her – things did feel uncharacteristically safe and familiar with Jeremy.

He got comfortable – or as comfortable as one could be in a wooden chair, stuck between a table, a wall, and a bed – took a deep breath, and began.

"I assume by now you've read about the lost children?"

"The bad guys' kids? Yeah, they were mentioned," she replied.

Jeremy winced. "There is a reason, they're called the Fallen's first abandoned experiment. They aren't evil," he explained. "They never followed Lucifer. In fact, they live in their own secluded communities, deep in territories humans avoid. They stay entirely out of our fight. But the angels look down on them. The truth is that they think them inferior due to their lineage."

"Oh. So, angels are racist. It's just not about skin color," Lyla replied, disconcerted.

"It's about wing color actually. On their planet, the hive had black wings. As part of the Gods' punishment, their wings were turned white – presumably to make them more recognizable, and so they'd have to see what they'd done every single day for the rest of their existence. As I've told you before, our wings are deeply ingrained in our identity. What was meant as a symbol of shame for The Ten, became a point of pride for their descendants. Meanwhile, the Fallen's descendants are still born with black wings to this day. And those black wings are the reason angels despise them," he explained.

"But you said, they aren't evil, that they keep to themselves," she replied, indignant.

"They do. And they aren't. The younger generations of angels are more tolerant. But we're long lived and many of us are stuck in tradition and in conservative paradigms. Azrael's mother was a priestess of Hermes'. His father is one of the lost. So, he was born with grey wings," Jeremy continued.

Remembering people's reactions to Azrael, she asked, "Is that why everyone here looks at him the way they do? It's like they're scared of him or something."

"They are. Azrael is here not because of his blood but because of his power. In terms of magic, he's the most powerful priest of Hermes' this temple has seen in over two millennia.

Which is why Hermes made him his general. People fear him. But they also loathe him."

"So, they need his magic, but they don't respect him?" Lyla answered, appalled.

"Oh, they respect him. They respect his power. And they follow his command without question. It's more that they don't invite him to family dinners, and they'd never want their daughters to breed with him."

Lyla wouldn't have thought it possible, but she felt such indignation on behalf of the big guy it made her want to scream. He may be an ass, but he didn't deserve such unfair treatment.

"Where would he be if he wasn't that powerful?" she asked.

"Mixed children are rare, but the lost always take them in. Some of them don't want to be a part of a world in which their two sides are so at odds though. So, they give up their wings forever and go live with humans instead. I lived with five of them during my year in the human world, actually..."

Jeremy adjusted his position and stared out the window for a moment. The look in his eyes was bittersweet.

"So, you don't think they're inferior then," Lyla interrupted.

Jeremy's head snapped right back to her. "Of course not! Azrael is my best friend."

She stored this away, deciding she'd have to unpackage the fact that this kind person in front of her was best friends with the king of grumps some other time. Instead, she asked, "How can you let them treat him like that?"

Jeremy sighed. "It's not as simple as it sounds." Sensing she was about to interrupt and tell him just how simple it was, he held up a hand, and continued, "The conflict between us and the Fallen is worse than it's ever been. Read this book I brought you and you'll understand. Where historically the Fallen would only have had armies of humans on horseback to play with, these days it's chemical weapons and the bomb. There's a reason human history has gotten exponentially bloodier in the last century and a half..."

He trailed off, staring into the distance. "The point is that we can't risk dividing our ranks with an inner revolution. As much as I wish I could advocate for change, I don't have that luxury."

"And Azrael? Why does he serve the angels when he could live with a people that wouldn't blink twice at letting him fuck their daughters?"

"Well, I didn't say Azrael was in short supply of casual sex... But that's really beside the point. He puts up with the angels' backwards ways because he knows that we need him. And he'd never walk away from this fight, knowing he'd be leaving his brothers and sisters to die. It's just not the kind of male he is."

Begrudgingly, Lyla respected Azrael's stance. It didn't make him any more pleasant, but it did explain a lot. And the fact he hadn't left meant he had character.

"I should probably apologize to him..." she started.

"I'd advise against it," Jeremy answered. When she raised an eyebrow, he added, "You didn't do anything wrong. You couldn't have known what your question would bring up. Mentioning it again... Azrael gets enough reminders of the blood that runs through his veins as is. Leave it alone."

It was the most adamant she'd ever seen the healer, which, in turn, brought up a dozen more questions. Before she could ask any, he stood up, gave her a small smile, and left. She couldn't help noticing that he didn't seem entirely steady on his feet.

Lyla stared at the wall for a long time, thinking through everything she'd learned about this place in the last few hours. Suddenly, she remembered an important piece of information Jeremy had dropped: Azrael was Hermes' general.

Her father had assigned his second in command to be her instructor. Why?

8

The book Jeremy had brought over turned out to be the history of the world, from the angels' perspective. It recounted every human conflict she'd ever heard of and some she'd never known about, but – as opposed to her high school history books – described the involvement of the Gods, the Fallen, and the angels in every single one of them. This meant that she wasn't the only one who'd never had control over her own life. The entire human race had no idea of the strings that were being pulled behind the scenes. They were all pawns on a giant chessboard created by aliens who'd picked this planet as one of their playgrounds. She knew that wasn't an entirely fair assessment, but it turned her stomach to think seven billion people believed themselves to be the apex predator on this planet while being pushed around by invisible forces. She wanted to skim through the book as quickly as possible, but Jeremy had inserted a note in very neat handwriting, saying, "Study this in careful detail. It's a tedious read, but you need to understand the inner workings of this conflict."

Tedious was an understatement. It took her three hours to

study the first fifteen pages of the book. Not only did it describe every large conflict humanity had ever known. Most of them had been orchestrated in the shadows and had started long before what her human history books had claimed, snowballing from smaller conflicts into larger ones.

As she read on, Lyla realized that – in the same tradition as the Gods and the Fallen – the angels all named their children after fictional angels from human scripture. And indeed, they had no last names. Reading in more depth about an angel named Dumah, she noticed a mistake in the quoted dates. According to the book, Dumah the First had been a priest of Hades' for over three hundred years. Wrong dates seemed like a bit of a problem for a history book... But as she kept on reading, she saw more and more mentions of centuries old angels.

By the time she made it to her first magic lesson with Azrael, her head was spinning. She walked to the gym, in which male and female angels alike were working out, their wings folded away, which made it look shockingly similar to a human gym, and, as she stepped in, she noticed that every single one of them was looking at her. They knew who she was. Then she realized why they were all frowning: they'd probably heard about Hermes' appraisal of her. Feeling color rise to her cheeks, she ducked her head and crossed the gym to the room in which Jeremy had said her lessons would be taking place.

She pulled open a sliding door and found herself in a small room with a very high ceiling. It had the height of three stories - probably to allow for flying - the floors were covered in comfortable mats, and the lighting was low and soothing.

Azrael stood in the middle of the room, arms crossed, facing her. Did he ever relax? She turned around to slide the doors shut, keenly aware of the fact that she was turning her back on this male she neither liked nor trusted and who generally looked at her like he'd rather be anywhere else in the world than in her presence.

"Whatever it is, get it off your chest. We have work to do," he grunted, without preamble.

She hadn't meant to ask yet, but he wasn't giving her a choice. "I have a question about something I read..."

"Oh great," he answered, sarcastically. "More questions."

Apparently, he hadn't forgotten their earlier exchange, nor had he forgiven her faux pas about his wing color.

"Some of the priests mentioned in the book Jeremy gave me have birth and death dates centuries apart," she began, ignoring his jab.

"And?" he answered, impatiently.

So, he'd make her spell it out, then...

"Well... did they really live that long?"

"By the nature of what priests do, we rarely make it past two hundred. But, yes, occasionally a priest will make it into old age," he replied, as if that was the most normal thing to say.

"Old age? Wait, what exactly is old age for an angel?" she replied, getting dangerously light-headed.

"We've been known to live up to three hundred years," he replied. Seeing the dismay on her face, he added. "Don't worry about it too much. As a priest, your life expectancy is much closer to that of a human. And considering you're still a fledgling at twenty-five, I give you five years tops."

For a moment, she got so hung up on hearing that word again, that she almost didn't register he was telling her that he didn't think she'd survive past thirty. When she realized what he'd said, her face fell. He may think her a lost cause, but that was no reason to be cruel.

Without a smile, Azrael added, "That was a joke. I'm just trying to lighten the mood. Get your shit together, and you'll be just fine."

Now he just pissed her off. Nice of him to try to make a joke, but that was a poor attempt, and he'd gone from his dry brand of humor back to patronizing her so quickly, it gave her whiplash.

And made her want to punch him.

Squaring her shoulders, she stepped further into the room, and said, "Whatever. Aren't you supposed to be teaching me something?"

For a moment, Azrael looked unsettled. Then he sighed and said, "Right. You must start by learning how to pull your wings in and out at will. Is your back still sore from yesterday?"

So, he knew about Hermes' visit. She tried to brush off the heat rising to her cheeks again. Shrugging, she murmured, "It's fine."

"Did Jeremy check on your scars?"

No, he hadn't. He'd been too busy assuaging her unreasonable skittishness to actually do his job. Lyla had a feeling she was about to regret that.

"No," she replied, her voice smaller than she wanted it to be.

Azrael frowned. "He should have. It's rare, but sometimes a fledgling's wings don't come out right the first time, and they wind up with crooked scars on their backs. When that happens, they need to learn to unfold their wings in the exact same way for the rest of their lives. Even the smallest deviation from a straight line, can pose complications."

She thought she'd seen two perfectly straight lines, but would she have noticed any imperfections in her state of mind this morning? Wouldn't it be just her luck to wind up with crooked wings?

"I need to take a look at them," Azrael interrupted her thought-process. Feeling her heart rate speed up, Lyla looked up into his face. Now she definitely wished Jeremy had taken a look. She felt decidedly uneasy about offering her back to the ill-tempered angel.

What she found in his face gave her a measure of comfort though: whatever the reason, he looked just as wary about the prospect of scrutinizing her back.

Controlling her breathing, she slowly turned around. *Get a grip, Lyla, he may act like an ogre, but he hasn't actually tried to hurt you,* she thought to herself. But another voice in her head added a foreboding *yet...* At that, she closed her eyes, and reminded herself, that it didn't really matter whether her front or her back was to Azrael; there was little she could do to defend herself from him, if he wished to harm her.

Fighting to keep an oncoming panic attack at bay, she felt Azrael's huge presence invade her space. His breath tickled her neck as he carefully moved her braids out of the way, causing her throat to close up. But then he opened up one of the slits in the back of her fighting garment with the gentlest of touches. His fingers were calloused, but she hadn't expected them to be so tender. As tense as the situation made her, there was something surprisingly comforting in Azrael's touch. She slowly felt her airways open back up and her breathing even out again.

He carefully traced the line of one scar all the way to her middle back, before moving to the other one and doing the same. Then he stepped away and said, "They look great, you'll be just fine."

Relieved, Lyla turned around to find his face colder than she'd seen it all day. Clenching his jaw, he said, "Enough time wasted. Sit down, and let's start."

Predictably, Azrael began with a lecture. Apparently, no matter how well things progressed with her training, she was not to practice magic on her own, or anywhere outside this room, or with anyone other than him. She was not to speak of it to anyone and she was to keep her training strictly confidential. She wanted to make a joke about not getting his feathers all ruffled, but she had a feeling she'd regret it very quickly if she did.

After the week she'd had, Lyla didn't imagine things could get any more tiresome. But she spent the next three hours sitting cross-legged on the floor, trying to picture her wings growing out of her back, while Azrael insisted she wasn't focused enough.

She had been for the first hour. Hearing her mantra in her head – *Keep moving* – she'd thrown all her energy into focusing on the task at hand. But the more he'd told her that her efforts weren't good enough the more she'd lost her focus, until her thoughts started drifting dangerously close to Max. By the end of their lesson, it was all she could do to keep breathing and try to clear her mind of the painful memories invading it.

Needless to say, she didn't sprout a single feather.

By the time they were done, even Azrael knew better than to berate her. He grunted something about seeing her in the morning and walked out, while Lyla shuffled to her room and fell into bed.

But sleep wouldn't come. Though she was dead tired, she kept thinking about the people she'd left behind. People she could theoretically outlive by centuries. What did Julia, Tania, and Daisy think had happened to her? She hadn't worried about the friends she would have left behind had Max and her run off together, but now it felt like she was failing yet more people.

In theory, she was free to run back to her old life, but she'd be endangering them if she did. It didn't really matter that she didn't have the power the Fallen believed her to possess. They were after her one way or another. And after everything she'd read over the last few days, she knew that anyone she got close to in the human world would wind up just like Max.

Max. The gaping hole in her chest was unrelenting. How much could someone hurt, before it killed them? In a desperate attempt at denial, she imagined herself snuggling into his embrace one more time. She could almost feel his warm chest on her back... his long pale arm thrown over her side, holding her close... his slow breathing on the back of her neck... She closed her eyes and waited until sleep finally came to her.

9

A fter that first day, Lyla started getting into a routine. A mournful routine, but a routine, nonetheless.

Her morning training sessions were the one time she could forget her pain. Listening to the continuous music of priests perfectly hitting their targets, she'd spar and wrestle with the big ogre. Occasionally he'd show her an escape she didn't know. Sometimes he'd even ask about techniques she'd learned from Max. And the combination of continuous motion and endorphins made it impossible for her to think beyond the moment.

She ate her meals in silence in the dining hall, sometimes alone, sometimes staring past Azrael's shoulder.

And in the afternoons, she read and read about every part of history she'd never heard about. Jeremy always visited for at least an hour. She knew he was doing his job, making sure Humpty-Dumpty wasn't shattering into a million pieces, but she appreciated the company, nonetheless. She'd first met him disguised as an old lady who'd seemed in need of company, but now their roles had been reversed. She was holding on by a thread, and he was the one offering her the kindness and patience that was keeping her from breaking entirely.

Her evenings were the most frustrating part of her day. Every night, she'd meditate, focus, and visualize her wings. And every night, absolutely nothing happened. And all the while, Azrael's ever scowling presence made those the three longest hours of the day.

By the time she went to sleep at night, she could barely stand. And yet she could still cry. So, every night, she entered her denial bubble and curled up in bed, pretending Max's loving arms were holding her.

After a few days, Azrael gave up on trying to get her focused and using her imagination, and just decided to piss her off instead.

It had been two days since Jeremy had visited. At his last visit, Lyla had noticed that he looked worse and worse every time she saw him. The last she'd seen him, there had been dark shadows under his eyes, he'd been slouching and absent-minded throughout his visit, and he had almost toppled over when getting up to leave.

As soon as she walked through the door to the practice room, she asked where Jeremy was. Azrael had answered that he was there to train her and that she was, yet again, wasting his precious time. But Lyla couldn't let it go.

"Where is he?" she repeated. "Is he ok?"

The large angel stared at her with those unsettling gold-green eyes, then bit back, "He'll be fine."

"Did something happen to him?" she asked.

"Lyla, let it go," he roared back, his voice rising dangerously now. "Sit down and focus on your wings!"

"No," she dug in her heels, "not until you tell me what happened to him!"

"Lyla, this is your last warning. Sit down and focus your

mind right this minute," he replied, in a dangerously low voice.

Instead of obeying, she crossed her arms and stared at him defiantly.

"Fine. Be like that," he barked. "Jeremy is sick. He's in the hospital. And you'd do well to stay away."

"Stay away? He's been holding my hand through all this shit. I'm not going to stay away when he's the one in need! What happened to him?" she answered, outraged. It was one thing for this troll to rudely boss her around during training hours, but he certainly wasn't going to dictate her comings and goings outside their sessions. She sensed the rage mounting inside her until she was ready to launch herself at him.

"YOU are what happened to him! And over my dead body am I going to let you see him!" he growled back, stopping her in her tracks.

"What's that supposed to mean?"

"It means," he said, slowly stalking toward her, "that he's been trying to heal you and you sucked him dry. It means that you're a needy little fledgling who needs to stop feeling sorry for herself and start dealing with her shit on her own. It means that you better let my friend recover fully or you'll find out just how mean I can really get," he finished, towering over her.

The word "fledgling" was what pushed her over the edge. Using both her palms with full force, she pushed him back a step, startling him, but not stopping to notice.

"You keep calling me that like it's a dirty word," she began. "But a fledgling is just a baby bird. What else am I supposed to be when no one ever told me what I was?"

She was now the one yelling in his face. She was a good head shorter than him, but in this moment, she didn't feel it. "Tell me!" she went on. "When was I supposed to turn myself into a proper adult angel? Was it when I was orphaned at five? Or maybe in one of my nine abusive foster homes? Perhaps between a brutal beating and a foster brother touching me and whispering that I better keep it a secret? Or was it when I was living on the street with my only friend in the world, barely able to eat one meal a day between the two of us? I'm so fucking sorry that I'm an inconvenience to you, Azrael!" she spat, "Believe me, you wouldn't be my first choice of people to spend time with right after I lost everything I ever built for myself and everything I ever cared for. But here we are! So yeah, I've been holding on to Jeremy's kindness, because he's the only one here who gives a shit if I live or die! You clearly have no heart, so you may not realize, but us "fledglings" need just the bare minimum of nurturing to survive."

Azrael blanched with her words, but he quickly recovered. In a gentler voice, he said. "Lyla, look to the side."

"What?!" She was taken back by his words but turned her head reflexively. And at her side, she saw a pristinely white wing, held at perfect tension. The shock made half of her anger disappear. Clearly it had been her rage that had called up her magic, because as soon as it dissipated, her wings fell to the ground, and she nearly toppled back over them.

Azrael caught her in time and helped her into a sitting position. He sat down across from her, looking down at her. As good as it had been to yell at him, she now felt like a deflated balloon. What was she doing telling off this huge male when she couldn't even hold herself up without tripping over her wings?

"I was harsher on you than I needed to be," he started, cautiously. "I apologize."

She lifted her eyebrows at him.

"Don't look at me like that. I admit my wrongs. Truth be told, I'm glad it led to this. You manifested your wings, and flared them in my direction to boot," he added, with a smile.

She bit back the instinct to apologize and appease him. She had meant every word she'd said, and she wouldn't take it back. Instead, she replied, somewhat sheepishly, "So now you just have to piss me off enough every day that I'll pull out my wings?"

Azrael let out a full-throated laughter. "No, I think it'll get easier from here. For now, I'm clearly in the way of your concentration. I will leave you alone for the next couple of hours. Meditate and try to make them fold back in again. I'll be back to check on you."

As he stood, she asked something that had been bothering her for days. "Where do we store them? They're so big..."

"That's because they're partially metaphysical," Azrael answered in his teacher voice. "If you could look into an angel's back, you'd see small baby wings inside their torso. But when we manifest them, they grow in size, more or less proportionally to our magical power."

She couldn't help noticing that his were only second in size to Hermes' own wings. And she'd just screamed in his face. Looking at the beast towering over her, Lyla swallowed and reminded herself that she'd been in her right to express her frustration.

As if sensing her discomfort, Azrael gave her a reassuring smile, and turned to walk away. At the door, he spun around and said, "Jeremy is going to be fine. Just give him a few days to recover." Then he slipped out and gently closed the door behind him.

By the time Azrael returned, Lyla had successfully folded her wings away, confirming her theory that she could focus a lot better without him scowling at her.

Thankfully, his attitude improved over the next few days, and, by the end of the following week, her wings would appear and disappear at will. Her excitement was short-lived though.

At their next lunch, Azrael pointed out that it was now time to learn to stand, walk, and ultimately fight with her wings.

They were waiting in line for food. As usual, most people avoided any proximity to Azrael, but Lyla had started noticing that some of the glances thrown her way had morphed from insulting to assessing to flirtatious – some more overtly than others. She was checking out a male angel, who was blatantly looking her up and down from the other side of the room. He would certainly make for a great distraction from everything that was still weighing on her every time she closed her eyes to go to sleep.

She'd been called promiscuous before, though she didn't entirely understand why being honest about her needs and desires and having them fulfilled by a consenting adult was deemed problematic behavior by others. Deep down inside, she knew that most of her sexual encounters had been a means to regain control over a part of herself that had been taken away from her so long ago. She was still heavily damaged by the things that had been done to her in foster care, as exemplified by her recent freakout over being alone in a room with Jeremy. But every time she chose to have sex with someone felt like she was taking a little bit of her power back – though she knew, it might never be enough.

"Are you listening to me?" Azrael interrupted her train of thought.

"Yeah, yeah," she answered without taking her eyes off the muscled angel in the corner. "Learn how to walk, and then how to fly, like the little baby bird I am."

Azrael let out an exasperated sigh, and took his plate to their table where he ate his entire meal in silence. As he got up to leave, he leaned in close to her and whispered, "Just a word of warning: the angel you are so blatantly ogling? You couldn't have picked a bigger asshole."

Lyla smiled sweetly at him, pretending to weigh his words, and replied, "I think I could have. I could have picked you."

He scoffed, pulled back and left, throwing a "Suit yourself!" over his shoulder.

10

Her morning training hours had been replaced with what felt like physical therapy. Mornings and evenings were now the bane of her existence. Azrael had decided that fighting without wings was insufficient in their work anyhow, so, instead of training in hand-to-hand, they'd walk out of the compound into the dark and cold nearby woods where she'd pull out her wings and proceed to try to lift and flare them, as well as stand, sit, and walk without toppling over. She felt like an old lady being held up by her nurse, and all thoughts of sex with strange angels dissipated as fast as they'd come.

The worst of it was that the physical exhaustion was only a part of her plight. Every time her wings were out, she felt energy seeping out of her. It reminded her of the feeling she'd experienced when reading people's cards or doing healing rituals for them. Back then she hadn't known if it was real or imagined, but she'd always felt as if she was leaking energy out into the world. But now it was amplified a thousandfold, and she could barely hold her eyes open by the time she made it to her second evening session.

Azrael frowned when she met him in the snowed over courtyard. "What's wrong?"

"I'm fine." Her insistence was mitigated by the fact her voice wavered.

"You don't look fine," he growled back. "You look like you're burning up."

She looked up at him and blinked. His outline was blurry, and she couldn't quite form the words to assure him that she needed to train, if only so she wouldn't have to sit alone and think of Max. He put a hand to her forehead and swore. "I knew it. You've been bleeding out your magic and made yourself sick. The Ten be damned, do you have a death wish?"

Lyla wanted to answer that she did, but her legs wouldn't hold her up. Before she knew it, Azrael had scooped her up and was flying toward her balcony.

When she opened her eyes again, she was tucked into bed, the big guy sitting on the edge, holding a freezing cold towel to her forehead and neck. He was murmuring under his breath, but she couldn't make out his words. She was freezing. Why was he torturing her? No, wait. She remembered this. He was trying to lower her temperature. But why him? They had healers here.

"Jeremy," she got out between chattering teeth. "I want Jeremy." As soon as she said it, she felt how true it was. She yearned for Jeremy's touch so badly it ripped something open inside her, and hot tears ran down the sides of her face and into her hair.

Azrael gave her a pained look. Did he hate tending to her that much?

Leaving the wet towel on her forehead, his hands slowly framed her face and started wiping the tears off her temples. More followed, but she couldn't have stopped them if she wanted to.

"The fever is making your emotions run havoc. I'm sorry,

but Jeremy isn't well enough to tend to you. And I'm under strict orders not to let any other healers near you. I'm afraid you're stuck with me." He kept wiping away her steady stream of tears, giving her a pained smile. "You're going to be all right, little one, I promise. I may be a surly bastard, but I would never let anything happen to you."

She wasn't sure why he was being so nice to her, but she let his voice take away the pain. Before she knew it, it lulled her to sleep.

Her dreams were disjointed. She was in a burning house. Then she heard a familiar laugh from the other room. She followed it deeper into the flames, turning the corner to an eight-year-old Max, panic-stricken, struggling against a cop.

They'd been caught, trying to run away. Their first home had been bad, but it was so much better than what was to come. Max had convinced her to escape, but the police had caught up with them within days. They'd talked themselves out of being returned to their previous family. Instead, they'd been sent to separate homes, which is where the true horrors had begun.

She turned around. Max and the burning house were gone. Instead, she was in a freezing cold attic. A boy, years older than her, stood at the door of the room, his back to her. But it wasn't a room, it was a freezer. There was ice crusting her blanket. She knew what the boy wanted. She knew what he'd make her do. She tried to retreat, but it was too late. He turned around, and, as his face came into focus, she realized it had been replaced with Max's.

As she tossed and turned, Lyla kept dreaming of the worst moments of her life and seeing Max's face everywhere. It was the most excruciating torture, seeing her tormentor's faces replaced with his. His grin was twisted into something evil, manipulative. Everywhere she looked, he was luring her deeper into her demise, laughing at her as he did.

Finally, she found something to hold on to, something to pull herself out of this pit of despair. Her right hand was touching something soft. She reached out and dug her hand into that softness. And there, was that voice again. The one that sounded like coming home. She almost drifted off again, until she heard Azrael say, "Please take your hand out of my feathers."

Lyla opened her eyes. It took her a moment to focus them and remember where she was. Azrael was sitting on the edge of her bed, bent over her, his wings draped around her body. She felt cocooned into the safety of his protection. Or maybe she was just that delirious. Then she realized that her right hand was buried deep into his left wing. She let go, but a couple of his grey feathers came off as she did.

Lyla gulped. She'd just torn out Azrael's feathers, and his face was inches away from hers. Surprisingly, he smiled at her. That smile was more genuine than anything she'd ever seen from him.

He pulled back and said, "Your fever broke. At last. Thank the Ten." He closed his eyes and briefly lowered his forehead to hers before straightening out and folding his wings back in.

Lyla was bathed in sweat and starving, but the big guy wouldn't let her go anywhere. For the next two days he sat by her side, brought food to her, and insisted she not lift a finger. He was no less bossy or crotchety than usual, but it was nice to have him take care of her. They barely spoke – what would they have spoken about? – but it didn't bother her to quietly lay next to him.

Two days later, Azrael finally broke the silence to discuss her training. "We need to add a step before we can train your muscles to carry your wings," he told her.

"Oh goodie, another step."

Ignoring her slight, he continued, "You can't seem to help

seeping out magic whenever your wings are spread. We need to work on that, or you'll accidentally kill yourself. I've seen it before. It happens to angels after they survive terrible events. They can't separate from the fear, so their magic tries to shield them against invisible enemies, and they wind up at best getting sick, at worst inadvertently killing themselves."

Lyla blushed and looked away. He was matter-of-factly telling her that she was so screwed up, she couldn't tell safety from danger, and constantly expected the latter. She'd read about the human version of this, people whose post-traumatic stress disorder was so bad, their nervous system was on constant overdrive. This wasn't a conversation she wanted to have with him.

But Azrael wouldn't have it. He grabbed her face and forced her to look at him. Holding her gaze, he said, "There's no shame in having survived hardship. All it means is that you're strong enough to still be standing."

She really didn't want to have this conversation with him. It was bad enough that she suspected Jeremy poked around her heart at will. But she hated it even more when Azrael saw her weaknesses. Grinding her teeth, she held his gaze and nodded, so he'd let her go.

"I need to check on Jeremy," he said, getting up to leave. "I'll see you in the courtyard tomorrow morning. Get some rest."

He turned around at the door, as if to make sure she'd be all right without him, hesitated for a second, then shook his head and walked out.

II

Over the next weeks, Azrael made a visible effort to be less cantankerous. He'd replaced her morning and evening sessions with trust building exercises. From rock climbing, to wrestling, to walking through obstacle courses with her eyes closed and nothing but Azrael's voice to guide her, he was trying to get her to trust him enough that she'd be able to fully relax around him - and ultimately around others. A few days in, he started interrupting their activities time and again to have her manifest her wings. At first, she could only hold her magic in for a few seconds before she'd switch back into survival mode. But over time, the increments in which she could stay centered, focused, and relaxed slowly began increasing. When she was able to keep it up for five minutes at a time, they added her physical therapy to the regimen.

She still spent her afternoons reading, and Jeremy was back to visiting every day. At first, she was more careful around him, but she had a feeling there was nothing she could do to stop him from using his ability on her. So, one day she decided to steer into it instead.

"Jeremy, are you waiting for me to open up? I mean, you come here every day and, unless I have questions about your world, we talk without really saying anything. Are you waiting for some sort of breakthrough where I'll start telling you about my childhood and my nightmares?" she asked him.

"It's your world too now," he answered, thoughtfully looking at her.

"You're dodging my question," she pointed out.

"No, I'm not. I'm just reading you," he answered, slowly turning his head to one side, then the other, as if he was indeed reading her like a book.

"I'm not a human therapist. I'm a healer," he finally said. "Though I do believe that understanding your past is an important tool in freeing yourself from trauma, in my experience there's only one thing that helps people fully heal and move on."

"Yeah? What's that?" she asked, more sarcastically than she'd intended.

"Love."

She wanted to scoff at him, but she knew he was right. They sat in silence for a moment, before he added, "But if you ever want to talk, I'll listen. If you'd like to tell me about your childhood... or about Max..."

The silence grew heavier. Finally, she gathered her courage, to address his offer.

"I don't know if I can. At least not yet," she answered, looking out the window at a pair of angels fighting each other at the level of her room. "I avoid thinking about him all day, so I can keep up with all this - so I can survive. And if for nothing else, so that he didn't die for nothing. But at night-"

She cut herself off, her throat closing up. A tear rolled down her cheek, but she didn't try to hide it from Jeremy. Vulnerability wasn't shameful to him; it was a cherished gift.

"At night," she started again, taking a deep breath, "I imagine that he's holding me. It's the only way I can go to sleep." She turned to look at his eyes, where she found nothing but understanding and acceptance. He didn't say anything. Just looked at her and waited, giving her the choice to keep going or to stop.

"I don't think I'll ever heal from this. He was everything to me. He was my brother. And my best friend. I was in love with him, though I didn't realize it until it was too late. He was who I'd go to when something important happened, who I'd celebrate with, or commiserate with. He was who I planned the future with. He knew everything about me. I felt safe around him. He would have done anything for me. I wish I could be angry at the world for what happened. Or even guilty that it was my fault. But I just really miss him."

It felt good to speak her thoughts, but that was as much as she could air at once. She wiped her tears on her sleeve, and turned back to Jeremy, who waited a moment longer to see if she'd say anything else. Then he replied, "Thank you. For the gift of your thoughts and your trust." He hesitated, before he added, "Feelings morph over time, but we can't change or cancel them. There is one very important thing I need you to understand though: it wasn't your fault."

Lyla shook her head, looking at the floor. "But it was," she said, through new tears. "The demon was there for me. If I hadn't been what I am, it wouldn't have come for me, and Max would never have been in its way."

"I assure you, that Max was bound to die the way he did. There is nothing you could have done to prevent it. Nothing, do you hear me?" She wasn't sure why he spoke with such intensity, but she couldn't help nodding... though she didn't agree with his statement.

"And the last thing you should feel is shame or guilt over

'what you are', as you call it," he continued. "You are in no way responsible for what happened to Max. Or to your parents. Or for any of the things that were done to you."

He kept holding her gaze, and she found it impossible to look away. Then, with a smile, he added, "And you sure aren't responsible for Azrael's foul mood. How is the old curmudgeon treating you?"

Relieved about the broken tension, she smiled, shrugged, and answered, "Better these days. As irritating as he is, he's actually a great teacher."

Not wanting the conversation to circle back to Max, she hurriedly asked a question that had been on her mind for a while. "Did you know Aphrodite?"

Surprised, Jeremy leaned back and took a deep breath. When he didn't immediately answer, Lyla added, "I read that she only died twenty-five years ago. I was wondering if-"

"Yes," he interrupted her, in a low and uncharacteristically sad voice. "I knew her. I knew her rather well, actually."

Lyla felt like she'd stepped onto forbidden territory, but as soon as she wanted to retreat, Jeremy stopped her. "It's all right. You're learning as much as you can, and I'm happy to tell you of my experiences."

He waited a moment, seemingly weighing out where to start with his tale.

"I knew her my whole life," he finally began. "She was killed in a raid on her temple while I was away for my year in the human world. In their myths, the humans focused on the erotic aspect of love, and they turned Aphrodite into the goddess of beauty. Which she was, though she shared the Gods' alien features. But she was so much more than that."

He paused again, seeming lost in distant memories, more affected than Lyla had ever seen him.

"She was love incarnate. It's hard to describe, but her love was... It was like a truth, an unquestionable fact. When someone loves something or someone, there is always the time factor, the changeability of emotions and feelings. Even the most profound love — be it between angels or humans — can be fickle in nature. But Aphrodite's love simply was."

He seemed lost in thought for a moment, before he went on. "She had the power to look into people's minds and hearts - she knew everything that was going on inside you — but by the nature of what she was, she would never have abused her power. She was such a singularly focused force; she could have taken over this world all by herself. Except that she never would have done such a thing. Which is exactly why Ramiel killed her as easily as she did. Aphrodite never used her gifts to manipulate. She could have rewritten the Fallen's mind. But taking away her free will would have spoken against everything she stood for. And she wouldn't have allowed her priests to do anything other than fighting hate with love either..."

He was silent for another moment, before he concluded, "Love may be the most powerful force in the world. But it isn't enough against evil."

Tears were now running freely down Jeremy's cheeks. Lyla had rarely seen men cry, but he didn't seem to think anything of his tears.

"Ramiel overran the island with a horde of demons in the middle of the night. We still don't know how they found the temple, or who betrayed us... The Goddess... she was pregnant with her last heir when I left. That night, she went into labor..." He swallowed. "It was a massacre. No one survived... The only priests of Aphrodite's left are the ones who were in the human world or working in other temples at the time."

For a long while, Jeremy looked down at his hands, regaining his composure.

"I'm so sorry," she said, lamely.

Jeremy smiled, sadly. "Me too," he replied.

Lyla couldn't fathom the loss it had been to the world, for dozens, hundreds, of people like Jeremy to die, let alone their progenitor – love herself.

12

A couple of days later, Lyla and Azrael were trudging through two feet of snow, when he told her he'd come up with a test for her. If she passed, he'd move on to teaching her about actually using her magic, rather than just keeping it in. As much as she wanted to move back indoors and stop coming out into the freezing cold every day, Lyla had rather enjoyed the array of trust-building activities Azrael had come up with over the last few weeks. He was still a hard-ass, and sometimes just a straight up ass; he never failed to remind her that her gaining control over her magic was a matter of life and death, and the more her efforts flagged, the meaner he got about it. But he was overall more pleasant to be around, and he was a master at coming up with dangerous but fun activities to train her control: from climbing trees, to scaling steep cliffs, he kept her on her toes and made it impossible for her to think about her broken heart.

Besides, with Halloween around the corner the days on the island had become extremely short and they'd walk out and back to the temple under the most incredible lights she'd ever seen. The Aurora Borealis was strong here and its magic never ceased to amaze her. Azrael was used to it and didn't seem to realize that the colors and shapes in the sky were mesmerizing, but he allowed her to stare at them for a few minutes at the beginning and end of every day.

When they arrived in a clearing, he ordered her to manifest her wings and approached her with a black cloth in his hand. "Today, your wings are staying out. I'm going to blindfold you and guide you through an obstacle course of sorts. The only thing you need to focus on is not letting your magic leak out of you. Do you trust me?"

He waited for her to lock eyes with him and nod before he walked around behind her, tying the blindfold around her head.

Lyla focused on her breathing. She was safe. Azrael had taught her how to feel into her adult body, to make the distinction between the present and her traumatic memories. When she used his techniques, even the traumatized parts of her brain understood that she was no longer defenseless.

And so, they began. She listened to his calm voice, as he guided her step by step along a path she knew well. She hesitated for only a split second when he diverged from the path and took her into unknown territory, but she proudly realized that her magic hadn't even attempted to manifest.

Next, he made her climb up and down a large tree, guided only by his words. The trickiest part was to keep her wings from getting caught in the branches. She was balancing fairly well now with her new limbs, but she still forgot to take the size of them into account when in tight spaces.

After the tree, Azrael took her to a cave. It was significantly warmer than the outside temperature, which was rather pleasant, but the humidity and the sound of dropping water freaked her out ever so slightly, and her heart rate rose. Remembering the breathing exercise he'd shown her to help slow down her pulse, Lyla stopped and waited until the roaring in her veins slowed.

"Well done," Azrael commented. His rumbling voice, echoed in the cave, and she could tell he was further away now. As he led her deeper in, she sensed the space growing smaller, until he asked her to get down on the ground and belly-crawl through a tight opening. She stopped halfway through, feeling stuck. She'd never liked tight spaces, they reminded her too much of being pinned between a wall and a person. Breathing became difficult, but she didn't allow her magic to flare up.

Azrael didn't make a sound. She knew he was waiting for her on the other side. That he wouldn't leave her there. Realizing that his much larger bulk had made it through this space, she noticed that she wasn't nearly as tightly boxed in as she'd thought, and she continued crawling through to the other side. When Azrael spoke again, telling her to stand up, his voice came from behind her. He told her to keep walking straight, though he himself didn't move. She felt air hit her face and realized that they'd come out on the other side of the cavern. Smelling the ocean, she wondered if she was on a rocky beach, though the waves sounded too distant. Finally, he ordered her to stop and not to move an inch.

"Do you trust me?" he asked again.

"Yes," Lyla answered, not needing to think about it.

"Do you trust that no matter where I led you, you're safe?"

"Yes," she said again, knowing it to be true.

"Take off the blindfold."

She slowly reached up and unbound the cloth from around her head. As she opened her eyes, terror struck her heart. She was standing on a ledge only twice as large as her feet, fifty feet in the air. Under her, the ocean was crashing against the cliff edge. She'd been so razor-sharply focused on Azrael's voice that she'd entirely missed the salty cold winds now hitting her face. Lyla focused, flared her wings to keep her balance, contained her magic, and made a concise effort to look straight ahead and not lose her balance.

"Do you still trust me?" Azrael asked, in that same impassive voice.

"I do."

"If I told you to jump and that I'd catch you, would you do it?" he asked, stepping closer.

She would have. He wasn't her favorite person, but for the last few weeks, he'd safely guided her and caught her every time she'd fallen.

"I would," she answered, her voice steady.

"Jump."

Before thinking about it, her body obeyed his command.

As she looked at the cliffs she was plummeting toward, Lyla's heart jumped into her throat. She'd been on roller coasters before, and her body reacted with the same panic, finding itself in uncontrollable freefall.

But she didn't release her magic. Before she could fully give in to the panic, Azrael flew up behind her, grabbed her by the waist, and they slowly glided toward a snowed over beach where he carefully put her down on her feet.

"Congratulations. You're ready to start working with your magic," Azrael said, giving her one of his rare smiles. "I didn't feel like walking all the way back. This is a short cut to the village. And I'm famished."

Said village reminded her of movies set in medieval times. Every house was old and solid, as if to withstand centuries of weather and life. She noticed that none of the houses were excessively big, but that they all had rooftops and terraces upon which angels could easily land. In fact, while some of them were walking down the cobblestone streets, many angels flew overhead, cutting straight to their destinations. Inside shops, people politely folded their wings away, so as not to take up too much room, but as soon as they exited a store, they'd manifest them and take off into the skies.

There was something so pure and innocent about the beings in this town. She'd read about the God's islands and the villagers. They were the angels who'd opted for a quiet life, away from the fight. They'd lived in these small towns since the very first generation of angels, never knowing war or famine, only ever living in peace and harmony. Though these angels knew the history of their kind, they'd never experienced evil, malice, or greed.

And at the same time, every single one of them was intimidatingly graceful, their white wings lending them an otherworldly intensity, their magic reaching far beyond their physical bodies. These were the true cherubs of the Gods, the purest testimony to their supremacy over flawed humans.

Lyla smelled the tavern, before she spotted it. The scent of wood fire in its multiple chimneys mixed with that of fresh meat and herbs, making her mouth water. It was roomy and loud inside the main room, where many angels leisurely sat. While the compound was always busy and tightly regimented, the angels in this village lived a much more carefree life, though here too, they averted their eyes and went silent when Azrael walked through. He either didn't care or he pretended that he didn't, as he guided Lyla toward a table near a large fireplace where she sat down, the fire warming her back, and realized that everyone was staring at her.

"They aren't used to angels not displaying their wings whenever possible," Azrael explained. Indeed, though the villagers were conscious of tucking them away in tight places, the roomy tavern had specially designed low-cut chairs and stools, from which everyone draped their wings. At a nearby table, two angels flared theirs in rhythm with their heated argument. Lyla almost expected them to start flying off their stools and up toward the high ceiling, until she noticed the placards nailed at intervals along the walls. They read, *No flying allowed. You WILL be expelled if your feet leave the ground.*

She wasn't fully comfortable displaying her wings in front of a crowd, but they wouldn't stop staring, so, ignoring her impostor syndrome, she called them up and lazily draped them over the back of her chair. At that, she saw rounded eyes quickly avert themselves from the pair of them.

"Show off," Azrael said, gesturing to the waitress.

Lyla frowned at him, and he chuckled, "Someone's so busy feeling self-conscious about her wings, she doesn't realize she has the proportionally biggest ones in the room. Present company excepted."

He proceeded to order for the both of them and they waited in silence, unsure what to talk about. This made her so uncomfortable that she attacked her food as soon as it arrived just so she'd have something to keep her hands busy.

Azrael laughed at the vigorous way she inhaled her food. "You really hate uncomfortable silence, don't you?" he said, shaking his head. Embarrassed, Lyla tried to slow down, but it turned out this was the best meal she'd ever had.

Bypassing the awkwardness, she moaned, "I've never had meat that fresh... and..." She interrupted herself, taking another bite. "It tastes like green pastures and sunshine, but that's not possible," she continued, her mouth embarrassingly full.

"It is, when it was killed by a God," he replied. He leaned back and looked at her, gauging her reaction.

"Hermes killed this... venison, I'm eating venison... You're telling me that he personally killed the deer?" she asked.

"Yes," Azrael answered, clearly amused by her confusion.

"But he's running this entire place, and leading an army in a battle for the soul of humanity..."

"He is. And at night, he goes hunting in our woods. The Gods are predators. They have a lot of energy to offload and being cooped up in an office or training guardians so much less powerful than himself leaves him... restless."

"When you say "hunting"," Lyla started, dropping her fork back to her plate, "do you mean with weapons, or do you mean..." she trailed off, waving her fingertips around and gesturing to her own teeth.

Azrael laughed. "I mean with the claws and fangs, yes," he managed, through his chuckles.

It was unsettling thinking that her father truly was a predator through and through. That the Gods were unrivaled both in their magical and physical power.

Azrael finally dug into his food, and said, "There's so much leftover meat from his hunting trips, he provides most of what the tavern serves. Though he usually brings the best cuts to the orphanage on the other side of the village."

"There's an orphanage here?" she asked, starting to eat again.

"Yes, at the foot of the Sacred Mountain. Most of the fledglings there are the children of priests who fell in battle," he said around a mouthful of venison.

She'd noticed the mountain he mentioned. It was high, though on flat terrain, surrounded by small canyons, cliffs, and sharp rocks and seemed to be in constant motion from how much wind surrounded it. She'd been meaning to ask him about it, but this new information about Hermes seemed more important. If he brought the best meat to the village's orphans, he couldn't be all that heartless. And yet, she'd wanted to run screaming from him when she'd met him.

"We rarely get any of the meat at the compound, except on holidays and formal functions..." Azrael interrupted her musings. "Speaking of which... there's a dinner you need to attend tonight," he hurriedly finished.

He looked at his plate, casually cutting his meat. Too casually.

"What sort of dinner?" she asked, carefully.

He avoided her eyes as he said, "The eight remaining Gods get together and strategize a few times a year. This time, it's at our temple. Tonight, they'll wrap up their palaver with an official dinner. All priests must attend."

"Why didn't you tell me sooner?" Lyla asked, wondering what it was, he wasn't telling her.

He looked up from his plate, sighed, and said "Because I didn't want to give you time to overthink it." He paused, swallowed, and pushed his plate away. "It's nothing terribly complicated, but there are a few rules you need to follow. There is a reception of sorts before dinner. The Gods will be sitting on a stage, and – as one of the most recent recruits – you'll be formally introduced. Whatever you do, wear your wings proudly. As you enter the room, head straight toward your father, get down on one knee at the foot of the stage, bow your head and wait. Don't speak unless spoken to, and make sure to use some sort of honorific for your father."

"I feel like I'm meeting the Queen. Am I also not allowed to show them my back?" she joked, though the idea of being presented to Hermes' seven siblings made her wonder if the venison would stay down.

"I'm not sure which human Queen you're speaking of, but there are no greater predators than the Gods and the Fallen. I'd very much suggest not showing them your back, and not look-ing them straight in the eyes either," he answered, now wear-ing his serious face. "The dinner will take place in the adjoin-ing ballroom. The Gods sit at the center table. Everyone else is seated at tables in concentric circles – in pecking order. The most respected warriors and family members are placed nearest to the Gods, so I assume that's where you'll be placed."

She pushed her plate away and closed her trembling hands to fists.

Azrael bit his lip, then said "Just think of it as a mandatory celebration. You passed your test today, you're ready," he added with an encouraging smile. Then he got up, left some coins on the table and headed to the door. They walked back through the cold darkness in silence. When she tried to head to her cell, he stopped her with a hand on her shoulder. "Whatever happens tonight, do not under any circumstance talk to anyone about your training."

He was back to using that aggravating commanding tone of his, but Lyla was too anxious to call up any snark. Instead, she nodded and headed back to her cell, where she found a dress in a garment bag, hanging on the door, and a note in Jeremy's neat handwriting: *I'll pick you up at six.*

13

Lyla hated to admit it, but the dress was magnificent. It looked like a cross between the angels' fighting gear and a human's idea of an evening gown. In the human world, she'd always made sure to go out in clothes she could still fight in. Similarly, this dress allowed for all the motions she'd need to punch, throw an elbow, or kick. It was tight around the front of her torso, close around her neck, but left her arms fully free for motion. Her entire back was bare, allowing for a proud display of her wings. The bottom half flowed just enough to still seem formfitting while allowing her to easily throw a knee or kick out. Her legs being on display made her want to wear a pair of leggings, but angels clearly believed in the freedom that came from showing skin.

A human would have worn high heels with such a dress, but she'd always believed them to be highly impractical. Luckily, Jeremy had dropped off a pair of lace-up boots made of a supple leather. While their heels still gave her backside an attractive curve, the boots didn't much impede her balance.

Keeping with the theme of practicality, Lyla pinned her

dark hair up. She didn't have any makeup, but come to think of it, she hadn't seen any of the angels in the compound or in the village wear any either. Looking into her green eyes in the mirror, she called up her wings and reminded herself, "You're ready for this, Lyla. Azrael and Jeremy wouldn't let you walk into the wolf's den if you couldn't handle it."

As if he'd heard his name, Jeremy knocked on the door. "You look beautiful," he commented simply, before walking her to the top floor in silence, where they got in line behind other angels, some single, some in pairs, some in trios, in front of a large set of wooden double doors.

"I'll walk in with you, then peel off to the side. Azrael told you what to do?" he asked. Lyla nodded.

The angels around them all had a look of serious formality on their faces as they waited their turn to enter, spines straight, wings on display. By the time they reached the large wooden doors, Lyla's heart rate was going through the roof and Jeremy quickly squeezed her hand, whispering, "It's only a formality. Nothing to fear. I'll be close throughout."

Finally, he pushed the door open, and the crowd inside went silent. On the other side of the room were eight Gods, sitting on a stage, Hermes in the middle. Behind them stood eight warriors. Azrael stood behind Hermes, and Lyla realized that they must be the Gods' generals, ready to pounce on any threat.

The sight was breathtaking and terrifying. Lyla felt her pulse thrumming in her neck but kept walking toward them.

All eight of them looked entirely alien. Their white wings were so large, they draped on the floor next to them. They all looked similar to Hermes, but with varied features. One of them, a female, had jet black eyes all the way through, and where her father's hands ended in fingers and claws, hers sported talons. Another, Ares she guessed, sat on his chair in full armor, including a helmet that hid his face entirely. She'd seen pictures of Artemis, she knew that antlers grew out of her head, but nothing had prepared her for the sight of a seven-foot tall, winged female, with predatory cat eyes and sharp antlers sprouting from her forehead.

Yet, the one who unsettled her the most, was the God sitting right by Hermes' side. He didn't have any animal features, beyond his wings and the down on the top of his head. Indeed, he looked like a magnificent human male, tall, muscular, with a chiseled, handsome face. Until he closed his eyes. While his regular eye lids remained open, an extra lid closed over his beautiful blue eyes, like a shutter closing from the outside in. And on this extra lid, there was a second pair of eyes: purple with red pupils, they moved at such a fast speed it was impossible to follow them.

As the combined awe and horror of the various creatures she was looking at shook her to her core, she remembered Azrael's warning, and averted her eyes. When she finally made it to the stage, she dropped to one knee - thankful for the cut of her dress - and bowed her head as her wings draped around her body. The entire room stared at her, and she was glad not to have to look back at those alien, predatory eyes.

"You look bewitching, child," Hermes addressed her in that echoing voice of his.

Feeling the silence as a palpable danger, she answered, "Thank you..." in a small, shaky voice. "Sir," she quickly added, remembering she was supposed to use an honorific.

"Sisters, Brothers," Hermes slowly drawled. "I present to you, my youngest daughter, Lyla, or Lailah."

He put a slightly different emphasis on the second name, catching her by surprise. She wanted to look up at him and ask what he meant but remembered it would be considered an affront. Had he named her himself, before she'd disappeared into the human world? Was hers an angel name too?

Before she could recall the angel names she'd learned about, Hermes went on. "She finally carries her wings with pride. Her training, on the other hand, has been grossly disappointing." He paused for emphasis, then addressed her directly again. "You'd do well to work harder and prove yourself worthy, daughter." The last word was spat out with such dismissal, it made her want to run out of the room. Instead, she controlled her breathing and the angry tears that made their way up her throat, and answered, "I'm sorry, Sir," putting just as much loathing into her address as she'd heard in his.

Hermes turned away and lazily dismissed her with a hand gesture. On shaky legs, Lyla stood, looked at the Gods for a dreadful split second, and walked toward the crowd on her left. By the time she was out of ear shot, she had trouble standing, but a familiar hand snaked its way around her shoulders to hold her up.

"You're doing great," Jeremy whispered in her ear. "Let's check the seating arrangements. I'm sure we won't be sitting too far from each other."

There was a good old fashioned seating chart, hanging in a corner. Her anxiety made her giggle as she looked up at something so trivial. Then she finally found their names.

They were not sitting together. Jeremy was sitting right behind Hermes, while she had been placed on the last circle, as far from the Gods as possible.

"What the–" Jeremy began.

"Whatever. It's ok, I just want this evening over with," she replied, making her way into the mostly empty dining room and taking her seat. Jeremy sat with her until the crowd arrived and loudly took their places.

"This will change, Lyla. I promise. He's just trying to make a point," the healer tried to assuage her.

"Jeremy, it's fine. I don't really care. I just wish I didn't have to attend in the first place. Now go sit with the good kids, will you?"

Jeremy sighed and stood up. Before leaving, he said, "I'll walk you back to your room tonight. Wait for me, all right?"

Lyla sat silently throughout the entire dinner. She noticed the curious eyes on her, as every angel in the room was, yet again, weighing her father's dismissal of her. But she didn't look at them. Not at the angels at other tables, nor at those right next to her. She didn't care what they thought of her. She just wanted to make it back to the comfort of her cell.

Occasionally, she threw an eye at the center table where the Gods spoke loudly, ignoring the presence of dozens upon dozens of their subordinates. Their plates were heaped high with raw meat only, and Lyla almost gagged when she saw them wolf it down. Some were too fast to even watch: one second their plate was full, the next, all that remained was red blood. Others slowly sucked on the flesh they held between their claws or talons.

What infuriated her the most, was that Azrael had not even been granted a seat. Instead, he stood at the door, arms folded in front of him, a common guard dog. Hermes used him for his power but didn't even deem him worthy to eat a meal with the angels.

As soon, as the seated part of the event was over, and Gods and angels started mingling again, Lyla slipped away, avoiding Jeremy altogether. Quietly closing the large wooden doors behind her, she stood in the top floor corridor, tears of rage burning her eyes.

She returned to her cell, and changed into her most comfortable clothes, but her racing mind wouldn't let her sleep. After a couple of hours of tossing and turning and staring at the ceiling, she got out of bed and ran downstairs to sneak into the kitchens.

Though she'd barely touched her food, the meal had been delicious. And she couldn't get the image of Azrael standing watch while they all stuffed their faces out of her head. She'd get him some food. Maybe it was silly, but she knew what it was like not to be allowed to eat good food; she had lived in homes in which she'd been served leftovers while everyone else had a fresh meal, and she'd vowed never to allow such an injustice again.

By the time, she'd made a plate, and poured a glass of wine, the party had long been broken up and she could hear and see the last priests returning to their cells. Slowly enough not to spill any wine, she made her way to Azrael's room on the fifth floor. He'd told her his cell number, in case she ever needed to find him, but she'd never been there.

When she arrived, she hesitated, her heart suddenly beating furiously. She could hear heated voices behind the door, though she couldn't make out what they were saying. God, what if she walked in on Azrael and a female? Or male? She didn't really know what he was into. She felt as if she were intruding, but she carefully placed both food and wine on the floor, gathered her courage and knocked.

Azrael answered the door a moment later. He seemed surprised to see her, but his surprise quickly turned to annoyance. Scowling at her, he sharply asked, "What do you want?"

"I... It was unfair that-"

"Stop," he growled. "The last thing I need right now is a self-pitying fledgling. Go to bed!"

Lyla's stared at him, mouth gaping, for what felt like an eternity, before he closed the door. She thought about leaving the food, but not feeling like being mocked for it the next morning, she crouched down to pick it up. As she stood back up to leave, she heard the door open again. Jeremy slipped out, threw a "Fuck off, Ass-rael" over his shoulder and shut the door behind him.

Jeremy turned toward her, looked at her inquisitively, then noticed the food. He cocked his head to the side and asked, "What's the plate for?"

Lyla sighed. "It's dumb," she replied. "I hated seeing Azrael stand there like a guard dog, while everyone else stuffed their faces."

Jeremy frowned. "What makes you think that—... You know what, never mind. Give me that."

He reached for the plate and glass, which Lyla handed over, confused.

"I'll be right back. Don't go anywhere."

Without an explanation, the healer went back into Azrael's room. Lyla had no idea what was going on, and she couldn't make out their hushed voices, but not wanting to disobey Jeremy, she stood rooted to the ground and waited for his return.

"I'm sorry about all that," he said, stepping out and gesturing back in the general direction of Azrael's room. "He's been a real ass-hat all evening, it's not your fault."

As much as that might be true, it had been no less painful to be called self-pitying yet again. It hurt because she knew it to be true from his perspective. He made enormous sacrifices every single day to serve a people who didn't give much in return. But she couldn't think that selflessly. She'd been at the temple for almost two months, yet she still lived with both feet firmly planted in the past and no desire to belong. Particularly after tonight.

"Is there anything you'd like to talk about, Lyla?" Jeremy

interrupted her thoughts.

"I'm fairly certain you can read my mind, so why do you ask?" she snapped back, more rudely than she'd intended.

"Yes, I can," he answered. "But it isn't polite, so I avoid doing so whenever possible."

"Why are you kind to me, even when I'm being a jerk?" she asked, guiltily.

Jeremy laughed. "Honestly, I can't entirely help it. Besides, I honed my patience skills on that one," he added, hooking a thumb back toward Azrael's door. "You're a kitten in comparison. Now, can I at least walk you back to your cell?"

"Sure," Lyla answered, mollified.

They walked down the stairs in silence, and were about to turn onto her corridor, when they heard raucous voices around the corner.

"...Did you see her introduction? Hermes as good as trashed her in front of the Gods. There's no coming back from that."

She'd heard that voice before. It belonged to the red-haired angel who'd been staring her up and down in the cafeteria that day. He'd been flirting with her since, though she ultimately always turned him down. His name was Michael and he struck her as just as big of a dick as Azrael had warned her, though it was always enjoyable watching the latter's scowls whenever she gave him the time of day.

Lyla immediately halted and pulled Jeremy into the alcove of one of the cell doors. Breathing hard, she glued her back to the door, hoping they wouldn't turn around and notice.

"I knew she was struggling to adapt, but I didn't expect him to send her straight to the bottom of the pecking order. That was brutal," said an unfamiliar voice.

"Weren't you trying to fuck her, Michael?" asked a third voice.

At that, Jeremy stepped away from the door, a fury on his face she'd never seen before. Lyla flung out her arm to hold him in place. The last thing she needed was for the three angels to know they were listening.

"Not anymore, I'm not!" Michael replied, laughing. "You couldn't pay me to fuck a Hermes reject!"

Lyla had to physically restrain Jeremy, who was ready to pounce on them. She looked him in the eyes, through tears of humiliation, and mouthed, *Please, don't*. She felt his muscles reluctantly relax, and he stepped back into the alcove, pulling her into the corner, and enveloping her in his arms, effectively shielding her from view, but – more importantly – attempting to shield her heart.

"Coming from you, that's saying something," the first angel said. "I didn't think anyone was below your standard, Michael!"

The three angels guffawed, and Jeremy's arms tensed around her. Lyla closed her eyes against his chest and thought, *Keep walking. Just keep walking. Get out of here!*

Thankfully, they did, laughing all the way down the corridor. Finally, Jeremy let go of her. She knew all he wanted to do was help, and he was the only person she knew who actually could help, but she couldn't stand any one person – even Jeremy – seeing her that humiliated. "Good night," she whispered, and ran off to her room, closing the door behind her before he could follow.

14

Lyla had to drag herself out of bed the next morning. Any progress she'd made in her training, in her student-trainer relationship with Azrael, in accepting this place, had evaporated overnight. She knew her broken heart could never heal, but at least she'd been able to distract herself these last few weeks. At times she'd even enjoyed her training and her lessons with Azrael. Now she just wanted to go home, crawl into Max's cold bed, and never wake up again.

She knew that if she didn't go down to the yard, the troll would come find her and make it that much harder on her, so she reluctantly put on her gear and walked down. On the way, she mentally prepared for a lecture from the big guy. She expected him to chide her on being late, on having skipped breakfast, and – of course – on being a needy fledging who'd made last night all about herself.

What she didn't expect to find was a gathering of angels all focused on one of the fighting rings. There was dead silence in the yard, as all eyes swiveled between someone standing outside the ring and... Azrael. That was Azrael standing in the middle of the ring, grey wings flaring behind him.

"Come on, Michael!" he shouted, his voice carrying across the yard. "I heard you've been running your mouth again. Since you don't seem to learn basic decency the easy way, let me beat it into you."

Reluctantly, Michael stepped into the ring, keeping a safe distance from the much more skilled angel who prodded him with his words. Lyla stayed as far away as possible, so no one would notice her presence.

"Don't worry, rook, I'll go easy on you. You can use any weapon you want, while I'll fold away my wings."

Their wings were essential in the use of magic. He was allowing Michael the use of his body, his magic and any of the weapons on the walls, while he would only use his arms and legs. To drive his point home, he pulled off his training shirt despite the biting cold, revealing the muscular chest and abs Lyla had suspected underneath. Their training and combat clothes were made of a material that was both highly resistant to stabs and slashes, as well as magical attacks.

Azrael was demonstrating just how little he feared the red-haired, big-mouthed angel.

And the latter made exactly the mistake Azrael had warned her about. He'd told her that hand-to-hand and weapons training were key because of the many situations in which they couldn't afford to use their wings – be it because they couldn't risk depleting their magic, or because they had to keep their identity hidden from unknowing humans. Apparently, many a battlefield had seen flocks of angels fighting alongside oblivious humans. In his arrogance, Michael chose to rely on his magic alone.

He started throwing it at Azrael before the latter's shirt hit the ground, and Lyla's heart skipped a beat. Something about seeing the beefy angel under attack infuriated her. But Azrael was far from defenseless. She'd known he'd gone very easy on her in her combat training, but she hadn't realized just how easy he'd gone on her.

In Lyla's experience, bulk tended to go hand in hand with a lack of speed and agility. But the big guy proved that theory wrong. Michael kept throwing magical attacks at him, trying to keep his distance, but Azrael was too fast. He dodged the blows easily, all the while closing in on Michael, his footwork as fast and as graceful as a bullfighter's.

In theory, his opponent could have taken to the air, but that would have made him look like a coward to the entire yard. Instead, she saw panic in Michael's eyes as Azrael closed in, a grin on his face. This was easy for him. As he dodged one of his opponent's strikes, ducking to his left, he came back crashing into Michael's ribs and immediately followed through with an uppercut to his chin. The three beats were so fast and seamless, they flowed into one motion. As Michael's head snapped back, Azrael stomp kicked him in the gut. The former's armor may have protected him from blades and magic, but it couldn't protect him from the full force of impact of the big guy's boot. The red-haired angel doubled over and fell to his knees, his wings instinctively folding back in.

He had been bested. And it had taken Azrael all of ten seconds to do the besting. Holding his side, Michael bowed his head, reluctantly acknowledging the fact.

"Apologize to the female you insulted. She's standing in the corner," Azrael growled, towering over him. At no moment had she noticed him looking at her or even realizing she was there, but as soon as he revealed her presence, the crowd turned toward her and parted to let Michael through.

He reluctantly stood, slowly exited the ring, and approached her. She could see Azrael standing in the ring, his wings now unfolded again, ready to pounce if he disobeyed. What Azrael couldn't see though, was Michael's face. Although he was still holding his side and struggling to catch his breath, he threw her a look so hateful, it was clear he barely contained his rage and his desire to murder her. But that didn't intimidate her: she'd seen that look before, and before there had been no Azrael standing by.

Michael stopped six feet from her and said "Apologies, Lailah, I was out of line last night." She wasn't sure why he used the same name Hermes had called her by, but before she could piece anything together, Michael closed the distance between them on his way out of the yard. In passing, he murmured, "Quite the champion you got yourself there. I guess scum attracts scum."

Azrael did not relax his stance until Michael was gone. Then he picked up his shirt and put it back on, strolling over to Lyla and yelling "Spectacle's over. Get back to work!".

He didn't speak to her. Instead, he cocked his head toward the exit, implying she should follow him out of the yard. As they silently stomped through the snow, Lyla didn't know what to say. She was mildly embarrassed that Jeremy had clearly caught him up on last night's events. But she was even more surprised by his reaction. She hadn't expected him to defend her, though it made sense: much like she couldn't stand him not getting fed at the party, he'd probably experienced so many insults and so much humiliation, he didn't allow it to happen in his vicinity either. In that sense, she could have been any of the priests at the compound.

Once they were out of the temple, Azrael stopped, and turned to her. "May I fly you to a place where we'll have the privacy to talk?" he asked, hesitation in his voice.

"Okay," Lyla answered, unsure of what they had to talk about.

"Hold on tight," he said, as he grabbed her around the shoulders and under the knees, holding her close to his body and taking off. She held on to his muscular neck, unsure where to look. It wasn't uncommon to see angels carrying fledglings or injured people, and since she couldn't fly yet, this was the most practical way to get places quickly... but there was an intimacy to this position that went far beyond how close they got when they wrestled during training. Her face was in his neck, she could smell the sweat from his fight with Michael and feel his abs shifting as he soared through the air. Thankfully, she was quickly distracted by the fact that he headed straight toward the Sacred Mountain. As they got near, he started flying in a way she hadn't witnessed before, twisting this way and that, pulling in one wing while flapping with the other, and similarly bending his body around the many jagged rocks on the way up the mountain; he'd pull in his knees, or twist to the side, all the while shielding her body either with his own or with one of his soft wings, expertly avoiding the treacherous currents of wind that surrounded the mountain.

When they arrived at the top, he gently dropped her on a patch of green grass, under a large tree. Oddly, there was no sign of winter up on the mountain. The winds they had flown through weren't active at the top, as if there was a curtain shielding the mountain from intruders. Snow and ice hadn't made their way up here either. Noticing her quizzical look, Azrael explained, "Hermes anchors his power on this mountain. I'm not sure how any of it works, but at this point, the Sacred Mountain is more magical than it is natural."

Lyla turned back around to where they'd come from, and said, "That looked like a really hard flight," awe bleeding into her voice.

Azrael smiled, almost shyly. "It is. In fact, no one's ever made it up here alive. The currents are extremely dangerous, and they'll throw any angel up against the rocks. You're the second person ever to see the top of the mountain."

"How come you can do it?"

"Easy. I've been practicing since I was a fledgling. At the time, my wings were so small it wasn't that risky, and as my wings grew, I adapted my flight to currents I knew like the back of my hand. I actually built a cabin at the top, though I don't spend much time in it, seeing as I'm the only person who can fly up here."

"Your mother let you fly up a path that has killed everyone who ever tried it?" Lyla asked, remembering that Azrael's father was a lost child and that he probably grew up without him.

Azrael sat down in the grass, leaning against a large tree, and Lyla followed suit. He didn't seem angry, but she could tell he rarely spoke of his childhood. After a moment, he took a deep breath and said, "My mother died giving birth to me. I didn't exactly have a caretaker in the traditional sense."

He looked at her, as if gauging her reaction. It wasn't so much about satisfying her curiosity; more so she could tell that he wanted her to keep asking questions, so she proceeded.

"Where did you grow up?"

"At the compound. My grandfather lived in the village. My mother was a priestess of Hermes' in training. When she was sixteen, she ran away without explanation. When she came back, she was pregnant with me. I was told she refused to tell anyone who my father was. At her age, my grandfather could have made her get rid of me, but she knew that if I was born, the angels would have no choice but to allow me to live."

He paused for a moment, clearing his throat. She could tell, he never spoke of this. He seemed lost in thought for a moment, before continuing.

"When I was born with grey feathers, my grandfather left me with a nursemaid in the village. I found her, years later, to thank her, but she told me she hadn't done it out of the kindness of her heart. My grandfather had paid her handsomely enough to erase the taint of nursing a grey-winged hatchling... On my third birthday, he took me back and dropped me at the compound. I knew how to speak, walk, and fly, so he figured it was time for me to be of use, and priesthood was, after all, in my blood. He sold my services in the kitchens in exchange for my room, board, and education."

He paused again, looking into the distance and chewing on his lower lip, a nervous habit of his she'd noticed a couple of times before.

"They asked him my name when he dropped me off. I hadn't been given one yet. He chose Azrael. A not-so-subtle way of reminding me every day that I killed my mother on my way into this world."

She didn't know what was worse, that he'd lived for three whole years without anyone calling him by any name, that no one had cared enough to take on a parental role in his life, that he'd been asked to work at such an early age in exchange for things that should have been given to him for free, or that his grandfather had been cruel enough to blame an innocent child for his daughter's death.

She'd seen the occasional kid at the compound, but she couldn't quite picture what a three-year-old's life in the temple would look like.

"Where did you live?" she asked.

Azrael's attention snapped back to her. "There are more children than you know at the compound. They live on the other side of the yard, the side I didn't show you."

She'd assumed there were just more cells there.

"Priests with families live in apartments over there. They have their own kitchens, library, and training rooms for the fledglings. I was placed in the cell I still live in, but I'd go over to study and train with the other fledglings every day."

She knew what the cells looked like. Jeremy had told her that they were all exactly the same. With a sudden shock, she realized that Azrael had been living on his own at an age where children still regularly woke up crying or sometimes wetting their beds. He'd eaten and trained with the other kids, but he'd gone to sleep alone in a tiny room every day.

"Did you have friends?" she dared ask.

"Not until later. Sometimes I played with the other fledglings, but their parents didn't want them associating with me. My teachers, however, treated me fairly in class. One of them even gave me my first knife."

He pulled a knife out of his boot and handed it to her. She took it out of his hand. Somehow, she knew no one else had touched that knife since the day Azrael had received it. His first gift, she assumed. It was a minuscule, two-inch blade reminiscent of some of the pocket knives humans gave their children, except that it was made of a much tougher magical metal. She made a mental note to ask Azrael what Hephaestus' priests forged their weapons out of, but now wasn't the moment. The handle was a tiny sheep horn – black like his father's wings, she noted. A very young child could have curled his fist around the handle, but the male in front of her probably couldn't even get two fingers around it.

She'd thought him cold and unemotional all these weeks, but he carried a blade in his boot that was of no use to him other than as a reminder of his childhood.

"Once I had that, I started carving some toys. I was never bored again after that," he told her, a smile on his face.

Christ, he'd had to make his own toys. And she thought she'd had it bad. She wanted to tell him how sorry she was, but she knew he'd hate her for it. No one wanted to be pitied for their past. She knew that all too well. It was part of the reason she'd always felt Max was the only person to understand her. Instead, she waited, allowing Azrael to continue or stop his tale.

After a while, he continued. "Things changed when I was fourteen. Jeremy's father was sent here to work in the hospital. Jeremy was eighteen. He was still in training, but there is no better place to learn than at a hospital in either Ares' or Hermes' temple. So, he came too. He took me under his wing, so to speak. I don't think Jeremy is capable of not loving someone, and his father didn't mind him spending time with me. On the contrary, he'd invite me to their apartment for dinner, whenever his busy schedule allowed for it... Jeremy's father died of heartbreak after his mother was killed, but he was the kindest angel I've ever known... Other than Jeremy of course. Before his arrival, I'd still run into occasional trouble with larger, older angels. No one ever messed with me again after Jeremy made it clear that he considered me a little brother. Mostly they wouldn't dare lay a hand on a priest of Aphrodite's, but he didn't mind the cuts and bruises whenever someone was dumb enough to try it."

"Sounds like someone I used to know," Lyla mused.

Azrael lifted an eyebrow.

"There are a lot of things Max couldn't save me from, but he sure tried," she reminisced.

Something flickered over his face, which she couldn't place. Disapproval?

"He must have been a brave young man to place himself between you and danger," he replied, but she could tell he didn't mean it.

Instead of probing, she said "Thank you for reminding me what that feels like."

"It was nothing. In truth, I owe you an apology... When you came to my cell last night, I assumed you were upset about your father's treatment of you... I was an ass to you, and I'm sorry. Jeremy told me why you'd come. And then he made me eat the food you brought, which would have tasted delicious had it not been for the side of guilt he served it with."

Despite his large size, he somehow managed to shyly look up at her, waiting for her reaction.

"Apology accepted," she said, smiling at him.

"Thank you, Lyla," he answered seriously. Then he added, "As for Michael, I told you he wasn't worth your time."

She appreciated the lightness with which he handled the conversation. It helped her forget the profound humiliation she'd felt the previous night.

"I should thank you really," he added. "I've been looking for an excuse to teach that vulture a lesson for years."

Lyla laughed, feeling giddy for the first time in a long while.

They took the rest of the day off. Azrael didn't show her around the mountain. Instead, he flew them to the village and gave her a tour of each and every shop on the main street. Jeremy's presence had been healing, but this too was a wonderful distraction from her pain. For the first time since she'd arrived on the island, she had fun.

She tried on various outfits at a female clothing store. Azrael offered to buy her favorite one since she had no money of her own, but she refused. They visited a furniture store, where each piece was hand carved out of wood from the island. Many of them had symbols and sigils carved into them - for the protection of the household, Azrael explained. Her favorite store housed knickknacks of all kinds. Having for the most part grown up with no more than the strict necessary, she loved owning objects that were of absolutely no use other than bringing the owner joy. She explained it to her chaperone, but he thought it very odd to care for cumbersome objects that served no purpose whatsoever. Diplomatically, she refrained from pointing out the knife in his boot.

Their final stop was a place called "Arms and Armor". It was his favorite shop. No surprises there. The blade smith was a priest of Hephaestus'. Between him and Azrael, many of her questions were answered. Their training garments were made of dragon hide. At first, she thought they were pulling her leg. But they explained to her that, while rare, dragons were in fact one of Lucifer's experiments. They stayed to themselves for the most part, living in caves so high up in the mountains that humans couldn't reach them, but they allowed the Gods to use the skin they shed every few months to make their armor. Their weapons were also made of creatures. Indeed, they used the claws, fangs, and shells of demons and any other creatures related to Lucifer to make all their weapons. There was a magic in using the enemy's very blood to hurt them, the priest explained.

While she kept quenching her curiosity with the kind store owner, Azrael meandered off into a small corner, where he began handling small knives, stabbing, and slashing the air with them. Finally, he picked one and brought it back to the merchant.

"Good choice," the latter said, "a double-edged boot knife made of vampire fang. It has just enough weight to feel substantial, while being thin enough to slip right into a boot, or under your enemy's armor."

Azrael bought the knife, and they left the store. Outside he handed it to Lyla.

"This is for you."

"What? No. I'll buy things when I have money," she answered, uncomfortable.

"It's a gift," Azrael replied, shaking his head. "I want you to have it."

There was something so serious and determined in his expression, she couldn't refuse him. Besides, she remembered his childhood boot knife and realized that giving her one of her own was probably the most meaningful gesture he could think of to mark the moment.

"Thank you," she said, taking the knife out of his large hand and crouching down to attach it to her boot. It fit as if it had been made for her.

As they walked back toward the temple, Lyla asked, "What's your boot knife made out of?"

"Lucifer's left pinky claw," he answered.

She stopped in her tracks, and Azrael roared in laughter.

"I'm joking! I think it's werewolf claw."

"You, my friend, have the strangest sense of humor," she replied, trudging beside him through the snow.

This time, it was Azrael who stopped in his tracks.

"Friend? I like that..." he said.

She turned around and saw a warm smile on his beautiful warrior face.

That night, she sat up in bed, pulling her new knife in and out of its sheath, scrutinizing it under every angle. She was still gripping it in her fist when she fell asleep.

For the first time in months, she forgot to think about Max as she drifted off.

15

Now that she and Azrael were befriending each other, Lyla's life and mood greatly improved. She still missed and mourned Max, and she felt guilty whenever she forgot to do so. She still held on tightly to the lifeline Jeremy provided. But the many hours she spent training became truly enjoyable. The healer had been right: Azrael's bark was worse than his bite, and now that she'd peaked past his gruff exterior, he didn't seem nearly as intimidating.

He told her that she was proficient enough in hand-to-hand combat that it was a waste of her time at the moment, except for weekly upkeep sessions. As for weapons training, he had decided that it could wait for now. Instead, they spent their mornings in a wide field outdoors, where he began teaching her how to fly under the stars and the Northern lights. Since she could now hold up and move her wings rather well, he began slowly showing her the various motions needed in regular flight - from a sitting position. Next, he gave her exercises to practice, and the more she repeated the series of motions, the more she could feel her body wanting to propel itself into the airs, as if it had been made to do so. Well, it had been, she realized.

After that, he told her to run down the path and to take off. She felt a bit silly playing airplane – even more so since she'd never traveled on one – but he assured her that it was easier to gather speed first, adding that, at least he wasn't teaching her by making her run off the edge of the compound's roof. She laughed, thinking it was one of his bizarre jokes, but he gave her that impassive look of his and informed her that that was exactly how he'd perfected his flight skills.

On her first few tries, she took off, but couldn't sustain her flight for much longer than a few seconds. But with every day, she climbed a little higher and flew a little longer. Until one day, she soared over the tree line of the nearby forest and got her first full view of the island.

It looked entirely untouched by the world. Jagged cliff edges surrounded most of it, with rocky beaches here and there. The village and the compound took up a third of the island. Now, in late Fall, they looked like a magical wonderland, snow covering the rooftops, and many chimneys sending smoke into the air. A smoke which, in these temperatures, meant life and warmth on the most primal of levels.

The compound towered over the village, with its many stories. It wasn't gaudy or luxurious in the way of the European gothic cathedrals she'd seen pictures of, but in comparison to the simple stone houses in the village, it looked like a castle. Her favorite feature from inside the temple were the large picture windows that offered a view of the outside landscape in various parts of its architecture, but now she noticed the outside artwork too: though the structure was a simple square, with a tower on each corner, there were enormous statues reminiscent of human gargoyles sculpted into the outside walls and towers. They seemed to tell a story of Gods and Fallen battling each other – yes, that was a statue of her father vanquishing an army of demons on the Western tower. She'd have to take a closer look someday.

The rest of the island consisted of farmlands, woods, and the occasional green pasture. She noticed that there were no farm animals, no abattoirs; the angels only ate hunted meat. She'd never had the luxury of being a vegetarian, but the thought that no animal was raised for slaughter in this place, was an unexpected relief.

Lyla's endurance needed a lot of work, so she landed back in the field before falling and getting skewered on one of the trees. Getting her fill of the aerial view of the island would certainly be a great motivation for her to keep on working hard.

Their afternoons and evenings were spent studying magic in the same training room in which she'd first manifested her wings.

"Magic is nothing more than will power. The more you have of the latter, the better you are at the former," Azrael explained on the first night. "For us it is something we have to practice and grow, whereas the Gods or those that inherit their mantles simply are their magic through and through."

"What do you mean, those who inherit their mantles?" she asked.

"Poseidon's descendants scattered to the four winds, so his mantle has essentially become irrelevant, but when Aphrodite died, she passed her power on to her youngest direct heir. The Gods are in agreement that that is indeed how their power is passed on. Aphrodite's heir is a little less powerful than she was, seeing as he was born into an angel's body, and he is still learning how to contain so much raw power in it, but the mantle lives on in him."

It was a relief to hear that Aphrodite's legacy lived on,

though Lyla assumed it was only a small consolation for Jeremy who'd lost both his parents in the attack and in its aftermath.

"We all have basic magic," Azrael continued, "which is to say the ability to apply our will to the world. Beyond that, each God passed on a specific magical gift to his or her descendants. Hermes gave us two types of powers so to speak: combat magic and mild telepathy. You could say that our powers lie somewhere between Ares' and Aphrodite's, which sounds counterintuitive but might be the reason humans imagined them to be in a romantic relationship. We don't have the raw power of Ares and his priests, but we have more than all the other angels. And while we aren't allowed to make others do things, and we certainly can't access their thoughts and feelings as directly as Aphrodite's priests can, we can empathize with their surface emotions as a tool in helping guide them. Our job is to use those gifts to put souls back onto the righteous path."

Lyla cleared her throat. "That sounds uncharacteristically religious..."

"It does?" Azrael asked. At her raised eyebrows, he shrugged and added, "I wouldn't know. The point is that our job is to reform monsters, be they angels, Fallen, spawns of Lucifer's in one form or another, or humans."

"Humans?"

"Occasionally. If their sphere of influence is large enough. That's why it's important for you to know how to fight without using your wings or your magic. We only use magic on humans as a last resort. Whoever we are going after, the most essential part of our mission is to give them a chance to repent," he said, as if that were indeed a creed he lived by with every breath he took.

"Repent?" she asked. Bitterly, she remembered all the monsters she'd met long before encountering an actual demon.

"Why? They made their choices."

Azrael looked at her for a moment. She didn't look away. Maybe he judged her for not thinking everyone deserved a second chance, but she didn't care what he thought. He'd suffered a terrible childhood of isolation and loneliness, but he'd been protected in ways she never had been. He didn't know what it felt like to be twelve years old and scared to close your eyes and fall asleep at night.

"We give them a chance at redemption, and we offer them the gift of our faith in them, because that's what distinguishes us from them," he answered slowly. "If we simply avenged their victims, we'd be no better than the monsters. We don't do it for them. We do it for us."

Lyla frowned, peeved, and tried to turn away. But Azrael caught her shoulder and turned her back to look at him. She could feel the angry tears in the corners of her eyes. His words rang foul in her ears.

"Let me ask you, Lyla, outside of defending yourself in the moment, have you ever hurt one of the people who harmed you?"

She shook her head, avoiding his gaze.

She hadn't. She'd never given them what they deserved. And it made her a coward.

There had been that one time.

Her last foster father had fallen down the stairs, drunk. He'd broken a leg and couldn't stand on his own. She remembered it like it was yesterday: it was the middle of the night, no one was home, and he was lying at the foot of the stairs in a crumpled heap. His phone was nowhere in sight, there was no one in shouting distance of the house, as she well knew, and he'd somehow succeeded in stabbing himself in the femoral artery with a pair of scissors he'd been carrying.

She'd lived with him for six months, and the man had terrorized her. Worse than the physical abuse, he'd played such awful mind games with her that she'd started to think she was going insane. But she'd persevered, mostly thanks to Max's presence in her life. Max would skip school every day to find her and make sure she kept her head on her shoulders, reminding her daily that they were simply counting down the days until she turned eighteen.

The crash had awoken her from a fitful sleep. Fully clothed, she'd gotten out of bed to find him at the bottom of the stairs. The thought had crossed her mind to go back to bed. Or to run away. To just let him bleed out on the floor. All she'd had to do was to do nothing.

But she hadn't been able to. Instead, she'd walked down the stairs, made a tourniquet for his leg out of her belt and called the ambulance. She'd avoided eye contact and stayed out of reach the whole while, but she'd known he was at her mercy. She'd known how easy it would have been to let him die. But she hadn't been able to do it.

She'd waited at his side, just out of reach, until she'd heard the ambulance. And then, she'd run up to her room, grabbed her few possessions and climbed out the window like a coward.

She'd allowed a monster to live another day, to hurt others after her, instead of putting him down when she'd had the chance.

Pulling her out of her memories, Azrael's hand gripped her shoulder tighter and said, "That's a good thing. Hermes' capacity for forgiveness is the root of his power just as love was that of Aphrodite's. And it's the core of our power to. Don't ever think it a weakness." His voice was stern, his piercing eyes unwavering. "Whatever you were just thinking of... you followed your nature by not taking revenge. It's when we act rashly, when we play avenging angels that we start losing ourselves and we fall."

Lyla found it hard to breathe around the knot in her throat. She'd always felt guilty for that night. Even Max had chastised her for allowing such a monster to live. But the way Azrael spoke of it, she'd done the right thing. Seeing the sincerity in his eyes and focusing on his comforting hand on her shoulder, she allowed the anguish, the fear, the guilt, the shame she'd held on to so tightly all those years to flow out of her grip as she let them go. After a moment, he dropped his gaze and let go of her shoulder, giving her a moment to compose herself.

Next, Azrael explained how one's magic was as wide as their imagination. Humans believed in magical spells: one spoke the right words and used the right ingredients in order to effect a specific result. Real magic, Azrael explained, was all in the imagination: angels learned to use their wings to control the amount of power they threw out into the world, but it was their minds that shaped the power into a "spell" so to speak. If they imagined it to beat their opponent back like a strong blow, it would hit them like a truck; if they imagined it to create a defensive barrier, that's what it would do; if they imagined it to wrap around their enemy's limbs like tight bonds, it could do that too. In theory their magic could move planets. However, the mental aspect of shaping magic was a delicate affair, and anything beyond simple battle magic was rather difficult for Hermes' descendants to form. The most complicated and intricate ideas took years to practice – if one was at all even capable of shaping them into a reality. Besides they also needed a proportional output of energy. So, while Hermes' priests were theoretically capable of moving land and sea, few of them could have uprooted a single tree.

Ares' priests were for instance quite incapable of using their magic for any purpose other than to enhance their strength, power, and speed in combat. The very way Demeter's priests were trained to think, pertained to the natural world and the manipulation of plants and elements only.

Aphrodite's priests, on the other hand, had some of the most incredible magic, Lyla thought, as they could directly affect, influence, and change other people's thoughts and emotions. No wonder, the Fallen had gone after her.

Hermes' priests were a little more flexible than most, Azrael explained, in that their magic could extend beyond combat enhancement to anything that was useful in the realms of either combat or persuasion.

"Or so in theory," he explained. "The fact that our magic is more malleable than most makes it more difficult to study. It gives us the longest learning curve of all angels, and some never make it very far. We'll begin with something simple."

He set up a row of wooden figurines on a shelf and told her to knock them down from a distance, using the power of her wings only. Violent magic was the simplest type of magic there was. In that sense, they were hybrids between the most brutish and the most graceful of angels.

Things had been going so well recently, Lyla assumed she'd get the hang of this quickly.

After a couple of weeks, she hadn't moved a single figurine. She flapped her wings, she tried to channel her magic through them, but nothing much happened. And certainly nothing intentional. Her magic leaked out, sure, but she was incapable of directing it and completely at a loss as to how to shape it to fit her imagination.

On the fourteenth day, Azrael sat down in defeat and said, "I think we should try something else."

"Oh, thank god," she sighed, kneeling across from him.

He shook his head. "I'll never understand why you say that,

when you know that there is no such thing."

"It's a habit. Habits are hard to break," she answered, bewildered.

"Work on breaking it. Your habit is stupid," he sternly replied.

Trying to put a crack in his composure, she smiled and said, "Your face is stupid."

Azrael looked at her sharply. She saw affront and ire in his eyes, as well as a smidgen of pain. But mostly, he looked pissed. She felt her heart lurch and her eyes widen. "Sorry," she quickly fumbled for words. "That was a joke... Human banter."

He frowned. "Humans find it funny to insult each other's faces?"

"Not exactly... Well, yes... Sort of? I'm sorry, Azrael..." she trailed off, then hastily added, "I don't think your face is stupid."

He looked at her so intently, she felt herself blush, before he changed the topic. "The first time you used your magic, you used your voice- "

"About that..." she interrupted. "I thought we needed to unfold our wings to be able to use our magic. But my wings weren't out that day..."

Azrael bit his lower lip for a few seconds before answering. "I'm not sure what happened. I've never heard of an angel using magic without their wings. On the rare occasion, an angel is born with the capacity to use other parts of their body to focus and concentrate their magic, which I suspect you are capable of doing with your voice. But I've never heard of one sending out focused magic without wings. All I can think is that your survival instincts kicked in. You were in mortal peril and your magic defended itself in whatever way it could, even without your wings."

"You speak of magic as if it's a living entity," she noted.

"It is. It's our very life force. We are so closely connected to it that we can't live without it."

Lyla let that sink in for a moment.

"You weren't exaggerating when you said I almost killed myself that day…"

"That day, and the day you fainted in the courtyard," he replied seriously.

That was a sobering thought.

"So, how does this work?" she asked, standing up and turning toward the shelf. "I scream at the figurines?"

"Do you remember what you did the last time?" he asked, rising to his feet. "What you thought of? What you felt?"

"Yes," she replied, swallowing.

"Do it again," he said, and backed up to the door.

Lyla stood, facing the row of figurines, remembering that most horrible of days. Max's cut up body, his curled fingers lying next to the rest of his hand. Those fingers that had run through her hair mere hours before. His glassy, horrified eyes. Eyes that had always been so alive, always with a hint of amusement in their corners, now so full of terror. She remembered pouring all her rage and despair into that one scream.

She closed her eyes, took a shaky breath, and her stretched wings started thrumming with power.

Her pain was at the surface at all times. She was busy and distracted enough to be functional, but she missed Max with every breath she took. She missed the life she'd never meant to give up. It was a constant ache in her chest, a nagging feeling at the back of every thought, it was the sharp knife lurking in the shadow of every laugh she shared with Azrael. Max would always be the price she'd paid for her legacy. She felt the wound she so carefully covered up every morning when she got out of bed gape open to its full extent, as if every emotional stitch

Jeremy had sewn through it was popping, letting the blood and pus flow freely.

And then, she screamed.

The figurines didn't fall off the shelf, as Azrael had requested. They were pulverized into particles so small, they simply vanished. As did the shelf. But she didn't stop. She couldn't stop. Her pain flowed out of her, and the more she released, the more she found inside the limitless well of her heart. Mixed with her magic, her pain took shape. It became something. It became life itself, rather than sitting and festering inside her chest, growing and growing, until someday it would choke her in her sleep.

She screamed and screamed, losing awareness of her surroundings.

Until she felt a hand on her mouth, and her scream, as well as her magic, were cut off. Another arm snaked around her waist, and she was pulled back against a big, barreled chest. She blinked in sudden fear and tried to struggle against the iron bands of those arms, but her muscles obeyed the soothing voice in her ear instead: "Shhh, stop struggling. Please. Please, stop. It's me. It's Azrael."

Azrael. Azrael was holding her. Begging her to stop. His voice was wavering, his arms shaking around her. She fell limply against him, her body giving up the struggle, her wings folding back into her body, and they both slid to the ground. Slowly, he removed his hand from her mouth, but he didn't loosen his tight hold on her. Now that her pain had no magical release, it transformed into tears and sobs. And Azrael held her through all of it. He didn't caress her hair and hold her hand as Jeremy had, nor did he speak reassuringly to her as Max had always done. He simply held her tightly against his body, his own face buried in her hair.

They sat like that until her tears stopped and her breathing steadied, and until Azrael's own trembling ceased. Finally, he lifted his head and asked, "Are you alright?"

She nodded.

"Well, I guess we don't have to look for your magic anymore. Just help you control it."

He was still holding on to her, and she felt his chopped breathing on her neck as he laid his forehead against the side of her head.

Finally, he said, "After you destroyed the figurines and the shelf and every single object in the room, right down to the mats, I wasn't sure if you'd kill me or yourself first. I could barely walk through your magic to get to you. Gods, you scared me, Lyla."

When he finally let her go and stood up, Lyla realized that he'd spoken the truth. Nothing was left intact in the room. She knew it to be soundproof and she assumed it had somehow contained her magic, but she'd destroyed every object in it, and – if Azrael was right – her magic would have turned against the people in it next. She turned to him to apologize, but what she saw in his eyes stopped her in her tracks: there was a vulnerability there she'd never seen before.

He gave her a weak smile and said, "You're one powerful angel! Pain can be a dangerous emotion to siphon," he explained slowly. "You never know how much of it you've been covering up. Starting tomorrow, we'll work on channeling different things and on controlling the amount. We'll get your magic focused. Believe me it's easier to reduce powerful magic than to increase a weak flow. But for now, it's dinner time."

They ate most of their meals at the tavern. She was happy to avoid Michael and his cronies in the eating hall, and the informal atmosphere helped further strengthen her budding friendship with Azrael.

The main room was so large that there were five wide fireplaces warming it, and they generally picked a spot near one of them to warm up after their long hours in the cold. But they also enjoyed the occasional meal at the bar that ran along the entire right side of the room. Whenever they did, Azrael would strike up a conversation with one of the two waitresses.

He'd told her that they were twins and the daughters of the owner. Artiya and Jegudiel were their names, and Lyla had learned that Azrael had saved their lives when they were very young. Their mother had been a priestess of Hermes'. When they'd been five years old (which must have been about ten years ago from the look of them), she'd taken them into the human world to show them everything that lay beyond the safety of their island. She'd intended it to be a weekend between mother and daughters, hiking, camping, and interacting with their charges, but one of her recent enemies had laid a trap, intent on revenge. They'd fallen prey to a pack of angry ghouls, who'd wanted to see her suffer for having taken one of their own recently. She'd tried to argue that he'd been rabid and had needed to be executed, but they wouldn't hear reason. By the time Azrael had found them, she'd been tortured so badly, he hadn't been able to save her, but he'd brought the fledglings back to their father, who now let him eat for free at the tavern, feeling he'd owe him for the rest of his life. Azrael, who still insisted on at least tipping them, felt responsible for the lives he'd saved. He often checked in with the twins, who were some of the very few angels around treating him like a full equal. Their kindness appeared to extend to any of his friends and so they repeatedly assured Lyla that she was welcome on her own any time she liked.

The food was divine. Artiya had once explained to her that Hermes killed the animals so quickly, they had no idea it happened, and that his magic infused them with bliss in their final moments. She would have called bullshit on such a theory, but the meat tasted so much like life itself that she figured her father really did have the magic hunting touch. It begged the question of what it would be like for a human, an angel, or a creature to be killed by him, but she tried not to dwell on that.

Lyla was still getting used to her new life, so she often felt that she was in one of those fake mead halls humans reconstructed for Renaissance Faires. The large room was mostly made of wood with stone chimneys, and if she lowered her eyelids just so, it looked like it was simply populated with costumed humans wearing fake wings, props they'd bought for cheap at a stand nearby. But those places had always looked just as fake as they were. As much as theme parks and faires tried to recreate the real thing, there was always something missing, something giving away the illusion. That something tended to be the lighting. Like the temple, the village had no such thing as electricity. Azrael had explained to her on one of her first days that the island was "powered" by Hermes, but she'd never asked him for details.

By the time, they finished their meal, Lyla was exhausted from the magical outpour of her evening lesson, but the remnants of fear and pain had been diffused by the nutritious food and the good company.

Azrael told her he needed to slip out for a minute to take care of something. Sitting alone at the bar, she looked around at the roaring fires, the torches decorating the walls all the way to the very high ceilings and the candles sitting on every table. They gave off a warm and beautiful light. She'd once heard that couples ate dinner by candlelight because it was more forgiving on their looks than electrical lighting was. She could now attest to that. But one thing still bothered her.

"How is there this much light in here?" she asked Jegudiel, who was on shift today. "It's the same at the compound. There's more light than the flames should provide."

The waitress dropped the towel she'd been drying the counter with and answered, "Hermes' power enhances them."

It must have shown on Lyla's face, that she had no idea what Jegudiel was talking about. So, she continued, "On their planet, the hive went through similar technological milestones as humanity. Someone discovered fire, someone invented the wheel, and someday someone built a computer. They never explained how it happened, but it would seem that technology almost destroyed all life on their planet. In fact, some scholars have speculated that the hive developed their more predatory traits and their magical abilities as a survival mechanism in the aftermath of such an apocalyptic event. At any rate, they forsook technology. Now on their islands, each God continuously powers a veil, a portal, and an enhancement spell on the mechanisms we use instead of electricity."

The more Lyla learned about magic, the more obvious it became that such an output of energy was far beyond the angels' power. In fact, the angels were nowhere near the ballpark of the Gods' magical abilities.

"I'm starting to understand why the Gods and the Fallen can't simply have it out with each other. That in itself would be the end of this world, wouldn't it?"

"Precisely," the bartender answered. "Their sheer power would annihilate so much of the planet, it would hardly be worth the effort. The Gods want to protect humanity from it, while the Fallen wouldn't want to lose their playground. Excuse me," she finished, coming around the bar with a notepad and pen to go seat a couple of priests who'd just entered the room.

Lyla looked at her leave and noticed that the newcomers

wore different robes. They weren't priests of Hermes'...

...and something was very wrong.

Their clothes were torn, and they were injured. In fact, they were holding up a third angel who seemed barely conscious between them. The tavern was so crowded, no one had noticed their presence yet, but Lyla instinctively stood up. Before she could think of what to do, Jegudiel returned, pulling her behind the bar and shoving her down a short ladder under a secret trap door.

"Where are you taking me? What's going on?" Lyla demanded.

"There's been an attack. Artemis' temple has been destroyed; no priest was left alive. I swore to Azrael to protect you with my life if there ever was a need. Please stay down here until we know there's no danger to the island."

And with that, Jegudiel disappeared, closing the trap door behind her, and leaving Lyla in the dark.

16

The panic hit her instantly. She was in a small, pitch-black, cubic space. A cold tomb carved into damp rock. Instinctively, Lyla climbed the rungs of the ladder and pushed on the door Jegudiel had expressly told her not to touch. But she needn't have said a thing: the door didn't open from the inside. She was locked in.

Was she though? She'd pulverized an entire room with her voice alone just a couple of hours ago. No, she could blow through that door if need be.

The realization calmed Lyla's nerves and her claustrophobia receded enough for her to listen to what was going on upstairs. She could hear a commotion in the tavern. She guessed that the priests were leaving to assess the situation, while civilian angels were hiding in the backroom Jegudiel and Artiya had once shown her. She could have hidden with them, but Jegudiel had insisted on making her a higher priority. As grateful as she was for a safe hiding spot, Lyla couldn't help wishing she was among the other angels right now.

Jegudiel had promised to put herself between her and danger. Lyla wasn't sure how she felt about anyone taking that kind of risk in her name. The waitress had a twin sister and a father who loved her, a job at a family-owned business. The entire village knew and adored her. If Lyla had interpreted the furtive looks she exchanged with one of the young priests who frequented the tavern at least as regularly as she and Azrael did, she had a lover who was crazy about her. She had a future. Lyla's broken life shouldn't have been leveraged against that. She'd give Azrael hell for extracting such a promise from Jegudiel.

Azrael. Shit.

A renewed wave of panic hit her. Azrael didn't know of the attack. What if someone got to him? What if there was an attack on the island right at this moment and Azrael wasn't prepared. After all, that's why Jegudiel had hidden her: in case this island too was under attack.

Her knees buckled and she had to reach out to the sides and hold on to the walls lest she crumple to the ground. The cool water running down the walls counteracted the clamminess she suddenly felt at the back of her neck. She hadn't felt like this since -

Since Max. Suddenly, she saw that door, the apartment door. Broken in. Something terrible had happened. Something terrible was happening. Max, mutilated, cut to shreds, throat torn out. But it wasn't Max she saw in her mind's eye. It was Azrael. Azrael with dead, glassy eyes. Azrael missing all of his fingers. Azrael cut up by a giant pair of scissors. Azrael with his throat torn out, his beautiful grey feathers soaked red.

Lyla couldn't remember how she got there or how long it had been, but by the time the trapdoor opened, she was rocking back and forth on the ground, hugging her knees, her eye sockets pressed deep into her kneecaps, trying to banish the sight of Azrael's lifeless shell of a body.

It took her a moment to register what the incoming light was. Someone had opened the door. Someone had come to get her. For better or for worse. Slowly she lifted her face and peered into Jeremy's distressed eyes.

"Lyla. Lyla everything's all right. You're safe, Lyla. Lyla, please listen to me..." she heard him say as if from a great distance, realizing he'd been talking to her for a while now, but that her brain hadn't registered the words.

Now that her flashback abated, she noticed that her entire body was trembling. More accurately, it was spasming, every muscle twitching uncontrollably. She slowly uncurled her arms from around her knees, but she could barely control her movements, or straighten out the fingers that were curled into tight fists, nails digging deep into her palms.

"Lyla, there isn't enough room for me to come down there to get you," Jeremy said, slowly enunciating every word, as if speaking to a child. "I'm going to need you to stand up and climb the ladder. It's only a few steps."

She stared at him for a while before she understood what he was asking of her. Ever so slowly, she got to her feet, almost keeling over with nausea.

"There's a brave girl. Now the ladder."

Lyla banished the rivers of blood running through Azrael's wings from her mind, and grabbed a rung of the ladder, but her sweaty hand slipped. Breathing hard, she tried again. She had only taken a couple of steps up the ladder when Jeremy extended his hands toward her. The moment she was within reach, he grabbed her under the arms and lifted her out of the pit as if she weighed nothing at all.

And then he gave her a bone-crushing hug, holding her so tight it would have cut off her breathing had she had any to begin with. One hand around her back and the other curled around her head, he held her close. "You scared me, sweetheart, you looked... haunted down there. What had you so alarmed?"

Jeremy's loving presence cracked something deep inside her, giving her tears free flow. "Azrael," she sobbed. "Is Azrael safe?"

Jeremy pulled back to look at her, not fully letting go of her. He gave her a puzzled look. He hadn't expected her to ask about her teacher.

"We were never under attack, sweetheart. Azrael is fine."

"Are you sure?" she insisted, her voice trembling, wondering what was hiding behind those deep blue eyes.

"Of course, I'm sure. He asked me to come get you," Jeremy replied, scrutinizing her face as if searching for something, an answer to a puzzle she wasn't privy to.

Feeling like she could finally breathe again, Lyla gasped as if she'd been drowning. She blinked at Jeremy, and the words uncontrollably poured out of her. "I thought he was dead. I thought they'd gotten him. I thought he was gone... It would kill me if he died, Jeremy..."

Jeremy suddenly went rigid, and she saw something like shock and sadness flicker across his face. Then he gave her a forced smile, and pulled out of their embrace, tugging a strand of her undone braid behind her ear like an afterthought.

"Let's get you home, shall we?"

She nodded and he took her hand, pulling her out of the now empty tavern.

"Do we have to trudge through two feet of fresh snow, or will you show me those new flying skills I've heard so much about?" he asked, grinning at her once they were standing in the icy winds.

Lyla was still shaking but flying home reset her emotions. Something about moving her body that way, about getting to feel the wind in her feathers, made her realize that even the darkest of emotions came and went, but her connectedness to this world was a constant. Her desire to soar through the winds was a constant. One born out of such depths within her soul, that it silenced even her aimlessness. Every time she flapped her wings, the wind seemed to whistle, *You are not broken. You are not done.*

They landed on her balcony. "Az wasn't kidding. You are a good flyer!" he said through a smile. He must have known that flying would take her mind off things.

The smile dropped as he added, "Lyla, we are safe here tonight, but what happened was awful. And you need to know." He took a deep breath before continuing, "Artemis was killed, and her entire island was annihilated. Three of her bloodline made it out. Barely. Only three. The rest are gone."

He paused for a long time, looking into the skies. She could see him swallowing hard; he was holding back tears. Finally, he continued, "I wish I could tell you that everything was going to be fine. But they've gotten to three out of the Ten. We're losing. That's the truth. We're losing and, if we don't get ahead, it's only a matter of time before they come for this island too." He paused, turning to her with a sad smile, and added, "I wish you'd seen this place before there was a constant threat looming over it. Before we were in this war. Make no mistake, Lyla, that's what it is: after a millennia long stale mate, we're back at war. And now, more than ever, it is crucial for you to train with everything you've got. Do you hear me?"

He said the last with such intensity, Lyla swallowed and nodded.

"Good," he said, grabbing her face with both hands and kissing her solemnly on the forehead. "Good night, sweetheart."

17

Things changed after that. For one, there were black banners hanging off all the balconies, making the yard feel like a dark pit of grief. On that first morning, Jeremy brought Lyla her own banner to hang from her room. He told her they used black to remember the dark wings of the Fallen who had taken their loved ones and allies, and that the banners would stay for sixteen days - which was the time it had taken the Ten to pull away from the hive and come to Earth's rescue after the Fallen's arrival.

Sixteen days to grieve before the angels would go back to working and fighting harder than ever. In that time, strict silence was to be observed in all common and public places. People were only to speak behind closed doors, or if strictly necessary. They weren't to use their wings if they had a choice either; instead, they had to walk everywhere, a reminder of the charges they protected, of the enormous burden the Ten had been saddled with for their original sin, of the sacrifice they made every single day. And there was no training allowed – though Jeremy informed her, that an exception had been made for her. Azrael would continue teaching her, but – out of respect – they'd take their sessions up to the Sacred Mountain, where it wouldn't disturb anyone.

The temple was oppressively quiet, every single footstep echoing into the silence. And the courtyard, usually bustling with energy and endorphins turned into an empty, sad, snowed over tomb. But worse perhaps was the village. People still needed to shop; some still ate at the tavern. But none of them spoke, or laughed, or smiled. The sorrow was most palpable here, among the angels who'd inherited Hermes' blood and wings, who lived in a world entirely separate from the rest of the planet, but who hadn't been gifted with enough magic to protect themselves against the kind of assault Artemis' Island had just suffered.

Humans spoke of grief, but they had long since forgotten how to mourn. Instead, they danced to the "Life goes on" tune, always keeping up and pretending they felt alive no matter how much sorrow crushed their hearts. The angels, on the other hand, took time to mourn their dead. They not only followed the rituals and traditions, but every single mind on the island was focused on what had been lost.

It made Lyla feel less alone. Less misunderstood. As fucked up as it sounded, she was no longer the only one crying on the inside, she was no longer the only one slowly bleeding out. Everybody else's outpour of pain allowed her to give her own emotions free reign.

Along with all her unlocked pain came a flood of other emotions she hadn't known where there. She could no longer deny the fact that flying made her feel more alive than she ever had before. Nor could she pretend she didn't care for both Jeremy and Azrael. She deeply enjoyed the latter's company. Somehow, she'd even grown to like his "grumpitude", as she called it when he got impatient and his attitude deteriorated.

Most of all, she finally acknowledged the growing fire in her heart. The damage Max's death had caused her psyche would never heal. And yet, something had been born and grown inside her without her realizing. Something had made her get out of bed every single morning for weeks, no matter how screwed up she felt. Something had been driving her and she could no longer ignore it.

As much as she'd struggled against it, as much as this world still felt new to her, she belonged here. For the first time in her life, she felt a profound and unquestionable sense of kinship. She only knew parts of the angels' history, she barely knew anything about their traditions, but she had wings, and they rooted her to this place in a way nothing in her old life ever had rooted her anywhere. Not even her parents.

Not even Max.

And now, she knew, at the most primal of levels, that she and these people had a common enemy. After sixteen days, the angels would return to the fight with a fury. They would go to war with the black-winged monsters who'd taken their sisters and brothers. And Lyla too wanted their hide for taking a piece of her own heart.

With that realization, she began training in earnest. She spent fourteen-hour days with Azrael on top of the Sacred Mountain, every single day. He offered her breaks and days off, but she stubbornly refused. Much like her combat skills, her flying skills had become good enough for now. Besides, she practiced flying from outside the temple to the bottom of the mountain and back every day. Azrael carried her the rest of the way to his sanctuary, where they exclusively worked on her magic and her control.

When she'd first used her voice, she'd channeled the amount

of raw pain available to her. Little had she known how much more there was where that had come from. Pain and anger. Azrael first taught her how to use them in a measured way - *like a faucet you sometimes need a drop out of, and you sometimes need to transform into a torrent*, he'd explained. And so, she played with the amount of emotion and magic she siphoned out of her body, as well as with the vocal levels of her sonic attacks.

Once he was satisfied that she knew how to safely use her destructive magic, they moved on to "creative magic" as he called it, leaving the empathic powers with which they sometimes manipulated their enemies for last. He told her that was the most difficult magic to channel and that she wouldn't be ready for it for a long while. They began with invisible protective shields for themselves, and shackles to hold their enemies. Thinking something up and bringing it to life was after all everything creation was about.

Apparently, his skill with such magic was one of the things that set him apart from most priests in his generation: he was simply capable of a much more intricate and detailed layering of magic, which made him a significantly more skilled fighter. As they spoke over their lunch breaks, she found out that Hermes had watched him from afar as a child and stepped in to begin training him himself when Azrael turned twenty. Over the next few years, Hermes had not only helped him unlock the full capacity of his power, but had honed him into a capable second in command. Azrael admitted to her that he still wasn't the best strategist, and that his blind spots were a constant source of frustration to her father who deemed him too impulsive and heart driven. That didn't surprise her.

Once her shields and restraints had gotten passable, Azrael suggested moving on to telekinesis. She'd been surprised to find snow on top of the mountain that morning, but Azrael had explained that he'd asked Hermes to allow the snow to pass through the currents of his power, as he'd use it to teach her about telekinesis.

"Telekinesis? As in, moving stuff? I thought that wasn't anywhere near the wheelhouse of Hermes' brutes?" she asked, surprised.

"It isn't," he answered, smugly. "But it's in mine, and I have a feeling you might have a knack for it too."

In order to demonstrate, he used the snow. He brought his wings forward, almost cocooning himself inside them. She could see them flapping ever so slightly, like a gentle wave, allowing the smallest but most precise amount of magic to flow out of him. Their tips moved up and down, forward and back, as if they were extra hands, drawing a particularly artistic picture. And with the tip of those wings, he manipulated the snow right between them, invisible strings connecting his wings to the snow itself.

She had seen him angry; she had seen him joyful; she'd even seen him scared before. But she'd never seen him this focused. Very slowly, so as not to disturb his concentration, she started circling around him. He didn't seem to notice, as he was so absorbed in his magic. And as she observed him, she realized that she was looking at the little boy who'd carved his own toys with a tiny boot knife. The general was gone, replaced by an artist. The brute was nowhere to be found. In his stead stood a beautiful male, full of joy and love and wonder for the world. As she circled around the back of him, she noticed how every muscle under his shirt was rolling and twisting with extreme precision. And she finally understood why he was so accurate with his magic: he had full control of every minute movement of his wings; there wasn't a single extraneous motion, no wasted effort, and no room for approximation.

By the time she closed her third circle, he'd finished his work, and stood, arms-crossed, a broad grin on his face, awaiting a reaction.

In front of him stood a five-foot-tall snowman. One that had facial features sculpted into him, and arms ending in hands. For god's sakes, there were veins sculpted into those hands! Somehow, he'd used his magic to freeze the snow into place. One of the arms was stretched out toward her, palm up. And inside it, sat a snowball.

"For you," Azrael said. "If you can move that ball using your magic only, you get to throw it at me!"

"Azrael," Lyla responded, baffled. "This is extraordinary! It's beautiful!"

"Thank you," he replied. And blushed. Actually blushed. Well, that was a sight, she'd never thought she'd see!

"I would have given him wings, but I didn't want to waste too much time..."

Lyla spent an excruciating two days trying to move the snowball. Sometimes, she would lift it only for it to topple right over the snowman's hand and come plopping to the ground. More often, she'd simply explode the poor ball. Though, at least her control was good enough that her magic never touched the snowman himself – which, she assumed, was half the exercise.

On the third day, she had an idea. She'd been using her voice aggressively this whole time, but this wasn't combat magic. Standing six feet away from the snowman, she focused her mind, spread her wings, looked at the snowball, and ever so gently began humming, as she allowed her magic to trickle out of her.

As if pulled by invisible threads, the ball lifted off the snowman's icy hand, shakily at first, but steadying along with Lyla's voice. She didn't hum any particular song, simply the notes which came to her naturally, coaxing the ball up into the air and then carefully toward her. She let it float in front of her for a moment, her voice a constant thrumming in the air around her. She admired her work for an instant, breathing very carefully, so the music would keep carrying the snowball on her inbreaths, before angling herself toward Azrael – and making the ball fly straight into his face with a sudden crescendo of the note she'd been holding.

Having seen Azrael move against Michael, she knew that her ball hadn't been fast enough to hit him, had he been prepared. But he'd been as mesmerized as she was by the floating ball, and it took him entirely by surprise as it soared straight for his face and splashed against his forehead, leaving red patches on his skin and water drops in the free-floating strands of his long hair.

His eyes narrowed and, fast as lightning, he made a snowball with his hands and hurled it in her direction. She got hit in the hip and laughed harder than she had in months. As she did, she briefly lost track of her magic, and her laughter rebounded around the snow, lifting up individual snowflakes off the ground. They floated around her face, but as soon as she realized what was happening, her giggles faded and the snow obeyed gravity again.

"Magical snowballs only," Azrael, who hadn't noticed her laughter's effect, interrupted. "And I'll give you a five-minute head start to create some."

Lyla scrambled to make as many magical snowballs with her vocal cords and wings as she could. When he informed her that her time was up, she had a dozen, misshapen balls in front of her.

What ensued was pure mayhem. Azrael beat her in quality and speed - both of the creation and the aim of his snowballs.

Besides, he threw most of them from high up, using his flight to perfection, while she was scrambling on the ground, only occasionally nicking him with an unexpected blow. Unable to catch up to him, her hair dripping in snow, her face freezing from the iced water that melted off it, she finally sat down and wrapped her wings tightly around the front of her body, allowing only for a tiny space to peak through, letting him pummel her with his shots.

But while he was flying around victorious, trying to get past her shielding wings, Lyla began singing. At first, it wasn't loud enough for him to hear under the flutter of his wings and his boisterous exclamations, but bit-by-bit she gave her voice and her magic more room. And as she did, the snowman slowly lifted off the ground behind Azrael. By the time it was flying higher than him, she stood to her full height and spread her wings out behind her. Azrael saw her expression and looked around, confused as to what was going on. Lyla didn't allow impending victory to sidetrack her. She sang the word "come", calling the snowman toward her and steadily humming *mmm*, until it was hovering above Azrael.

By the time the latter realized that the one place he hadn't looked was up, she went silent and reeled her magic back in, allowing gravity to do its job. The entire snowman came crashing down on Azrael before he could dodge it.

Azrael himself fell to the ground and Lyla had a moment of panic, fearing she could have hurt him. Using everything he'd taught her about the intimate connection between magic and imagination, she'd made sure to imagine the sculpture melting back to the temperature of packed snow so Azrael wouldn't get hit with hard ice. But she couldn't tell if she'd been successful.

She had been. Azrael sat up in a pile of moving snow, roaring with laughter. When he'd finally calmed down and brushed himself off, he walked over to her, reminding her for a moment of just how much larger and scarier than her he was.

Before she could apologize or retreat, he grabbed her around the shoulders and under the knees and flew them off the mountain. Though he knew the path through the winds like the back of his hand, his eyes were always focused and alert on their flights up and down the mountainside. Looking at the grounds and at the currents twirling around them, he said, "It's been a really long time since an opponent took me by surprise. Well done! And you're done for the day. You're soaking wet and you did admirably today. You need a warm meal and a hot bath, not another six hours of training."

By the time they landed on the ground, Lyla's teeth were chattering wildly, and Azrael didn't seem much better off.

"We're walking home," he said, looking at her obliquely. "You're trembling so hard, people will think you're drunk if I allow you to fly."

So, they set off toward the temple, one agonizingly cold step after another. Lyla was so focused on dreaming up the hot bath she'd take, that it took her a second to realize Azrael had stopped walking. He stood a couple of steps behind her, looking back toward the entrance of the forest. She looked between him and the forest, wondering if he sensed danger. Their snowball fight had momentarily dispersed the grief and fear, but Azrael too had been somber and on edge these past couple of weeks. As she looked at him, his shoulders relaxed, as if he'd gauged that the presence he sensed was a friendly one.

When she saw who it was, her own body did the exact opposite.

Her father, wearing nothing more than what looked like a loincloth, emerged from the dark forest. His fangs and claws on full display, he was smeared with blood. "Smeared" was generous. He was covered in it. All she could guess is that he'd bathed in it: his down stuck to his forehead from too much blood, it dripped down his head, and pieces of furry hide hung from his claws. He trudged through the snow, unaffected by its temperature, slouching as if under a great burden, and heading straight toward them.

Lyla had to control her body and order it not to bolt. She stood near Azrael, trembling in the cold, and very much wishing she could just hide behind him.

When he arrived, Hermes looked Lyla up and down, ignoring Azrael. The look in his eyes was so wild, she was terrified to know what he was thinking. But he didn't say anything. Instead, he addressed Azrael.

"The sixteenth day is nearly over," he said, his voice not only echoey, but gravelly, rough, as if he'd screamed himself hoarse. "There is a rogue werewolf in Denning, New York, in the United States of America."

"Fucking Denning," Azrael simply answered, addressing her father more casually than she'd ever seen anyone do. "Why do you need me for the job? It sounds like something for a rook."

"Because I want you to take her," Hermes answered, a nod of his head in Lyla's direction his only acknowledgment of who he was speaking of. "She's ready to cut her teeth on a real fight. And afterwards, I need you in my office. We have some planning to do."

Before his voice had finished echoing, he started walking past them and toward the temple.

"Tomorrow, we go to war," he threw over his shoulder, his white wings dragging behind him, leaving a trail of red blood in their wake.

18

While Lyla waited for Azrael the next morning, she decided to practice her magic. He'd told her to meet him at the foot of the grand staircase, which was still abandoned, seeing as it was five in the morning. Azrael was late, so in her boredom she stood on the steps, wings unfolded, and started practicing her telekinesis on one of the torches hanging on the wall. Soon, the torch was hanging upside down and twirling in the air, defying gravity, controlled by Lyla's mind alone. She let it twist around her, dancing with the flame, when an idea occurred to her: could she control the flame itself?

She returned the torch to its sconce and carefully focused on the fire, shaping it into a ball of light, the tips of her wings moving in unison with her will. Once she was satisfied with her control over the ball of fire, she called it toward her.

Using magic was intoxicating. By the time Azrael arrived, she was rolling the ball of fire up and down her arms, over her back and the edge of her wings, never allowing it to quite touch her skin and feathers. She was so entranced by the use of her own power that she didn't hear his approach.

"Lyla!" he called, sharply.

Her concentration dropped for a split second, and the fire licked her shoulder, burning her. She winced as the flame burned through her training clothes and into her skin, before regaining her composure and sending the fire back to its torch.

Azrael stood in front of her, arms crossed and wings stored away, a fury on his face the likes of which she hadn't seen him display in weeks. Lyla flinched at the sight of him, forgetting all about the pain in her shoulder. This was not her friend; this was the alarmingly dangerous warrior who'd pulled her out of her human life. And he was livid.

Before she could say anything, he threw her the jacket she'd draped over the banister and headed up the stairs. She followed him in silence. He finally stopped in front of a door on the highest floor, schooled his features – or tried to – and said, "Fold away your wings and put on the jacket."

He stared at the door as he spoke, but she could see his jaw twitching in rage. The cold in his voice sent her right back to those first few weeks when he hated being in the presence of "the fledgling".

Swallowing and calming the pulse in the side of her throat, she obeyed him, suppressing a hiss as the material of her jacket came down on her burned shoulder.

Azrael waited until she was zipped up, before he opened the door onto a massive room. There were tables covered in maps, desks strewn all over the place, and the walls were covered in notes reminiscent of human investigative shows. In the center of the room, a disk-shaped something floated above the ground. It looked like purple smoke, morphing constantly, yet preserving its oval shape. In fact, it looked oddly similar to some of the currents of wind around the Sacred Mountain. It stood under a wide skylight. No, that was open sky where a skylight should have been: the magic disk was emitting waves that went straight up into the skies, not allowing the cold to enter in the opposite direction. It looked... exactly the way she pictured magic should look like.

This is the war room. And that must be the portal, Lyla thought, in awe of the energy the latter was pulsing with. On the Sacred Mountain, it was easy to pretend Azrael just flew her through strong currents of wind. But this was different: she was looking at a small amount of her father's concentrated energy, swirling away day in and day out, filled with a magic far beyond anything angels were capable of.

And behind it stood her father, dressed in full training gear, snow-white wings folded at his back. Gone was the wild look from his face, replaced by those cold, calculating raptor eyes.

As usual, he didn't waste time with niceties.

"As you have in the past, teleport to the East side of the territory. The vampire is waiting for you at the youth ranch with instructions. It should be an easy mission."

And with that, he turned his back to them and returned to whatever battle plans were laid out on the large table in back.

Without any more of an explanation, Azrael grabbed Lyla by the wrist, pulled her toward the portal and stepped in, dragging her behind him.

19

The instant she stepped into the purple light, everything went white and then a new landscape emerged in front of her, like one of those virtual reality experiences she'd heard about. Except that this was real.

It was at least fifteen degrees warmer than on the island, and it hadn't snowed here yet. It usually didn't until mid-December in the Southern parts of New York – though that was only a few days away. They were in a wooded area, surrounded by tall naked trees, leaves crunching under their feet. Lyla looked around and realized that they were standing in a parking lot, at the foot of a hiking trail. The map next to them said, *Welcome to Slide Mountain Trail – 6.2-mile loop.*

She wasn't prepared for the shock. She was home. Not only was she in the human world and in America, she was in New York. Where people did such trivial things as hike for the hell of it.

Before she could process the flood of grief that threatened to burst through her carefully constructed walls, Azrael turned toward her and unleashed his bottled-up ire. "One rule. The Ten be damned, there was one rule, fledgling! DO NOT SHOW YOUR MAGIC! You couldn't even obey one order? What is WRONG with you?"

"I'm not a soldier. I don't follow orders," she replied flatly, before she could think better of it.

Azrael blanched. "No," he answered, in an eerily calm voice. "And at the rate you're going, you'll never be."

She understood what he meant to say: she'd never be fit to serve as a guardian, as a priest of Hermes'. Her life lay shattered at her feet. All she had these days was her training. He couldn't have dug the knife in deeper.

"You're lucky I didn't tell your father about it," he rambled on. "The way he looked yesterday... he's hanging on by a thread... He would have pulled you apart if he'd known... But I WILL have to tell him. The Ten have mercy on me, I should have told him right away... Do you have any idea what could happen if anyone saw you?"

"There was no one there. I was all alone," she replied, her voice wavering from the blow he'd dealt her.

"The walls have ears and eyes in that place! Have you not realized that yet?" he continued, a wild almost desperate look on his face now. "Your friend was cut to pieces! You saw the THREE priests of Artemis' that survived an attack that killed thousands. What will it take for you to understand the gravity of your situation?"

She understood how serious their communal predicament was, but she didn't quite grasp why he seemed to think there was such danger to her in particular. However, Azrael didn't look like a male she wanted to try to reason with at this moment. He looked quite livid in fact.

The priest wiped a hand across his face and forced himself to slow his breathing. "If they find out how powerful you are, they'll come for you..." he muttered, more to himself than to her. "Please don't let it be my fault, if anything happens to her," he pleaded, sitting down at the foot of the trail.

Carefully, Lyla sat down next to him. If she didn't know any better, he seemed in agony over something. Though his words still stung, she knew she had to help get him back on his feet and onto their mission. She'd deal with her grief later. Shoving it away, she cleared her throat.

"I'm sorry, Azrael," she began, but he didn't look at her. She slowly wrapped an arm around his wide shoulders and saw his eyes close. "I didn't realize how much I was messing up. I promise it won't happen again."

He took a deep breath, opened his eyes, and slowly turned toward her. The rage was gone, as was the despair, replaced with a bone-weary exhaustion. "That burn better scar over as a reminder never to do anything that stupid again."

Part of her still wanted to argue that her playing around with a bit of magic couldn't possibly have been that big of a deal. Instead, she got up, smiled, and asked, "Where to next?"

20

"Explain to me, why we didn't portal in somewhere closer?" Lyla asked an hour into their silent hike through the woods.

She was in the best shape of her life and didn't mind the hike so much, but its smells and sounds reminded her too much of the few times she and Max had taken trips Upstate. They'd gone on day hikes time and again, enjoying the physical exertion and quiet from the city. But they'd only tried camping once, before concluding that their childhoods had provided them with enough discomfort to last a lifetime.

What would Max say if he could see her now? She'd kept living because he would have wanted her to, but she had a feeling that he wouldn't recognize her if he saw her in this moment. It had been about three months. Three months of hanging on to whatever sense of reality she could. The whole thing had been so dreamlike, it wasn't difficult to become a part of the dream. But now that she was back in the real world, she felt like her brain might short-circuit.

This was reality. These trees, the fall leaves crunching under her feet, the occasional deer crashing through the woods, the planes in the sky. That other world, the invisible island, was a dream. A nightmare some days. But it wasn't true. It couldn't be.

And yet, Azrael was here. Looking oddly human with his wings folded away.

Keep moving. Keep moving. Her mantra had been on loop inside her head for the past hour. She'd put one foot in front of the other, ignoring the tricks her mind was playing on her.

"Because it's rude just showing up inside someone's house," Azrael replied, keeping his eyes on the path ahead.

"So couldn't we have portaled to right outside their fence?" she asked, trying not to sound petulant.

"We did. We've been walking through their territory since the first step we took."

"Whose territory?"

"Everyone's." He looked around them, apparently uneasy to drop his guard, and continued, "All right. This isn't ideal, but it's time for a little history lesson. Keep your wits about you as we talk."

Lyla nodded.

"You've read about the Fallen's second generation of children at this point, I take it?" he proceeded.

"The greatest hits of monsterdom? Sure," she replied casually, but Azrael stopped in his tracks and leaned in, very seriously whispering, "Do not use the M-word around here. It's a great insult."

"Okay," she nodded, taken aback, and Azrael resumed both his hike and his tale.

"None of them ever served the Fallen. Instead, they live in their own communities-"

"Like the lost children?" she interrupted.

"No, not like the lost. The lost are isolated from both angels and humans," he said, sadly. "The second generation mingles with humans. They hide in plain sight. But every single one of their species forms packs that will live nearby each other for support. Well except poltergeists. Ghosts can't exactly interact with humans. It seems plain cruel to have created them in the first place, if you ask me..." he drifted off.

She hadn't really given it any thought, but ghosts were the one species she'd read about that had so little influence on the physical world, they really seemed like no more than a botched experiment.

"Why did they make ghosts at all?" she inquired.

"They probably didn't think it through. Thank the Ten, evil isn't always rational and organized. But never mind ghosts today, they are Hades' charge to round up and help move on. All others live under certain rules. They can do as they please, as long as they don't show themselves to or kill humans," he explained.

"Isn't that the whole-"

"No," Azrael interrupted her, emphatically. "That is what human fear has portrayed. The reality is that they rarely feed on humans at all. And they almost never kill. When they do, Hermes or Ares step in."

Azrael walked in silence for a bit before he continued. So, monsters were really just "monsters light". That was a relief, amidst the discoveries she'd been making about this gruesome world.

"But when they go off the rails, it tends to have disastrous consequences. Which is why we need to shut this werewolf down before he pulls in his entire pack. And Denning is a very special place, in that it's a large territory in which an ancient vampire pack coexists with werewolves, ghouls, shapeshifters, and skinwalkers. They're in a loose alliance, which in many ways has served them well. The vampires supervise the werewolves' monthly transformation in exchange for their blood. The ghouls feed off dead animals, hunted by the skinwalkers who transform into larger animals, and make all the corpses disappear. And the shapeshifters transform into humans and do all sorts of illegal things that make everyone happy...- Before you ask, no, we do not intervene for anything other than the endangerment of human life."

"I wasn't going to... never mind. Sounds like a good arrangement. Wouldn't that make everybody happy?"

"You'd think... But no. Tensions spark often. The various species are terrible at co-existing. But it's provided these packs with such a comfortable life that they each refuse to leave the region. Denning itself is a mostly abandoned town in the middle of these woods. But the territory reaches far beyond it. The roads leading up to Denning actually all have "Welcome to Denning" signs far, far out of town. It's a code, to let other creatures know that they've entered the territory... and that they better turn around. All of them are extremely territorial, in case that didn't bleed through in my story..."

Something suddenly occurred to Lyla. "Azrael, how come you all speak English? You guard humans all over the planet, there are thousands of languages in the world. Why English? For that matter, why don't you all speak whatever the Gods spoke on their planet?"

"We don't actually know that they spoke anything at all. They might very well have had a different form of communication," he began.

"Ah yes, I forget that they are all cagey about their past..."

Azrael ignored her snide comment. Maybe he didn't know the definition of "cagey". More likely, he didn't deem it worthy of an answer, good little soldier that he tended to be wherever Hermes was concerned.

"We speak the most internationally used language in the

world. It has changed over the course of history. Centuries ago, angels had to speak multiple languages, now English is sufficient. Athena's scholars still learn fifteen to twenty languages each, and they teach them to quite a few of our bloodline. Once upon a time, I wanted them to teach me. But they told me I spoke best with my fists," Azrael explained bitterly, before turning his attention back onto the path and motioning her to be silent.

They snuck through the woods for another couple of hours in silence, before coming out on a wide green lawn. The sun was rising now, making Lyla think that Hermes' Island must have been about two time zones ahead of Eastern Standard Time. Dozens of beautiful horses were grazing behind an electric fence nearby. They crossed a street and arrived on official private property. This wasn't just a ranch; it was a kid's camp. For very rich kids.

"Fancy..." she muttered.

"They run this place for humans. It's a family business," Azrael explained.

"By family, you mean the ones that rhyme with "empires"? Isn't that a bit..."

"It's perfectly safe. Now please shut your mouth before more disrespect comes out of it," he chided her.

Keeping quiet, she followed him across the parking lot and into the compound, where he asked for a Ms. Brown.

21

They were led through the wood-paneled corridors of the ground floor and into an office that screamed "wealth". Even Lyla could tell that the old books on the shelves were worth a fortune. But the biggest status symbol were the photos, casually strewn across the shelves, of a woman posing with everyone from Bill Gates to Mick Jagger. This person had wide-reaching power, and she wanted you to know it.

Said woman casually strolled in a moment later, walking around them and sitting behind her desk without shaking their hands. Lyla followed Azrael's lead and sat across from the vampire.

She wasn't what Lyla had expected. Having watched too many movies, she'd thought a vampire would be stunningly beautiful and captivate her with one look of her deep blue eyes. But this woman was... well, not even a woman. She looked barely out of her teens and was actually rather plain. She wore riding pants and boots, and had walked in holding a helmet and a crop. Lyla stared at them as she carefully placed them onto the desk between them.

"Keeping up appearances, you understand," the vampire said, sweetly. And as she did, something shifted. Something about how she held herself, how she spoke, how she flicked her wrist at the discarded helmet was captivating. Enthralling really. She radiated the power reflected on the shelves.

She also radiated something else: hostility. A whole lot of it.

"Mercy," Azrael addressed her. "I thank you for calling upon us."

"Oh, Azi, so formal and old-fashioned. And yet you're not even fifty. Nothing but a cute little duckling. There's no need to pretend around your elders," she responded.

Azrael's smile stiffened, as did Lyla's spine. She'd read that vampires were fast and strong – though not as fast and as strong as humans had made them out to be in their stories – and had a psychopathic lack of qualms for violence. But she was fairly certain Azrael could still take the bitch.

"Mercy, you called for our help, remember?" he answered, as politely as possible.

"Yes, yes, but I do love making you flutter through all those hoops..." she said sweetly, though there was no sweetness in her eyes, just cold, indiscriminate rage.

"Mercy, we've been through this before. I know you love nothing more than a good show of power, but the reality here is that you need me. And I don't particularly need you. So, are you sure you want to go down this road? Again?" Azrael said, an ever so slight threat in his voice.

"Fair point. But... there's that whole Hermes nobility that won't let you shed blood unless absolutely necessary. You wouldn't dare harm me, and that just makes it so fun to toy with you," she replied, baring her teeth.

No fangs, Lyla noted.

"Oh Mercy, I know plenty of ways to hurt you without leaving any permanent damage. See, the thing about not being allowed to inflict avoidable harm, is that it makes you really creative..." Azrael insinuated. His smile was gone, replaced with that terrifying combination of power and arrogance he sometimes displayed.

"Fine," Mercy conceded. "Don't get your feathers all ruffled."

Azrael leaned back and crossed his arms, letting her know he'd won the first round.

"Who's the gosling?" she asked of Lyla.

"Just an apprentice," Azrael answered, dismissively. That was the second time this morning he'd shown contempt toward her, though she was happy to have the heat taken off her in the presence of Mercy Brown.

"I see," the vampire replied, slowly turning her head toward Lyla. "I certainly hope she knows the risk she took, entering Denning."

"For the love of the Ten, get to the point!" Azrael exclaimed, ignoring her warning.

"You really do take all the fun out of it, don't you?" Mercy replied, all business. "Fine. The Alpha werewolf's youngest son has lost his mind. His name is Colin, he's in his early thirties, and he's been going around biting good townsfolk. The idiot got it in his head that human folklore was onto something about lycanthropy being contagious."

Lyla had read that none of the creatures could turn humans; their condition was simply hereditary but never contagious. Which also explained how well contained it was, since every single creature was born into the life and into a family of creatures.

"I would take him out myself," the vampire continued. "But I'd rather avoid a war with the werewolves... Hence the need for your delightful presence."

"Where is he?" Azrael asked, ignoring the disdain dripping from Mercy's voice.

"He's barricaded himself in that old shack in Denning proper. It's only another – what? two? - hour hike through the woods. Unless you walk along the road, in which case it's four. I could give you a ride, but I really don't want to."

"You're welcome, Mercy," Azrael replied, standing up. "It's been a pleasure, as always."

And he turned his back on her, leaving the room without another word. Lyla stood up and muttered an intimidated "Bye" at the vampire.

Before she was outside, the latter spoke again. "Learn everything you can from him. He knows what he's doing, that one." Lyla turned around and caught a glimpse of sadness in the vampire's face. It was quickly replaced with contempt, as she added a growled, "And now get the fuck out of my office."

A half hour of silent walking later, Azrael stopped, sat down, and offered her some water and venison jerky.

"I thought you said not to insult them?" Lyla whispered.

"I said, you shouldn't insult them. Mercy and I... We have our dynamic. It works for us. She likes to remind me of her power. But that only works if I give her something to push back against," he replied, wolfing down his portion of meat.

"I guess I get it," Lyla began, pensively. "Their taste for warm, human blood... It's what they are at their very core. It defines them the way our wings define us. Living their entire existence without being allowed to ever open a human vein... It would be like walking around with your magic bound. There at all times, reminding you of what you are, begging to be used, but forbidden... What's the harm, if it gives her satisfaction to bark at you, when you're a constant reminder that she may never bite?"

Lyla looked up. Azrael had stopped chewing and was staring at her. "I apologize for what I said earlier. I spoke in anger. You would make an excellent guardian. You just met a creature who openly threatened you, and you showed her compassion and understanding... And yes, that is exactly why I let Mercy sharpen her claws on me."

22

The final leg of their journey took the predicted two hours. By the time they made it into Denning, Lyla's sense of reality had gone on strike. She was walking around a regular American town in regular Upstate New York, and the idea of angels and monsters no longer computed. All of it felt like wading through a dream, someone else's dream. As she automatically put one foot in front of the other, she couldn't help the feeling that she'd wake up in her apartment, next to Max, to find out the big guy on the path ahead of her and his lessons in magic had been nothing but a very vivid dream.

Their training clothes were hidden by surprisingly human looking winter coats, and Azrael, his shoulder-length black hair tied off in a bun, almost fit into the human landscape. Though they needn't have worried about blending in: the town was deserted. Even for early afternoon, it was eerily empty. They walked down its one road, not encountering a single soul or vehicle. Though, occasionally, Lyla could swear that she heard whispering right behind her, only to turn back and see no one there. *Another sign that I'm dreaming*, she thought and almost started giggling.

But the further down the road they got, the more Lyla's cognitive dissonance disappeared, replaced by an eerie sense of premonition. As much as her brain struggled to grasp reality, there was magic in the air. She could sense it almost like a thin mist she was walking through, as it slowly brought her senses back to full alertness.

There were several run-down, collapsed, and abandoned houses along the road, each one creepier than the next. But the last one was haunted. Its moldy wooden slats needed a coat of paint twenty years ago, all windows were barricaded from the inside, making it impossible to peek in, and there was a hole taking out a large part of its roof and third floor, where a chimney had once risen along its eastern wall.

As they approached the house, Lyla's stomach started twisting into an uncomfortable knot. The closer they got, the less she wanted to be there. Finally, she reached out and grabbed Azrael's sleeve, who immediately came to a stop, looking at her quizzically.

"Wait," she started. "This doesn't feel right. There's evil in that house."

She didn't know how she knew, but that was exactly what it felt like: wrong. This was the same exact feeling she'd had facing the thing that had mutilated and killed Max.

Azrael turned to fully face her and gave her what he must have thought of as a reassuring smile.

"Lyla, you're hesitating because this is your first mission. That's normal. It happens to everyone the first time. Everything has been theory for you thus far. This is the first real danger you're facing since..." he trailed off.

"I swear that's not it," she interrupted. "Azrael, we shouldn't go in there. Whatever is in there, it's waiting for us. It knows we're coming!" She couldn't control the flutter in her voice, when every cell in her body was telling her to run in the opposite direction.

For a brief moment, the big angel seemed disturbed by her words, before shaking his head. "Mercy's information is good. She's always true to her word. She wouldn't set me up," he insisted.

Lyla swallowed, looking at the house across the street. She knew she shouldn't trip up Azrael, she knew her job was to obey and watch how a real mission played out. The worst thing she could do was to be a liability while he took care of the werewolf. Yet, she could barely control the shaking in her muscles.

"Okay," she said, keeping her eyes on the haunted house across the street.

"Lyla, I wouldn't let anything happen to you while you're in my care," he said, ducking his head and looking for her eyes.

Knowing how useless it would be to tell him it wasn't her safety she worried about, she answered, "I know," and took the first step across the asphalt road.

Azrael had explained to her on the way, that he planned on simply knocking on the front door. Once inside, he could easily use magic without witnesses and one lone werewolf was something he could fight in his sleep. Mostly, he'd explained, Hermes wanted her to experience the adrenaline of a real fight, as well as to observe how guardians persuaded their opponents to give up their twisted ways. She'd asked him what would happen if the wolf promised to atone. Azrael had replied, that this particular one seemed too far along. But, on the off chance that he could be redeemed, they'd take him prisoner and bring him to the Alpha werewolf to serve a prison sentence and be rehabilitated.

As they walked toward the house, which, oddly enough, stood alongside other houses on a large patch of green grass without any fence to demarcate the property, Lyla noticed that the front door had been left ajar. Her heart racing, she made her body put one foot in front of the other, her legs feeling like lead, as she kept the tears making their way up her throat from choking her.

True to his word, Azrael politely knocked on the door. "Colin?" he called.

Silence.

"Colin?" he tried again, louder this time.

Nothing.

"Colin! My name is Azrael, I serve Hermes and I've been sent to talk to you. I'm coming in. I strongly suggest you meet me with your hands in sight!"

Azrael sighed, shook his head, and slipped through the door, muttering under his breath, "Every time... When will they learn?"

Cautiously, Lyla followed, quietly shutting the door behind her.

Azrael immediately shrugged out of his coat, unfolding his wings, and she followed suit. The inside of the house was crumbling. Furniture pieces were sparsely scattered around, as if someone had left a few things behind and moved out in a hurry. Water stains covered the walls and ceiling, old wallpaper from the 1960's peeled off the walls. Once colorful, it gave the main living space a sordid quality. The fireplace was no more than a pile of crumbled bricks, light fixtures hung off the walls and ceilings, barely held up by a cable or two, and the smell of the place was unbearable.

As they turned the corner into a corridor – Azrael ahead, Lyla giving him enough space in all directions to maneuver quickly if needed – she beheld the cause: a dead body lay on the ground. It looked like it had been a man in his mid-thirties or so. Shirtless, he lay propped up against the wall, an expression of pain and terror on his face. There was an infected bite in his shoulder sending deep black veins toward his heart.

Azrael stopped for an instant, looking at the corpse. His jaw twitched, that mixture of anger and sadness on his face she'd seen there before. She saw his lips move silently, but she couldn't tell what he was mouthing. Then, in a split-second, his expression went back to neutral as he slowly opened a creaking door leading to what she could only assume were stairs.

Lyla made herself stop staring at the corpse. She knew it would haunt her dreams for months to come, but she also felt that perturbing sense of wrongness grow with every step they took deeper into the house.

She almost let out a shriek when she realized that someone was sitting on the stairs. A human boy in his late teens. He was holding his biceps, where she saw a similar wound as that on the corpse's shoulder. They were the werewolf's guinea pigs she realized, the humans he'd tried to turn. And his bite was killing them. Judging by how far down his arm and up his neck the black veins were reaching, she could only imagine what was going on under his shirt. He didn't look like he'd make it to a hospital in time.

What was even more telling was that he didn't have the energy to be surprised about the winged visitors. He just looked at them, eyes glazed over in his pale feverish face. As they approached, she realized he was trembling. She knew the chills were a symptom of blood poisoning, but he was mostly trembling out of fear. He knew he was dying...

Trying to hold his head up, he looked at Azrael and slowly pointed to the ceiling, mouthing the word *Upstairs*.

Tears in her eyes, Lyla paused and looked to her teacher for guidance. Azrael, who was only a couple of feet from the boy, gave him a confident nod and turned to climb the stairs. But just as he walked past him, the boy grabbed his arm with surprising force. For a second Lyla thought he'd attack them. Until Azrael calmly turned toward him and stepped back down. Never letting go of Azrael, the boy slowly lifted his shirt with his other hand, revealing black veins snaking their way all the way across his torso. The gesture seemed to have taken all the energy he had left. He looked like death itself, as his hands dropped and he looked up at Azrael pleadingly.

For the first time, she realized how in control of his emotions the angel was. His breathing had sped up ever so slightly, betraying the fact that it pained him greatly to watch the boy's plight. But he never let him know that, as he smiled and crouched down near him, taking his bloodied hand in both of his. It disappeared in his grasp, much as this boy's short existence would disappear into the grand scheme of things.

Azrael locked eyes with him, their faces intimately close to one another, and wrapped one of his grey wings around the boy's back and head, supporting him with the gentleness he'd show an infant. The tip of his other wing reached between them. As Azrael leaned in and kissed the boy's sweat-beaded forehead, his wing twitched against the latter's chest.

Lyla knew what he'd done. The magic he'd expelled at such close range might as well have been a bullet through the heart.

But, as opposed to a bullet, it didn't leave any blood in its wake. The boy simply went limp, collapsing against the wing holding him up, his hand slipping out from between Azrael's.

Ever so slowly, the angel of death lay the body down onto the stairs. Mouthing the same words he had before, a single tear rolling down his cheek, he stood back up and climbed the stairs without looking back.

Lyla felt like she had just intruded on an intimate moment,

a sacred moment. Walking past the body, she noticed that the scared little boy looked peaceful, relieved. He was smiling, his dead face the only flicker of brightness in the house.

There was a second door at the top of the stairs; Azrael didn't even bother to open it quietly. Instead, he barged in, Lyla on his heels, as they entered another large living space, a simple, bleak, run-down room, empty of any furniture except for a few bare, stained mattresses. Across the room, leaning against a wall, stood, she presumed, Colin the werewolf. He was tall and gangly, not at all the scary beast she'd imagined, an unkempt beard and a shaggy head of hair the only indication of his nature. His posture was entirely relaxed... as if he'd been waiting for them. As they stepped in, a wide, manic, tooth-gapped grin spread across his face, and Lyla realized that he wasn't evil. He was mad.

"Colin," Azrael began. "You have one chance-"

"Yes, yes," Colin interrupted him, the sinister smile never leaving his face. "But I have a surprise for you, birdies..."

His eyes widening, hands gesturing outward, he whispered, "Turn around!" as if revealing a wonderful gift.

Even Azrael didn't whirl around fast enough.

As the door was kicked shut, five creatures peeled out of the shadows.

To her horror, she realized that they were variations on the demon that had murdered Max.

For the first time in over three months, Lyla realized that some things were too powerful even for Azrael.

23

As soon as she registered the five presences, a switch was pulled inside Lyla. Gone was the foreboding fear in the pit of her stomach, gone was the trembling in her muscles, the palpitations of her heart. Instead, a cold peace washed over her. She took her first deep breath since they'd crossed through the town limits of Denning, as she looked at the five shapes. Three of them were built the exact same way as the first demon she'd encountered. The other two had obscenely deformed muzzles: like a dog's, but where a muzzle should have been, they split into two ends, each with a set of pointy teeth dripping with saliva. As for their six legs, they ended in overly large paws, tipped with claws so long they were clicking on the floor with each step. All five of them shared the elongated pupils of a goat's eyes, the crab like carapaces, and those curled horns atop their heads.

She vaguely registered that the mere sight of these creatures would have shattered a human mind. But she wasn't human. She'd never been. She was an angel, bred for this very kind of fight.

Instantly, Azrael summoned a domed shield around them.

As the five demons slowly walked around, positioning themselves in an evenly spread circle around them, he kept his eyes on as many of them as possible and calmly said, "Fight for your life. But, if you get an opening, I need you to run. Fuck discretion, fly out of here, if you can. As for these ugly fuckers, their carapace is impenetrable, but they're extremely vulnerable if you can get between the plates."

Lyla nodded. She didn't want to leave him behind, but she also knew that she was so far out of her depth, she'd only be a liability to him in a fight.

She'd do what she could though. One of the demons was more than enough to focus on for a novice like her. She knew she'd likely not make it out, but she didn't allow that knowledge to distract her. Instead, she flared her wings, squared off on the opponent straight ahead of her, keeping the closest two in her field of vision, and allowed her power to rise to the surface.

She'd greatly finessed her attacks in the last sixteen days, but she didn't know how long she could stay on the offense. As a martial artist, she'd learned that training was very different from actual fighting. Where one could keep up through the exhaustion of exercise for hours, they generally ran out of energy in seconds during a real fight. Even when she'd destroyed the training room a couple of weeks ago, she hadn't experienced the adrenaline of real life-threatening danger. Today, she might well deplete her resources in seconds. Which would be doing the demons' job for them.

Instead, she prepared to use the latest tool in her arsenal: telekinesis.

When Azrael dropped the shield, she was ready: she let out a quiet, high-pitched screech, pulling the hardwood flooring up from all around the clawed demon in front of her. Confused by the sounds she was making, and the fact that she hadn't at-

188

tacked him in traditional angel fashion, the beast wasted a split second before attacking. Which was all she needed. By the time it snapped back to attention, she'd pulled up enough of the flooring to create a tight cage around it. The planks had simply shot up all around it, curving inward and holding it tightly in place.

As it thrashed around in fury, trying to free itself of its unexpected prison, Lyla saw that another double-muzzled demon was launching itself toward her, on her left.

This time, she was the one who wasn't fast enough. She'd underestimated the energy it would take to cage Demon Number One: so far, she'd only worked with water and fire, two volatile but easily malleable types of elements; she needed to keep the pressure up against the wooden planks, or the beast would find a way to break them and escape. That meant sending a steady stream of her power in one direction, while being attacked from another.

Keeping her hold on the wooden planks, she sent half her power toward the floor in front of Demon Number Two, trying to raise the wood there and at least trip it up. But it was expecting her attack and easily jumped over the hurdle and straight at her.

As she saw it hurl itself through the air, Lyla realized that there was no point in saving her power. If she didn't do something, this would be the end of the road for her anyhow. The thing had leapt so high up, she could see its underbelly coming back down toward her.

She'd heard that one's last moments could stretch out into minutes if death was coming visibly and violently. And indeed, every millisecond elongated to a minute in her mind, as the beast stretched its six legs out to the side, gliding down toward her, where she guessed it would snap all six of those paws around her to shred her to pieces with those pointy claws that were gleaming in the few beams of sunlight that made their way through the wooden slats barricading the windows.

And as the sunlight made its way even into this dark hellhole of a house, hope made its way into her heart in this moment of final danger. The demon was so sure of itself, it didn't realize it was presenting her with its greatest weakness: as it stretched its limbs to the sides, the plates covering its belly pulled apart, offering her the smallest of openings, a tiny line of skin underneath its carapace at about the spot where a heart would be.

Not holding anything back, Lyla gathered the anger she felt at having been set up, at the danger Azrael's life was in, at having witnessed the gratitude of a teenager for his own mercy killing, and screamed it all right at a pinpoint she picked between Demon Number Two's plates.

It crashed in a heap to the ground with a yelp.

And time snapped back into place.

Lyla wasn't sure if it was dead or merely unconscious, but the amount of power she'd sent toward Demon Number Two had been so great that she'd let go of Demon Number One's trap. She turned around to see it stretching its body, free from its improvised cage, contorting its spine to unnatural angles. At the same time, it curled and uncurled its claws on the floorboards like a happy cat, literally licking its chops with what appeared to be a forked tongue that reached both of its muzzle tips at the same time.

Behind the eager demon, she saw that Azrael had dispatched one beast and was fighting the other two, wildly flaring around his magic and wielding two large knives that must have been hidden under his large coat.

Meanwhile, the wolf was sitting in a corner, giggling madly as he watched the display of violence unfolding in front of him.

Lyla remembered that demons liked to play with their food, and she realized that the thing in front of her was waiting for her fear to mount. She would have been grateful for the few seconds' reprieve, but as she caught her breath, exhaustion set in. She'd served Demon Number Two with everything she had, and she wasn't sure she could make a single floorboard rise, if she tried.

But the demon didn't know that. In fact, as the sorrow of defeat threatened to set in, she questioned whether it was playing with her or whether it was biding its time. She'd by far exceeded its worst expectations of her power, and maybe it didn't want to die at her hands.

Playing confident, she stared it down and cracked her knuckles. "What's up, pup? You scared to lose to a fledgling?" she sneered at it.

The demon growled, the sound somehow resonating in two different directions. At the same time, she saw that Azrael had been forced into a corner by his opponents. He'd dropped the longer of the two knives, and there was a bleeding gash in his arm, where one of the pincers must have closed on him. His wings were splayed against the walls to his side, still pulsing with energy, but the lobster-goat demons were closing in on him too quickly, dodging his strikes at lightning speed. As his back hit the corner of the room, he flicked his remaining knife at one of the creatures. Lyla didn't even see it tumble through the air. Instead, it seemed to go from Azrael's grip into the demon's neck in an instant, embedding itself right between the plate that covered its head and the one that covered its neck.

At the same moment, Demon Number One took advantage of her distraction and launched across the space separating them.

Before she knew what had happened, she was in its grasp.

It had simply taken her legs out from under her with a swipe of a paw, and was now sitting behind her, her torso in the tight clutch of its middle legs, pinning both her wings to her side, its front claws threateningly close to her throat. She tried to swing her elbows around, but all she hit was rock hard carapace.

"I wouldn't suggest that," it purred in her ear, with a suggestive scrape of its claws up and down her throat.

Hearing an intelligible voice out of such a monstrous creature should have broken her sanity. But fear never kicked in. Instead, she was met with cold, calculating reason. And her reason told her that this thing – much like its brother she'd met months ago – had orders to bring her in alive. It wanted her to think she was in mortal danger, but she wasn't. Unless it lost control of course. But no good would come from worrying about that.

Her arms were no help. Her wings and magic had been rendered useless. Feigning a scared swallow, she moved her neck ever so slightly, gauging how tightly trapped it was. No, headbutting was out of the question as well.

And then she remembered the one weapon she still had. It was poking into her leg at the moment. She'd fallen with her legs folded under her, the leather of her right boot poking into her left thigh.

As she thought about how to free her foot from under her leg without raising her captor's suspicion, she saw Azrael, panting, dodging a demon pincer and swaying too far to the left. The demons had known to keep their distance and to wear him out, which was exactly what she would have done with an opponent like Azrael. Another claw snapped down on his shoulder, catching on his left wing in the process.

Azrael fell to his knees, eyes wide, and screamed in pain, clutching at his feathers. There was a trickle of blood dripping down his shoulder and wing, but his scream sounded like nothing she'd ever expected to hear from him. Their wings were physically highly sensitive, but this was something else. The demon had cut into the part of the male's wing that was beyond the physical, it had cut into his power, his essence, his very soul.

And it had brought him to his knees.

As if in slow motion, Lyla saw the creature gleefully lift a pincered arm, pointing it toward Azrael's chest.

Before it could impale him, before she could think and remember that her own wings were trapped, Lyla screamed in anguish. At the sight of the kneeling angel, she let out a sound of such pure terror as she had never known before.

And the demon hovering over him vanished into red mist. She hadn't aimed for its weak points. She hadn't even thought of it. She'd simply thrown every last bit of her aching soul at the thing.

But there was one more thing left to do, before she could let go.

Demon Number One's grasp on her had loosened in surprise. And Lyla took the opportunity to squirm her foot out from under her, reach into her boot, and twist around in its grip. Before it knew what had happened, the demon collapsed onto the ground, two inches of vampire fang stuck in its belly.

"Are you hurt?" Azrael croaked out of the corner.

"No. Just spent... really spent..." she answered, panting on all four, the edges of her vision threatening to turn black. "You?"

"I'll be fine. Surface wounds. No permanent damage."

His voice sounded strained, but he got to his feet and walked steadily toward the werewolf. Lyla realized that the creature was still giggling maniacally.

Closing her eyes and dropping her head, she heard Azrael ask it three times if it was willing to change its ways. It just laughed through his questions.

And then it stopped laughing and silence fell upon the room.

A moment later, Azrael's hand was lifting her chin up, making her look at him. She realized that he looked healthier than she'd expected. Maybe she'd overestimated his exhaustion. Maybe he hadn't been nearly as out of his depth as she'd thought...

He stood up, bent over and carefully picked her up. "I'm flying us to the portal in case there are any more of them. There's enough of a cloud cover to hide us. Rest. You've earned it. You fought like a true priestess of Hermes'."

Azrael walked them to the third floor. She closed her eyes and rested her head against his unwounded shoulder. She felt him take off through the hole in the roof. Then, nothing.

Only blissful darkness.

24

The first thing Lyla saw when she finally opened her eyes, was Jeremy's intent face hovering over her, eyes closed as if he were in deep concentration. She was back in her bed; her limbs wouldn't move, and her eyelids felt like weights pulled down on them. Jeremy's hands were framing her face, his palms pulsing with magic. Unlike when he'd healed her in the past, she could feel his power seep straight into her. When she finally blinked her eyes fully open and cleared her throat, his eyes opened. For a split second, his dilated pupils looked like a bird of prey's, like the Gods' eyes. The vision passed as quickly as it had come though, giving way to Jeremy's kind blue eyes.

"Thank the Ten, you're awake," he sighed, letting go of her face.

"What's going on? I feel... heavy," she muttered through her muddled thoughts.

"I've been healing you all night. You were almost as depleted as the day we first met," he replied, gently helping Lyla sit up and propping her up. "Though you're healing much faster now."

Jeremy leaned back in his chair, rubbing a hand over his

sleep-deprived face. He took a deep breath and continued, "Sweetheart, I need to know exactly what happened yesterday. What did this to you? Who attacked you?"

Through the fog in her brain, Lyla started remembering Denning. The foreboding feeling in her gut returned as soon as she did, but she could barely keep her thoughts straight. "Ask Azrael," she murmured, closing her eyes to go back to sleep.

"I can't," he replied with uncharacteristic urgency. "Azrael left as soon as you got back. He and five of his best were sent to help Ares on a mission. He only had time to bring you to me."

The only thing keeping her from falling back asleep was the renewed twisting in her gut. She looked at Jeremy's distressed face, but all she could see were the demons' pincers closing on Azrael's wing, his agonized scream as he fell to his knees...

Jeremy took a shaky breath and continued, "Ares needed brawn, but it was supposed to be a simple and fast mission. They should have been back hours ago... I'm worried about him."

Lyla's brain was still lagging and she had trouble making sense of the words, but the apprehension she felt doubled. Azrael should be here. They didn't know where he was. He was in danger. She knew it. She could sense it deep inside her. And so did Jeremy. She'd never seen him this agitated.

"What happened in Denning, Lyla?" he asked again, barely keeping it together.

"It was a trap. The werewolf was just bait... We were ambushed by five demons," she replied, sorting through her thoughts with painful efforts.

"What kind of demons?" he asked, leaning in and grabbing her hand. He let some of his soothing magic seep into her, helping her breathe and gather her thoughts.

"The same kind as the one that killed Max... Three of those, and the other two were similar but with paws and muzzles. Split muzzles..." she told him, letting the ocean of his eyes calm her jumbled memories.

"That's not possible. Lyla, are you sure that's what you saw?"

She swallowed and nodded. Yes, that much she was sure of.

"Those are Princes of Hell. They're Lucifer's generals. They're nearly invincible. How did you make it out? Azrael couldn't possibly take on five of them and walk right into the next battle."

"He didn't," Lyla answered, pulling her hand away, as she remembered the blood running down her arm... blood too dark to be human, too thick, like syrup dripping down all the way to her elbow, as she pierced its heart... She peaked at her wrist and noticed that it was still there, dried black now, crusting her skin and her uniform.

"He killed two. I took care of the other three," she told him, staring at the wall. She'd done what was necessary. She didn't regret doing it. But suddenly she remembered something she hadn't noticed in the heat of the moment: she'd felt the creature's final heartbeats against her knuckles. One. Two. Then nothing.

Before Jeremy could swallow his shock and ask her more questions, there was a piercing scream in the yard.

And another.

And another.

And another.

Jeremy jumped up to look out the window.

"No... no... no, no, no, no, no, no..." she heard him whisper, as doors banged open all around them, running footsteps and screaming voices echoing through the compound.

Fighting through the last of her sluggishness, Lyla threw away the covers and stood up, dizzy with the sudden motion. Before half a minute had passed, her cell door slammed open and Hermes, a blur of motion, stood before Jeremy, grabbing his shoulder.

"Jerahmeel, the villagers! Get as many out of here as you can. Now! Go!" he barked at the healer, shaking him to alertness.

It took Jeremy a second to register Hermes' words before he turned around and flew off the balcony. As soon as he set flight, Hermes turned around toward Lyla, freezing her to the ground with apprehension.

"They're here for you, Lailah," he told her, taking a much more controlled step toward her. "I wish I had time to explain... I'm going to lift the currents off the Sacred Mountain for a few minutes. I need you to fly up there. As fast as you can, do you hear me? Whatever happens, whatever you see, you wait up there. Azrael will come for you. He'll keep you safe. Do not trust anyone else!"

His black eyes stared at her so intently, Lyla couldn't help nodding. "O-okay," she told him, promising to stay out of a fight she might very well be needed in.

Before her brain registered his motion, Hermes had pulled her into an embrace. He was so tall that her face was pressed against his barreled chest, one of his strong arms wrapped around her shoulders, his other hand covering the back of her head.

There was nothing in his embrace of the violence she'd associated with those clawed hands. On the contrary, they were gentle. Tender. Paternal.

Wrapping most of her body in his massive wings, he bent over and murmured against the top of her head. "I'm so sorry, Lailah. I wish there was more time. I wish..." He shook his head and sighed, laying his cheek against the top of her head. "Be strong, beautiful child. Be brave."

With that, he pulled back a step and gently kissed her on the forehead.

Stunned, Lyla just stared at him, the commotion outside forgotten.

"Go!" he yelled, bringing her back into the present.

Unable to find any words, she turned around and took off. She headed straight for the mountain, blocking out the screams all around her. Closing her eyes against the ashes in the air, trying her best to ignore her instinct to land and fight, her wings beating faster than they ever had, she flew over the village and up the mountain. Tears blurred her vision, but she knew what was happening down there. What she should be helping to stop.

As soon as her feet touched the top of the mountain, the currents went back up. She turned around and saw the fires scattered around the village. She saw angels trying to escape, falling from the sky. And she heard piercing screams. High-pitched screams. The screams of terrified children. Of dying fledglings.

And she, was trapped. Unable to do anything but watch, as the island was reduced to ashes.

PART TWO

25

Tearing her eyes away from the horror unfolding at the bottom of the mountain, Lyla stumbled toward Azrael's cabin. She'd never been inside; she knew it was a part of himself the angel locked away from everyone – including her. It was an invasion of his privacy, but she needed to assess her situation. Her father had sent her up here to be safe, and she wasn't going to wait around and pray that Azrael would come help her. Come to think of it, she didn't even know he'd be back at all. Though that was a thought she couldn't dwell on...

Slowly she pulled the heavy door open, stepping into a beautiful living room. Everything about Azrael was functionality, and yet this place was set up for comfort. She didn't look around to take in what made it so. More so, it was a feeling that hit her as she walked through the door. It felt like walking into a real home, the likes of which she hadn't had in two decades.

Tearing through the place, she found the kitchen and looked for supplies. She wasn't surprised to find the place stocked with food and water, knives stashed in every corner and enough wood to survive the rest of the winter.

As she turned back into the large living room after a thorough exploration of the small cabin, something grabbed Lyla's arm and smashed her into the wall, knocking the wind out of her.

Max had trained her for situations like this. He'd taught her how to use her body to her advantage and to fight with everything she had to get out of positions just like this one. But he hadn't trained her to go up against skilled fighters twice her size. Because that wasn't possible. Self-defense was only useful for the many situations in which one faced a smaller, untrained, sloppy, or distracted attacker.

It wasn't useful against an unleashed Azrael.

The angel pinned her against the wall with the full weight of his body, making it impossible to sprout her wings, his hands bands of steel around her biceps, allowing her no reach for a punch, his legs spreading hers, rendering her feet and knees useless. She tried to stomp on his boots, she weakly kicked him in the shins, she tried to thrash and headbutt him. But he didn't budge.

She'd been in similar positions with him before. He'd trained her to escape anyone weaker than him. They'd wrestled and practiced, to the point where his physical proximity had toppled over into the realm of the distracting.

But there was nothing amusing or arousing about this.

Azrael's face was staring down at her and, if she hadn't known any better, she would have said that he was in pain. The eyes that stared coldly at hers were unnaturally bloodshot, as if all their capillaries had burst at once, their pupils dilated all the way. The muscles in his face were twitching and his hands were loosening and tightening on her arms ever so slightly, as if he were waging a battle with himself.

As she looked at the pain etched deeply into his handsome

face, Lyla thought, *This is it. This is how I die.*

But she wasn't scared, or sad, or even angry. All she felt was pity for the warrior fighting the beast inside him. She didn't know what had happened, why he had an impulse to come after her, but she felt his agony as if it were her own.

She looked into his dilated pupils and heard his beautiful laughter ring in her ears, the light-heartedness with which he'd played during their snowball fight. She felt his tight embrace in the training room, when she'd almost annihilated them both and, in reaction, he'd grabbed her and held her as if he never intended to let her go.

And at the same time, she felt her father's immensely soft wings gently wrap around her, cocooning her in a parental safety she could never have imagined. She remembered the sensation of Jeremy's skin, as he injected his infinite love straight into her hands, his ocean blue eyes regarding her like there was nothing more important in the world than that she be heard. And through it all, she felt Max's wiry arms wrap around her sides, his chest seeping warmth and protection into her naked back.

But she also saw the backdrop of pain and hurt that had led to those moments, the darkness she and those people had battled every day – which made their love all the more precious, all the more meaningful.

Throughout her visions, she felt a fiercely burning love ignite in her chest. The love she felt in this moment of her impending death – for Max, and Jeremy; for Azrael, and even for her father – was all-encompassing. She saw them all in Azrael's eyes, and, in them, she saw beyond – to the entire world with its constantly reoccurring stories of hope and despair, of courage and love. For the first time maybe in her entire existence, she felt an unassailable love for life itself. She finally understood the need for pain, the purpose of suffering, its humbling contrast to the beauty and love in the world. She understood that creation and destruction were so intimately linked, that one could not exist without the other. And that there was nothing more virtuous than the hope and courage humans and angels alike showed in the face of darkness.

As Lyla closed her eyes, she felt a profound peace wrap itself around her.

She wanted to tell Azrael that things would be all right, that she didn't blame him. But she couldn't form words. Instead, her voice came out as a hum, a hum she filled with all the love in her heart.

Suddenly, Azrael's hands left her arms, and he stepped back. Lyla opened her eyes and saw him a few feet away, backed up against the couch, clutching its back as if to keep his hands from grabbing her again, lest they betray him and try to hurt her again. His chest was heaving with labored breaths and his eyes still looked unhealthy, but the madness in them was gone.

"Syringe... under the bathroom sink... bring it to me..."

With that, he stumbled past her and into his bedroom. Lyla rushed to the bathroom, where she found a large syringe amongst first aid implements. She carefully entered the bedroom. The angel was splayed out on the bed, his left wrist handcuffed to the metal bedpost, another cuff waiting on the other side.

"Give it to me, quick... I can't hold it off much longer..."

She approached him, her steps unsure, but he tore the syringe out of her grasp as soon as she was in reach, violently sticking the needle into his left biceps.

"I need you to cuff my other wrist," he said, stretching his arm toward the open cuff. Lyla carefully crouched down, keeping her distance from him. With trembling hands, her eyes on his face, she grabbed his thick wrist and snapped the cuff closed around it.

As soon as he was fully incapacitated, Azrael leaned his head back into the pillows with a sigh.

"That was a tranquilizer. And the cuffs are a lot stronger than they look. I'll be unconscious for a few hours. You're safe from me."

Lyla straightened out and nodded, slowly backing away toward the door. Before she could turn around and leave, he added, "I'm so sorry, Lyla."

"I know."

26

S tumbling into the bathroom, Lyla wished for a lock on the door. But the cabin had not been built for visitors. As soon as she closed it behind her, she crumbled to the ground, sobbing.

Through all the madness, life had quieted down these last few weeks. There had been a routine, a new normalcy to her days. But the last twenty-four hours had shattered all semblance of that.

Azrael had suggested that the Fallen would come for her again at the first sign of her power. She'd thought that she was safe on the island for the time being, but he'd been beside himself when she'd showed her magic, and he'd hinted that they'd come at her aggressively if they realized that her training was effective.

They had.

Twice in one day.

If Jeremy's information was correct, they'd sent five of Lucifer's strongest fighters to kill Azrael and to kidnap her. When that hadn't worked, they'd gone with Plan B, and taken Azrael and his best soldiers out of the picture in order to attack the island.

Her father had confirmed it too: they were after her. And they were willing to kill everyone in their path. God knew how many villagers and priests had died in the attack. If her senses were to be trusted, the entire island had been annihilated while she flew to safety. Perhaps including the father she'd never known, the father who'd hugged her with so much love... She still couldn't make heads or tails of that encounter, but she knew that, for a moment, it had felt like Hermes had returned a piece of herself to her.

And now Azrael had attacked her. Azrael. The male who'd repeatedly sworn to keep her safe. She wanted to believe that there was a reasonable explanation. She'd seen the struggle on his face, in his body. He hadn't wanted to follow through with it, and he'd fought to break the connection with whatever had a hold on his mind. But she couldn't help the little voice in her head whispering, *Maybe he's just another one of the monsters after all.*

It wouldn't be the first time she'd believed someone to be an ally, only to have them change in front of her eyes. She'd been the victim of too many cruel people over the years. It wasn't entirely impossible that the angel was one of them.

But Hermes had told her to trust him.

More importantly, Jeremy trusted him, Jeremy who was the only person other than Max who had never given her any reason to doubt him.

And, whether she liked it or not, she'd learned one other thing in her dreadful confrontation with Azrael: she loved him. She didn't know why, how, or what that meant. But she couldn't ignore the irrefutable bond she felt toward him.

Besides, she had nowhere to go. No choice but to wait for his explanation.

Lyla rocked herself back and forth on the bathroom floor, weeping for several long minutes, before she invoked Max, imagining his loving arms wrapping around her, his breath on her neck, as he whispered, *I got you, I got you, beautiful girl. You're safe. I'm not letting anyone near you. Not on my watch.* His memory rocked back and forth with her, pacifying her, patiently waiting for her to run out of tears, to cry herself to exhaustion.

But she couldn't afford exhaustion. She needed to get ready.

When she could finally think clearly, Lyla walked around the cabin, arming herself. She found two large knives to clip to her pants and slipped a pocketknife that was just the right size to double as a reinforcement for her punching fist into her right pocket. Then she proceeded to make a fire in the living room to keep herself from freezing. Finally, she made tea and a meal of rice, eggs, and what she figured was rabbit. She didn't feel like eating, but she knew she needed to stay strong for whatever was to come, and in the absence of Max or Jeremy to force-feed her, she made herself swallow every painful, unwelcome bite of nutritious food.

And then she simply waited, feeding the fire and emptying her mind of all the worries and intrusive thoughts that would be cleared up in due time.

Until, finally, she heard motion behind Azrael's door. It was the sound of metal clanking on metal. The handcuffs. His croaking voice followed soon after. "Lyla? Lyla, please get in here."

Reluctantly, she stood up and carefully opened the bedroom door.

Azrael was where she'd left him, still safely cuffed to the bed. But the tension had left his body and his face. His eyes were back to their usual green-gold, any remnants of the bloodshot, yellow-tinged, wild look gone.

"Lyla?" he asked, his voice trembling ever so slightly with

uncertainty. "Would you please uncuff me? The key is in the bedside table."

When she didn't move, he added, "I'm back to normal. I promise."

She looked at him for another moment, at his steady eyes that refused to look away, and slowly crossed over to the bedside table, removing the key while carefully keeping as much distance as possible between her and the bed. She proceeded to unlock his left cuff, keeping her eyes on his hand for any signs of quick motion. But Azrael didn't move a muscle. In fact, he seemed to avoid breathing too deeply so as not to scare her. His eyes followed her, as she carefully placed the key in reaching distance of his hand and backed away to the door.

Visibly pained by her mistrust, Azrael closed his eyes, chewing on his lower lip, before he spoke. "I'm going to undo my other cuff and sit up. I won't get out of bed until you feel safe... I know you have no reason to believe me."

Ever so slowly, avoiding any brisk motions, he did exactly as he'd said. Lyla waited, by the door, ready to bolt, if necessary, her hands near the knives she'd picked up. She felt so very weary standing in the door, waiting to see if the only ally she had left was going to try to murder her. She hadn't bathed or changed clothes since the ambush in Denning. Her training uniform was torn in places, covered in blood in others. She could tell that she wasn't fully healed from the demon attack, and the food she'd eaten had barely stayed down.

"Did I hurt you?" he asked, uncertain.

She quickly shook her head in response.

Azrael closed his eyes in relief. "But I scared you. Which is probably worse."

Lyla watched him chew on his lip in silence. What could she say? He had scared her. He'd broken her already very fragile trust.

"If I could go back and change things I would... Please believe me," he continued, desperation in his voice. "The last thing I wanted, was to scare you... I am so, so sorry-"

"Stop!" Lyla burst out. "Stop telling me how sorry you are. You're not the victim here! What the fuck happened, Azrael?"

Taken aback, Azrael sat up a bit straighter and took a deep breath. "You're right. You're right..." Shaking his head, he continued, "The Fallen didn't come for the island sooner because they didn't want to risk losing too many demons in the process. Hermes' priests are some of the most skilled in combat, it would have been a diminishing return for them. So, while there were spies who'd probably fed them our location long ago, they bided their time."

"Hermes said they were here for me."

"Yes, that too... When we came back from Denning, I was sent to help Ares on a mission with five of my most accomplished fighters. But there was no mission. It was another trap. They captured us and injected us with something. I don't know what it was. I'd never heard of it. But it made us do their bidding. They told me to bring you to them. And they told... they told my friends to... they told them to kill as many of their own as they could..." he finished, barely getting the words out.

The full horror of Azrael's words slithered over her, like a poison she was trying to unhear. It was a brilliant plan: in one fell swoop, the Fallen had taken six of the most competent warriors out of the fight, had made them do their dirty work and open the floodgates so the demons could march in and take care of whatever was left of the island. And if she'd learned anything about the code by which Hermes' priests lived, the Fallen had broken the minds and spirits of Azrael's friends. They'd never be able to forgive their own sins.

She was still wary of Azrael, but she knew the unimaginable pain it caused him to think of his friends' very souls twisted in such a way.

The latter's eyes were closed, a tear slowly rolling through his two-day stubble, his hands still palms up at his sides. A very loud and bothersome part of her wanted to rush over to him and hold him the way Max had held her so many times. But she could feel the tension in her own body, the fact that another part of her very much expected him to turn into a feral beast at any moment.

"What do we do now?" she asked, taking the middle ground instead.

"Now, you tell me if you can trust me again or not," he answered, a grave finality in his voice. "Your father entrusted me with your safety months ago. I'd do anything to keep you from the Fallen. But I nearly became the person who delivered you to them. I'd understand if you preferred to stay far away from me."

Lyla regarded him for a moment. The words pained him, but he meant them. He'd leave her life forever if she asked him to. But she could also tell that it was the last thing he wanted to do.

"I don't think I have much of a choice..." she replied, bitterly. "I appreciate your newfound respect for my boundaries... And, yes, I am mad at you by the way. But I couldn't even get off this mountain without your help. Let alone survive another attack..."

"Must I remind you that you killed three out of five demons in Denning?" he said, a slight smirk on his face.

He was trying to banter with her, and at the same time remind her of her power, so she wouldn't feel too vulnerable around him... Sometimes she forgot how sweet the big troll could be.

"Princes of Hell, you mean?" she answered.

"How did you-"

"Jeremy told me. Is it true?"

"Yes," he replied seriously, the banter now dead in the water. "Jeremy... do you know what happened to him?"

"Hermes sent him to the village. Told him to get as many angels off the island as he could. I don't know if he made it. Hermes ordered me to fly up here. I... The things I saw, flying over the village... I should have helped. I'm such a coward... I should have done... something."

Choked by the tears making their way up her throat, Lyla felt the despair of the last two days bubble up, threatening to unleash an eruption of emotion she knew they could not afford at this moment.

"Lyla, look at me," Azrael commanded her. She lifted her eyes to his, drinking in every word as he said, "You did the right thing. You couldn't have stopped what happened down there. But things would have gotten significantly worse if they'd captured you. I can see the currents through the window. That means Hermes is still alive. They must have him, or else he'd be here right now. But he's alive. Your father would be dead if they'd gotten you. You did the right thing," he repeated, "You are not a coward, do you hear me?"

He spoke with that intensity that made her nod her head in agreement with anything he said.

She also agreed to let him get out of bed.

He shuffled around the cabin, changing, eating, checking his wounds, and collecting some supplies. "What the fuck?" she exclaimed, when he casually handed her a stack of clean training clothes, including underwear, in her size. Throwing weapons and emergency food into a backpack, he threw over his shoulder, "I stashed some stuff in your size up here in case something like this ever happened. Glad I did," as if it was the most normal thing in the world.

Baffled, Lyla stumbled into the bathroom, where she took the quickest bath of her life and changed, finally getting rid of all the demon blood crusting her skin. She herself had gotten away without a scratch, though angry, purple, finger-shaped bruises had formed where Azrael had held her against the wall.

The angel was ready to leave by the time she finished dressing.

"I have to go back. There is something in your father's office we need to get," he told her. "And I need to check the village for survivors. I don't want to leave you up here on your own."

"What if they're still down there?" she asked.

"I doubt it. By now, they probably assume that you made it off the island."

27

Lyla didn't love the way her panicked heartbeat accelerated when Azrael picked her up and flew her off the Sacred Mountain. She knew that he'd never have attacked her in his right mind. She even knew that he'd somehow managed to fight against the serum he'd been given. But her body, with its decades of deeply rooted trauma, didn't know that as it screamed *danger* at the touch of his arms.

He flew them straight into the war room, where he took the backpack off Lyla's shoulders and strapped it to his chest so they'd both have access to their wings. The war room had been torn to shreds, but the portal was still floating in place, indicating Hermes' power.

Silently, Azrael motioned her to the back of the room where he opened a panel in the wall, behind which a secret room was hidden, housing a few bookshelves with what Lyla imagined must be valuable books, objects, and weapons.

He shut them into the small room, causing her a renewed wave of panic at being stuck in a small space, but Lyla breathed through it, reminding herself that he was her ally, not her enemy, that he was not the beast she'd seen a few hours ago, and that he certainly wasn't one of the many monsters she'd survived in her lifetime.

Azrael didn't pay her much attention, as he rifled through the shelves, throwing all sorts of random things into his pack—

Until they heard two voices on the other side of the wall.

He froze, and turned around ever so slowly, looking her straight in the eyes, communicating to her that they better be perfectly silent until the danger passed.

As the voices approached, she recognized one of them: Michael.

"...we got everything of importance here. I thought we might find some secret compartment where Hermes hides all the good stuff, but it doesn't look like it. Besides, that's not really what he is after anyhow."

"Why is he so unrelenting about the reject. I thought she was useless," answered a voice she didn't recognize.

"No clue. Don't care. I'm just glad this whole farce is over. Serving that self-righteous twit Hermes, obeying the grey-winged abomination... ugh, makes me nauseous to think of the years and years of service I gave them..."

Lyla felt her hands twitch toward the knives at her side, but Azrael's eyes widened in warning, stopping her from revealing herself and doing something she'd regret.

"Too bad we didn't find her. She must have left the island, but she won't get far on her own," Michael continued, coldly. She'd despised him before, but now she realized that any humanity he'd displayed in their previous encounters had been a thin veil for the psychopath that lay underneath.

"And they'll get Azrael too, which is the one I personally can't wait for."

"How so?" asked the stranger's voice.

"It's going to take the serum a few weeks to work its way out of his system. Meanwhile, they can track him, every time he uses his magic."

Oh shit.

"Clever."

"Yeah, I'm glad to be on the smart guys' team at last... Speaking of people I abhor, we'll get special treatment for having finished off the last survivors in the village -"

Lyla's stomach dropped, as she slapped a hand against her mouth, worried she might scream in horror.

"-but how many did Jerahmeel leave with?"

"Two dozen?"

"Via portal, you said?"

"That's what I heard. There never was a portal in the village, so I assume Hermes was with him and let them through."

"I thought he was fighting at the temple," she heard Michael muse. "Maybe I'm misremembering..."

No, he wasn't misremembering, Lyla realized. Hermes hadn't been anywhere near Jeremy. Jeremy had made that portal himself, she was sure of it. Indeed, she now remembered other things she'd never noticed before. How often had Jeremy used magic on her even though his wings were folded away? Angels couldn't do that. But he could because he was only part angel at this point. He was Aphrodite's heir. Jeremy carried the mantle. It was the only explanation.

She threw Azrael a quizzical look. Understanding her silent question, he nodded and smiled, visibly relieved that his friend, his brother, had made it out alive.

"Let's get the fuck out of here," Michael said at last, right on the other side of the wall.

They waited for many long minutes after the traitors' footsteps had disappeared, before coming out of their hiding space.

"I can't use my magic..." Azrael said, when they finally emerged from the tight, dark space.

"You always say it's important to learn to survive and fight without it..."

"Yes, but that means I shouldn't even fly. We're sitting ducks here. We can portal out, but then what?"

The answer came to Lyla as if it had been waiting in the back of her mind for months.

"The human world. We hide in the human world while we figure out our next steps. I know exactly where we can go. But first... there's one place we need to check for survivors. We need to go to the orphanage."

"Lyla," Azrael started, pity in his eyes. "You heard Michael. They killed everybody..."

But there was a nagging feeling in Lyla's stomach and this time she wouldn't budge.

"You didn't believe me, when I told you that something was waiting for us in Denning," Lyla insisting, the knot in her stomach intensifying as she realized it was the exact same sensation she'd experienced outside the haunted house. "But I was right. I don't know how, but I sensed it. And I have the same feeling now. Fledglings are small, they could have hidden. I'm not leaving until we check."

Seeing that she wouldn't give in, Azrael begrudgingly agreed to search the orphanage, as long as they walked there.

"If they tracked my earlier flight, they'd just assume I'm still here and haven't joined you in hiding yet, but there's no reason to tempt fate," he explained, folding his wings away and shouldering the backpack.

They walked through the temple in silence, their footsteps echoing through the big great tomb. Dead angels were scattered throughout the place. Most had been killed by magic. The lack of blood seemed grotesque to Lyla, as she walked past broken body after broken body, devoid of any gore to testify to their atrocious fate.

Keep moving. Keep moving. Keep moving.

Setting one foot in front of the other, she focused on the feeling in her stomach, the hope that someone had survived the carnage.

It was Azrael who broke down when they reached the ice-cold training yard. In the middle of one of the training rings, in a frozen pool of blood, lay four priests, face down in the snow. Stumps poked out of their backs where someone had cut cleanly through their wings. The frail corporeal part of their wings lay discarded at their sides.

Lyla knew that only a small part of their wings was physical. It was magnified when angels manifested them through magic, but she'd never seen wings without magic. They looked... misshapen. Like the stumpy little wings of a baby duckling. They were even covered in the same kind of down.

At the sight, Azrael ran into the ring and fell to his knees at his fallen comrades' side. Lyla followed him, carefully sitting near him, unsure what to do. He was openly sobbing, staring at his friends, his hand absently caressing one of the severed wings.

She'd heard Azrael's tortured scream when the demon had cut into his wing. She couldn't even imagine the unbearable torment these four priests had suffered in their final moments.

"Who would do such a thing?" she finally dared ask.

"Zadkiel," he replied, his voice raw. "She gave them the penance and death they asked for... with no one to do the same for her."

"Oh god," she gasped, realizing that these weren't just any four angels. They were four of the five who'd been kidnapped, drugged, and set loose on the island along with Azrael. They couldn't live with what they'd done, and they'd asked for the most painful and – having embraced the profound meaning of her own wings, she could only guess – dishonorable way to die. And the fifth of them had been the one to execute them, leaving her to keep roaming the earth with the burden of her compounded guilt and shame.

"They say an angel can't rest in the afterlife without their wings..." Azrael choked out between gasps.

She didn't know about any of the angel's beliefs and superstitions, nor did she know if Azrael himself believed in them. But she knew she couldn't leave the mutilated corpses to freeze and rot with the changing of the seasons. Besides, Azrael needed closure. Not only had he known, commanded and loved these priests, he was aware that he could just as easily have lain there with stumps on his back. His own guilt and shame were walking hand in hand with his grief.

Silently, Lyla pulled out a matchbox she'd seen him stash into the side pocket of his pack. He didn't move. He was cradling one of the wings in his lap like a child hanging on to a broken doll. Realizing she needed to snap him out of his pain lest he lose his mind, she stood, unfolding her wings, and focused on her magic.

It was much too soon to be using her power; she should have been careful not to tax herself too much, but she couldn't help it. She had to give Azrael peace. She had to give these angels the last rites they'd been refused. She had to give Max the funeral he'd been denied.

Gathering her focus, she began humming a Band of Horses song Max had introduced her to years ago.

I'm coming up only to hold you under...

Slowly she lifted the first body over the ring's ropes and placed the angel, on its back, in the center of another training ring, one covered in fresh white snow.

...Really too late to call,
So we wait for morning...

One after another she lifted the other three bodies, placing them in the training ring, at right angles, feet touching and heads pointing outward.

...At every occasion I'll be ready for the funeral
At every occasion, once more, it's called the funeral...

Slowly, reverently, she lifted each wing and carefully placed them on the angel's chests.

...At every occasion, oh, I'm ready for the funeral
At every occasion, oh, one billion day funeral...

Recognizing her intent, Azrael rose to his feet and began murmuring the same words he'd used in Denning.

...To the outside, the dead leaves lay on the lawn
For they don't have trees to hang upon...

Finally, she crossed their hands over the wings, so they hugged them tightly to their bodies.

...At every occasion, oh, I'm ready for the funeral
Every occasion, oh, one billion day funeral...

When Azrael went silent, finished with what she realized were words of tribute spoken in an ancient language she didn't recognize, she struck a match, instantly grabbing hold of the flame with her magic.

In near silence, humming one quiet note, she carried the flame over into the makeshift funeral ground and let it hover over the bodies. Then she switched to another tune, this one by Nick Cave and the Bad Seeds, using it to amplify the flame, growing and growing it into a large ball of fire.

...I don't believe in an interventionist god
But I know, darling, that you do...

She lowered the ball to the ground, letting it melt the snow between the fallen angels' feet.

...But if I did, I would kneel down and ask Him
Not to intervene when it came to you
Not to touch a hair on your head
To leave you as you are
And if He felt He had to direct you
Then direct you into my arms...

Intensifying the heat, she helped the fire spread over the four figures, and let it burn over them.

...Into my arms, O Lord
Into my arms, O Lord...

She watched the flames run along the bodies, licking their way up to their heads, kindling on the downy feathers of their small wings.

...And I don't believe in the existence of angels
But looking at you I wonder if that's true...

She watched the flames run along Max's body, his limbs stitched back together.

...But if I did I would summon them together
And ask them to watch over you...

The blood cleaned off of Max's skin. The skin of his throat back to its youthful perfection. His birth mark shining in the light of the flames.

...And I believe in Love
And I know that you do too
And I believe in some kind of path
That we can walk down, me and you...

His face serene. His eyes closed. He could be asleep. At peace.

At last, the flames engulfed the serene faces, giving them both much needed closure.

Lyla let her magic go with a sigh. The flames died down and

disappeared. They had burned so hot, all they left in their wake was a pile of small bone fragments and ashes.

Staring at the remains of the funeral pyre, Lyla reached for Azrael's hand and watched the ashes dance in the sky, her tears freezing on her face as quickly as they streamed down.

They stood like that for several minutes. Finally, they left the yard to find an enormous boulder almost blocking the entrance to the temple. Walking around it, she recognized her father's face. It was the severed head of his statue. Once towering over the temple, symbolizing the Ten's glorious defeat of the Fallen, it now lay in the snow, no more than a giant hulk of stone.

They walked toward the village, side by side, in silence, past charred houses and flocks of perished angels. They didn't stop to check faces. Neither of them could have borne to see Artiya or Jegudiel's face among the deceased.

28

The closer they got to the orphanage, the more distinct the feeling in Lyla's gut became. What had started as a knot of anxiety over the thought of leaving behind potential survivors, turned to hope with every step.

She'd never seen the inside of the orphanage, but she was familiar with its facade. It was everything that a human orphanage wasn't. It looked... charming... magical in some ways. It had been built to look like a tiny castle, reminiscent of adventure movies Lyla had seen growing up, the kinds of stories she'd held on to after her parents had died and she'd learned that there was no such thing as magic and happy endings.

The courtyard was a beautiful garden, with tall trees through which were built planks and ropes for fledglings to climb through. Lyla imagined what an afternoon in the yard would look like, with its small angels flying high and low as they played whatever make-believe games it was that angel children played.

But now the yard was a graveyard like the rest of the island, tiny bodies strewn across the ground, some hanging off the trees they'd gotten stuck in as they'd fallen to earth, half frozen in the snow and ice. She couldn't bear the sight of it, but she couldn't run from it either. If there was a chance that even one child had survived, she'd rescue them. Azrael on the other hand was simply indulging her. She looked up at him and saw the disgust on his face. He'd seen more death than most, but this was a whole new level of atrocity.

Taking a deep breath before he could turn around and leave, Lyla closed her eyes to the heinous sight and let the foreboding feeling guide her. She stood like that, in the middle of the yard, her eyes closed, slowly turning in place. Trying to use the meditation techniques Azrael had taught her what felt like years ago, she calmed her mind and let the images of slaughter and violence burned onto her retinas wash over her. Meditation wasn't about turning the mind into a blank slate; it was about focusing despite the constant mental assault of consciousness. So, she simply let the abominable visions of horror enter and exit her mind, as she searched for the feeling in her gut.

Imagining it to be a rope tying her to the surviving fledglings, she slowly followed it in her mind until she could almost feel the invisible chord throb with tension.

"That way," she pointed.

Scowling, Azrael shook his head and sighed, but Lyla sprinted off and into the building. Ignoring the dead bodies to the best of her ability, she followed her instinct down corridors and into a small second floor bedroom.

Instead of beds, there were four large hammocks in the room, leaving extra space for books, toys and writing desks. It was cozy, and yet something was missing. Though every possible surface had been decorated, there was an absence here. An absence Lyla knew all too well. It was the void left by too early an encounter with death. These fledglings had tried to the best of their ability to make a home in this room, to make it feel comfortable and safe, but every lovingly placed object, every drawing, every lifeless toy was a testimony to the parental love they missed from the first moment they woke in the morning to their last thought when they went to sleep at night.

"In here," she told Azrael, as he walked in behind her.

There weren't many places to hide. In fact, there was only the closet. Slowly opening the door, Lyla tried to put on the kindest face she could muster, not wanting to spook the surely frightened fledgling. She didn't know whether they'd seen them coming and hidden in the last few minutes or whether they'd spent the last day in the closet waiting for things to end.

What she didn't expect was for a small form to dart past her as she opened the door.

"Run!" said another shape inside the closet.

Lyla turned around and saw a blurry form try to take to the air to circumvent Azrael, who easily grabbed it by the waist. It was a male angel, maybe five years old with dark hair and golden eyes. He kicked and punched at the big guardian with all he had, but Azrael didn't let him down.

In the door of the closet stood the female who'd told him to run. She looked somewhere between ten and twelve, at that age that is difficult enough for girls when all is well, let alone when Fallen angels destroy your home. She stared past Lyla at Azrael, who scowled down at the little fledgling kicking and twisting silently in his arms, trembling from head to toe, dread filling her eyes.

Lyla couldn't blame them for being intimidated by the big guy. But something else caught her attention. Why were they so quiet? The female in the closet had tears streaming down her face and was suppressing whimpers, as if she was trying to be as silent as possible.

"Stop fighting, Raziel," she said, in a small trembling voice.

"We can't win against them. Let them do their worst." With that, the little boy went limp in Azrael's arms and looked back at his- friend? sister?

She stepped out of the closet, carefully shut it behind her, and stood with her back to it, as if protecting it. Why would she close the door? And why were they giving up so easily?

"What's your name?" Lyla asked.

The fledgling looked up at her, with her big brown eyes. Her curly hair was sticking to her tear-streamed, sweaty face, and she made a visible effort to keep her teeth from chattering.

"You don't need my name to kill me," she answered, drawing herself up to her full height.

"That's not what we're here for. We're here to get you out," Lyla answered, kneeling to allow the female to tower over her.

"You're lying."

"Why would you think that?"

"I'm not an idiot. I heard what happened. I saw it. And I've heard the stories of the Fallen. I don't know why you're doing this, but I know you're with them!" she exclaimed, still glued to the door.

"If you know so many stories, have you maybe heard some about a priest called Azrael?" Lyla asked and waited for the fledgling's eyes to widen in recognition.

"I have... They say he's good. But that he's scary. They say no one can best him in a fight. And that he can throw magic at you just by staring at you too long."

It was the little boy in Azrael's arms responding. Lyla turned to him and gave him a smile. "I don't know about that last part, but he is scary, all right. He just pretends to be big and tough though, so no one will know that he's a big softie on the inside."

She turned back to the female who still looked at Azrael very skeptically.

"This is Azrael. And my name is Lyla. We're here to help. What's your name?"

"Cassiel," she murmured, looking down, tears dropping to the ground.

"Cassiel, what's in the closet?" Lyla asked.

At that, the girl panicked. Like all children, she was a terrible liar. The more she protested that she wasn't hiding anything, the more her body language betrayed that the last thing she wanted was for Lyla to check the closet.

Until she woke up what was inside. Lyla finally understood the quiet, when she heard the cry of a baby that had just woken up hungry.

"What's its name?" she asked, distracting Cassiel from her alarm.

"Sarathiel. Please don't hurt it. It's only a hatchling. Please," she begged, and Lyla's heart broke.

It was Azrael who answered. He knelt down, still holding Raziel, and looked at both of them with as kind a face as he was capable of with his sharp features. "Nobody is going to hurt any of you. You have my word. I know a place we can take you, where you'll be safe. How well can you fly, Cassiel?"

"Well enough. Where are you taking us?"

Azrael turned to Lyla and bit his lip, as if debating how to answer.

"There is a tribe of lost children, living deep in the Catskills, North of where you and I went the other day... They'll take them in."

"Are you sure?"

"The lost take nothing more seriously than the safety of fledglings. Even when they aren't their own."

"But the lost are-" Cassiel started, and stopped herself, staring a little too obviously at Azrael's back where his grey wings usually stood out.

"The lost are kind and gentle. They have dark wings like me, yes, but it is the safest place you could be right now."

"What about another one the God's?" Cassiel pushed, in a small voice, trying not to anger Azrael.

"We can't be sure of their allegiance anymore. I'm not bringing you somewhere you could be vulnerable to attack."

"All right," Cassiel conceded, visibly upset but aware she couldn't possibly win a fight against Azrael.

Finally, she stepped away from the door behind which the hatchling was now screaming for dear life, defeat in her posture and a worried scowl on her face.

Neither one of the fledglings trusted them, but they didn't have time to reassure them. Lyla stepped into the closet and carefully grabbed the crying bundle she found on the floor.

"How are we going to get there?" she asked Azrael, who was opening the one large window that took up half of the wall.

"We'll portal. Let's fly to the portal. If they track me, we'll be gone by the time they get here."

He switched the backpack to his front, put Raziel on his hip and spread his wings.

"Look at my face while we fly to the compound," he ordered the little fledgling in his arms, and took off without further explanation.

Lyla made sure she held the hatchling safely in her arms as she unfolded her wings. Then she turned to Cassiel. "You too. Don't look down. Eyes ahead as we fly."

Cassiel nodded and they both took off toward the war room.

29

Lyla landed in the war room last, the hatchling in her arms now dozing. She hoped the flight had soothed it to sleep, but she reckoned the poor thing hadn't eaten in over a day at this point.

Azrael had put Raziel down and now knelt near the portal, looking seriously around at the four of them.

"The lost will take you in and they will keep you safe. But they won't make it easy." He looked at Cassiel, then Raziel. "Whatever happens, stay close to Lyla." Then he looked up at Lyla. "Let me do the talking. And keep your alabaster wings folded away," he warned her.

He stood, turned toward the portal, and reached his hand back without looking. Cassiel stood nearest to him. She looked up at him, hesitating, then took a deep breath to gather her courage and put her little hand in his. Raziel took Cassiel's hand, reaching his other one to Lyla.

Together, they stepped through the portal.

Once the brightness subsided and the landscape appeared around them, Lyla felt her ears pop. They were in low mountains, in a clearing in the middle of deep woods.

As soon as she'd looked around, figures emerged from the woods, circling them. They had a similar bronze color as the angels and shared their collection of disparate traits, but their wings were as black as a crow's. And they looked ready to fight.

How had they gotten here so quickly? Lyla had read up on the lost on a rare day off, and she'd found out that they hid all over the world, tucked away in communities humans never even stumbled upon. That is how they'd appeared so quickly: they kept constant watch; they'd survived by being invisible but aware of their environment at all times.

While Cassiel and Raziel huddled close to Lyla, Azrael went down on his knees and put both arms up in surrender. Lyla looked around at the animosity in the clearing and decided to follow suit. She knelt next to him, carefully placed Sarathiel in Cassiel's arms and wrapped her own arms tightly around the two fledglings.

One of the lost stepped forward, taking the lead. He carried a mean looking curved sword at his hip and a scowl to rival Azrael's on his face.

"Look who's crawling back to us. Tail tucked in and everything... What do you want, guard dog?" the lost angel spat at him.

"We're here to ask for asylum for-"

"Ha! You must be joking. You refused us once. We were very clear that there was no coming back from that," the male who carried himself like the lost's leader said, bitterness dripping with every syllable as he stepped closer. As soon as he approached, Cassiel and Raziel tucked themselves closer under Lyla's arms, trying to disappear the same way she remembered doing so often as a child when in the presence of someone large and threatening.

Circling Azrael, the black winged angel continued insulting him. "You chose them. You chose to be a servant to the white-feathered peacocks. You thought you were better than us, so instead you let that raptor put a collar and leash on you. But now you want asylum?"

Lyla sensed Azrael's patience dwindling. He'd told her that the lost were not to be messed with, but he'd had a long couple of days and every breath he took rumbled with the pent-up rage of a dormant volcano.

"And you come here with children? You bred with one of them and dare show up on our doorstep?" the ringleader continued, now crouching inches away from Azrael's darkening face. "Go die in a ditch, Azrael," he finished, spitting in his face and turning to leave.

Instead of wiping the drool off his cheek, Azrael closed his eyes at the insult and took a deep breath.

By now, Raziel was shaking so hard in her arms, Lyla could feel him battling his instinct to make a run for it. But Azrael simply turned his head, smiled, and winked at the fledgling. She felt the boy take a shuddering breath in response and his trembling let up ever so slightly.

"I request an audience with your Eldest. Unless things have changed a lot around here, that's not you, Marcus."

Lyla almost laughed nervously at the sound of such a common name for a winged magical creature hiding in the woods. But her guard went back up as soon as another figure peeled itself out of the shadows. An old male, wrinkled with a shaved head and wearing a long coat made of sewn together animal furs approached them, leaning on a thick cane but proudly displaying his raven wings.

"Clever," the Eldest said, walking up to Azrael. "Though you turned your insolent back on us, you still remember our customs."

He approached Azrael, squinting his eyes as he did, as if deep in reflection. Azrael hadn't moved other than to reassure Raziel. His arms were still up in the air, and Marcus' spit was running down his cheek where he hadn't bothered to wipe it off.

"But Marcus has a point, boy," the old angel continued. "You made your position very clear. We hear what goes on out in the world. We caught wind of attacks on the temples. But we cannot give you and yours asylum. We are not an encampment for wayward angels, and we do not take insults lightly."

Azrael politely let him continue, though Lyla could feel his patience fraying at the edges.

"I had expected more form you, boy! You and I may not agree on which battles are worth fighting, but I thought at least you'd see it through, not run to safety at the first sign of trouble. How distasteful..."

He shook his head and knelt slowly to look into Azrael's eyes. Everyone in the circle looked like they wanted to help but respected the elderly male too much to take his dignity away. So, he lowered himself slowly and, as he did, Lyla realized how weathered his face was. In fact, his eyes were covered with a blue sheen making him appear blind. And yet he looked at the big warrior's face as if he could see right through him to his soul.

"I didn't peg you for a coward, Angel of Death. What happened?"

"I'm not running, Eldest. And this is not my brood. These two fledglings and the hatchling are orphans, and the last survivors of an attack on Hermes' island. I am only asking asylum for them. This is the only place I can guarantee their safety," Azrael answered.

"Hermes' island has fallen too, then..." the Eldest replied, a shadow crossing his face. "Did he perish?"

"Hermes lives. And two dozen or so angels made it out," Azrael replied, swallowing around his grief.

"Priests?"

"I'm unsure, but I suspect the survivors were mostly villagers."

"Then it is happening, at last," the feeble Eldest said ominously. He turned on his heel, walking away. "We'll take the fledglings and the hatchling. They'll be safe with us. You have my word."

"What is happening at last?" Lyla asked, ignoring her promise to Azrael to keep her mouth shut. She couldn't pretend she hadn't heard the portentous words. Not after the two days she'd had.

The old man turned around faster than she would have imagined possible.

"The end of times as we know them. The legends prophesized the Gods would be toppled one by one, and that Hermes' fall would set about the beginning of the end."

Cocking his head at Lyla, he added, "Leave the little ones. Turn around and walk away before I ask questions you do not want to answer."

Lyla looked to Azrael for guidance. The latter slowly lowered his arms and wiped the spit off his face, nodding toward the fledglings. Gathering her courage, Lyla kissed Cassiel and Raziel's heads, handed the hatchling to the female, and murmured, "You'll be safe here. Take good care of Sarathiel."

Slowly, they peeled themselves out of her embrace and started walking toward the trees, clearly uneasy at the separation. But Lyla smiled at them reassuringly. She may not have appreciated the lost's hostility, but she trusted that it did not extend to the children.

The circle of warriors disappeared into the shadows, but

their Eldest waited for the fledglings, one hand stretched out toward Raziel, and leaning heavily on his cane with the other. At the last moment, the little fledgling turned around and ran back, swinging himself into Azrael's arms.

"Will we see you again?" he anxiously asked.

"I hope so, little eaglet. Meanwhile, I need you to do something for me. I need you to take care of your siblings. I'm leaving them in your charge, young warrior. And practice your flight. It's important."

He affectionately ruffled Raziel's hair and sent him on his way.

Just before disappearing into the shadows, the Eldest turned around and looked straight at Azrael with his cataract-heavy eyes. "Fight, son. Til the end. I may not agree with the battle you chose, but you need to see it through. The world may well depend on it."

And then, they were gone, as if they'd never been there. Lyla and Azrael stood in what now seemed like just any old clearing in the Catskills.

30

An hour later, Lyla was dozing on Azrael's shoulder at the Phoenicia bus stop. On the way back they'd made a plan to take the Trailways bus into New York City so they could grab everything they needed before disappearing in the human world.

She and Max had made arrangements for just such a situation. They'd have to grab the cash, food, fake IDs and other provisions from the storage unit and head to a car rental place. She'd be able to rent a car under a false identity and drive them to the cabin in California. She didn't look forward to driving all the way across the country, but they'd take breaks on the side of the road to sleep. Besides, Azrael refused to do anything until they were somewhere secluded that he could defend.

Once in California, they'd be safe enough to contact Jeremy and to start thinking of a plan.

In the meantime, Lyla was exhausted from the events of the last couple of days and she needed to save her strength for the drive. They'd bought the tickets and sat down to wait for a bus that only ran every four hours, which was plenty of time to rest up. She'd fallen asleep as he'd started telling her that the tribe of lost they'd just dealt with was excellent with illusion magic and enjoyed coming near the town borders to create illusions of more or less friendly black bears roaming the town. It kept tourists entertained, but wary enough not to venture too deep into the woods.

Thankfully the bus was relatively empty, and they snuck into the back without getting too many oblique looks for their unorthodox attire. As soon as they sat down, Azrael pulled out a leatherbound book he'd stolen from Hermes' office and handed it to Lyla.

"You should read this," he said without offering any further explanations. "I'm going to close my eyes. Wake me up if any danger presents itself."

At a loss, Lyla watched him lean back his oversized head and close his eyes. She opened the book. It was a notebook with neat, elongated, painfully precise handwriting. A journal. Hermes' journal.

Lyla turned around to ask what this was about, but the angel was already asleep, his head tilted back, his lips parted, giving him the slightest overbite. He looked oddly young and vulnerable in his sleep, like any innocent young man rather than a magical creature in his forties who'd been in battle and killed dozens upon dozens of times before.

She flipped to the first page of Hermes' diary and began reading.

August 14th, 2019 H.Y.

H.Y.... Human Years, Lyla realized with a jolt – that was how removed her father was from this planet. To him this was still a foreign land, one whose very calendar was alien.

I begin this journal on the day on which the search for my child finally ends.

For two and a half decades we scoured the earth for a magic signature the Fallen had covered up. I am not sure how they managed it, but it would seem that Lailah has no idea what she is. Her power is bottled up. Without it, finding her was like searching for a needle in a haystack, as humans say.

Jerahmeel found her in an American psychic shop, playing parlor tricks for humans, apparently oblivious to her actual abilities. She appears to have a sense of something extra-sensory going on, but no knowledge of the reality of magic.

Azrael now knows of her existence too. I have taken him off his usual duties and instructed him with her protection, while Jerahmeel studies her.

Lyla closed the book and took a deep breath looking at the winding roads through familiar-looking small towns. Up here, one town looked as picturesque as the next. Woodstock, Kingston, Cold Spring, Sleepy Hollow... from the back of a bus, they all looked like a movie set waiting to be populated by actors pretending to have unrealistically enchanted lives.

She'd not given much thought to the fact that Hermes had been looking for her. It wigged her out so much that the Fallen had had control over her upbringing, it was odd reading about the other creature on whose mind she'd been: Hermes. His writing sounded much like the God she'd met – cold, detached, clinical. And why would he care? How many children had he fathered over the millenia?

She'd read that the Ten had first procreated with humans who'd worshipped them as gods, actual priests and priestesses who'd willingly "lain with them", as her study books had euphemistically stated. Now that just gave her the creeps. Those humans had given up their bodies to beings that were so clearly alien and unattractive, simply because their religion had told them to... Thankfully, all further generations had been created by artificial insemination between Gods and willing angels. *Still gross, but at least it doesn't border on rape*, she'd thought when reading about it. But now she realized something else: as much as it may be an honor for an angel to father or carry the child of a God, none of those children were the products of love. Their existence was no more than a way to guarantee the propagation of the angel species.

That was all she was. An assurance that Hermes' line wouldn't die out.

No wonder he was detached, he may never even have met her mother. Overcome by a wave of loneliness, she looked at the sleeping angel next to her. She may still wear the bruises from his attack, but he was all she had at the moment. She missed Max and she'd already started missing Jeremy, but at least she had the big guard troll, as she liked to think of him.

Taking a deep breath, she continued reading:

August 15th, 2019 H.Y.

Jerahmeel is using illusion magic to get near Lailah. He spent many hours with her today and his report was encouraging. He tried asking her about her past, but she is lying to cover up some dark truths. I can only imagine what my Fallen brothers put her through in an attempt to win her over. But it would seem that they failed. Jerahmeel reports that she is kind and caring, that her blood proudly carries both her mother's attributes and mine own.

Meanwhile Azrael reports that she lives with another orphan, one she appears to care for and possibly be intimate with. We must be careful taking her out of her world. In spite of my brothers' treatment, she has

*loved ones and she will likely refuse leaving them. We will have to im-
press on her the danger she's putting them in.*

Lyla took a deep breath, her vision swimming before her eyes for a moment. *Keep moving. Keep moving. I got Max killed. KEEP MOVING!*

She continued reading:

In a couple of weeks, Jerahmeel will begin gently introducing her to magic until she accepts its reality. I hope she will willingly leave the human world for a training period. I cannot guarantee her safety at the temple, there are traitors in our midst. But I have asked Azrael to prepare his cabin on the Sacred Mountain. Only he and I will be able to visit her there, and he'll instruct her, safely away from any of Lucifer's spies.

Lyla stopped, perplexed. She'd been meant to live on the Sacred Mountain from the beginning? That was the real reason Azrael had clothes for her up there... And Hermes knew about the traitors? Why had he brought her to the temple? *Because you were injured*, she answered her own question.

And the out-of-control séance she'd experienced the day before Max's death - that had been Jeremy introducing her to magic. She'd landed on the island much sooner than Hermes had planned and had been tried by fire as it were.

Returning to the notebook, she realized that the next entry was from that day:

September 16th, 2019 H.Y.
I could have ripped off Azrael's wings for what he did today. Bringing my child within these treacherous walls. What was he thinking?
She was attacked by a Prince of Hell. It killed her companion and was going to take her back to Lucifer. My brother must have realized

we'd finally found her and decided to drag her away before we did. He had probably planned to break her in Hell...

Azrael says she mortally wounded the beast with a sonic attack. Her magic is finally coming out to play.

But she has no idea how to control its flow. He feared she might have drained herself entirely, so he disregarded our plan and brought her to the hospital to be immediately tended to by Jerahmeel. The fool!

There's no point in hiding her now. Everyone has either seen or heard of her at this point.

As for Azrael, he had the gall to respond that he'd never agreed to training a fledgling. As if he had a choice in the matter, or I cared about his feelings on the situation.

I cannot allow such poor judgement from my second in command. I let him know that, since he'd broken protocol by bringing her to the temple, she was now very much his problem.

She remembered Azrael's dismissive words all too clearly. They'd come a long way since, but it stung to hear that Azrael had tried to weasel his way out of being her trainer. And that Hermes had saddled him with her, instead of teaching her himself.

The next entry was from the day of their first encounter:

September 18th, 2019 H.Y.
I met her at last. She has her mother's eyes.

Lyla paused. Hermes had known her mother. Cared for her even, if that was a detail he cared to note and write about. The handwriting on this page was different. It wasn't neat like the rest of the journal had been. It was shaky, erratic.

I made a show of her supposed ineptitude. Hopefully I bought her some time... I treated her as awfully as I could think to. I thought it might break me to do so. But she believed it. What else has she been through that she'd so easily believe a father could treat his child that way?...

By blocking her magic, Lucifer had blocked my connection to her. For two and a half decades, I couldn't feel my daughter. Which was an affliction like no other, not being able to feel where she was or what was happening to her.

But today, when I forced her wings out, I broke through the wall... I can feel her now. And, by the Wheel, she is all pain.

She is grieving, but it runs deeper than that. Whatever my Fallen brothers did to her, her every cell is in agony.

The last word was scribbled almost illegibly, as if it had taken an insurmountable effort to put pen to paper.

Lyla's memory of that period was shrouded in a foggy veil, as if it had been so traumatic that she couldn't quite recall the specifics. In a way her new life had started with her friendship with Azrael. Everything before that was indeed pure pain and suffering. Looking back at it, she realized not only how far she'd come, but also that her progress wasn't natural: Jeremy, the son of Aphrodite, bearer of her power, had forcibly stitched her back together, coerced her to recover whether she liked it or not.

There was one last entry.

November 25th, 2019 H.Y.

Artemis fell today. It is only a matter of time before they get to us. They're coming for Lailah. We're running out of time.

Azrael and Jeremy know all the emergency protocols. As long as they can make it out... But I too must survive the attack. Lailah is not ready to carry the burden of leadership.

She has, though, shown extraordinary progress with her magic.
If her mother could see her, she would be so proud...

That last sentence hit her where it hurt most. In some bizarre way, Hermes cared. And so would her mother. *If she could see her, she would be so proud. Could. Would.*

But something else occurred to her, reading her father's notes. She was the youngest of Hermes' children. Unless he procreated again, she'd be the one inheriting his power. If Hermes died at the Fallen's hands, she'd get his magic.

She could barely handle her own. They needed to get Hermes back for so many reasons... not the least of which was that she needed answers. And she needed to see what these entries meant.

I made a show of her supposed ineptitude. Hopefully I just bought her some time... I treated her as awfully as I could think to. I thought it might break me to do so. But she believed it. What else has she been through that she'd so easily believe a father could treat his child that way?... was an affliction like no other, not being able to feel where she was or what was happening to her... If her mother could see her, she would be so proud...

Was the goodbye hug he'd given her... was that the true Hermes?

Did she dare believe it?

31

Before she could fully comprehend what it would mean to have a remaining parent who... loved... her, before she could think of what the Fallen were doing to him right at this moment, the bus pulled into the Lincoln Tunnel. She tapped Azrael on the shoulder, who was instantly awake and had a hand by the knife at his side.

"Hush. Hide that under your coat. We're here. And we have a subway ride ahead of us."

She shuffled him out of the bus, out of the sub-basement Port Authority terminal they'd arrived at and toward the subway. All the while, he walked a step behind her like a bodyguard, and hovered as she snuck under the subway turnstile and opened the emergency door for him.

He kept up his skulking on the platform, clearly uncomfortable with the amount of people in the crowd and the potential danger they represented.

"Why are we down here?" he growled.

"Because we're waiting for the train that will take us to the place where my stuff is," she answered, shaking her head.

"This is below the earth. Trains run above the ground. Hell is what is below ground. I don't like this. Are you sure we're in the right place?"

"Yes, this is the C train," she answered, just as the subway pulled in. "I've taken it for many years. And I need you to relax. You're drawing attention."

Azrael bared his teeth and openly growled at her in response.

"Azrael, I'm not joking. We're not dressed like humans, and you're behaving really suspiciously. Humans have cameras. There are half a dozen recording you right now. If the Fallen are clever, they'll look through footage anywhere in the city to try and catch a glimpse of us. So, chill, will you?"

"I only understood half the words you just said," he replied, gruffly, as he stepped onto the crowded train, continuing to eye everyone as if he wanted to throw them onto the tracks.

Thankfully, they got off two stops later, at 23rd Street, and he silently followed her all the way to her storage unit near the river.

The security guard hadn't changed in the last few months. He knew her face well enough to give her access to her unit without asking for an ID with which she could not have presented him.

As they descended into the bizarre bowels of the storage space, Lyla asked herself what it was that people stored there, hid there, hoarded there... But she didn't have time to think about it. She rushed to hers and Max's unit, opened the combination lock and immediately reached for two neatly packed backpacks. She passed one to Azrael, who pulled his own pack to his front and shouldered what had once been Max's bugout bag. She didn't dwell on that. She could not. Hermes' words had reawakened too many barely healing wounds.

But she did take the time to open a box of memories and to pull out one specific object: a picture of her and Max on top of the Wonder Wheel at Coney Island. That was where they'd celebrated her eighteenth birthday and their freedom from the system.

Without looking at it, she pocketed the photograph, pulled a fake ID and credit card from her bugout bag, shouldered it, locked the unit, and headed toward the nearest car rental place, the goofy looking angel in tow.

"Do you know how to drive?" she asked him on the way.

"Drive?" he answered, uncertain.

"A car. Do you know how to drive a car?"

"No. I've never been in a car."

"Never? How is that even possible? Doesn't your work take place in the human world?" she responded, disconcerted.

"I usually portal in and out of a location. And I have wings, remember?"

"Much good are those doing us right now..."

So, she'd have to drive all the way to California. By her calculation it was a four-day drive with very short breaks. It hadn't snowed in New York yet, but they needed to make their way South as quickly as possible. She could probably get them to the cabin by December eighteenth.

"I rode a horse once..." Azrael added, sheepishly. Lyla gave him her biggest "You're dead weight here" look and entered the rental agency, where she expertly asked for an economy car under a completely fake identity. Thank god for Max's shady contacts. Out of his element, Azrael, thankfully, kept the skulking to a minimum.

Once in the car, and once he was satisfied that he had enough sharp objects within his reach, she had to buckle him in like a child, because he had never experienced the miracle of seatbelts.

"Reach into the left side pocket of your backpack, there should be fake insurance papers in there, in case we get pulled over," she told him, pulling out of the lot.

Azrael opened said pocket and pulled out a bunch of printed paper.

"What's insurance?" he asked.

"It's a company that will pay the damages in case we have an accident. It's illegal to drive without it, because the police want to know that someone will pony up the money," she explained.

"And a lizard gives you this assurance?" he asked, rifling through her fake policy.

"That's right. It's a very rich, talking lizard," she answered, chuckling.

"I sense you are mocking me, but I don't understand the joke," was his disgruntled answer. "Also, you can't possibly be allowed to drive this fast."

They'd reached the West Side highway now. She was racing toward the George Washington Bridge at seventy miles per hour, and Azrael, clutching the dashboard like an oversized gorilla in the little car, seemed positively distressed.

"Finally found your weakness, demon slayer!" she teased him. "Sit back and relax, my friend. It's going to be a long trip!"

32

It took Azrael a while to loosen up, but by the time he did, Lyla had sorted through her feelings and was ready to talk.

"We went back for Hermes' journal. That was the real reason," she confronted him.

He didn't contradict her.

"Have you read it?"

"No," he replied, slowly. "But I knew Hermes was keeping a journal. I don't know what he wrote, but since every plan of his regarding you has been thwarted, I figured it was time you got to know some truths about him."

Lyla kept her eyes on the road, but she could feel him looking at her, gauging her reaction, trying to guess what she'd read.

"He mentioned my birth mother... I haven't asked all these months, because I wasn't sure I could handle the truth after everything... but I need to know..."

Azrael averted his eyes and quietly waited for her to ask the much-dreaded question.

"Jeremy told me that the Fallen took me from her," she added, with more urgency. "But he never said anything about who she was, or what happened to her... Is she... Is she-"

"She's dead, Lyla," Azrael interrupted, a quiet finality in his voice. "They killed her when they took you. I'm sorry. I thought you knew."

Lyla kept her mind busy, by passing the many eighteen-wheelers that now populated the evening freeways of Pennsylvania. Between her grief about Max and her pain at Hermes' rejection, she'd actively avoided asking herself what had become of her mother. But when she'd read about her, for just a moment, she'd dared to hope...

"Did you know her?" she softly asked him.

"No. Hermes never even told me who she was. You'd have to ask him."

"Tall order, at the moment..."

They drove in silence for a while longer, passing one truck after another, as the sky darkened behind them.

"What's his deal?" she finally burst out, unable to keep in the question that had been nagging her since the attack any longer. "Hermes treated me like utter crap every time he saw me, and then... the way he said goodbye... the things he wrote in his diary... he sounded like he... cared. It's giving me whiplash."

"He does. Care. He does care," Azrael slowly replied, as if searching for the right words.

"He has one hell of a way to show it!" Lyla yelled, finally letting the anger she'd held in flow out of her. "He physically hurt me. He made me feel less than. He humiliated me. In public. And you're telling me he cares?!"

"I don't think we should have this conversation right now," he answered, sharply.

"Oh, we are having this conversation," she replied. "You owe it to me. I put up with Hermes' shit. I put up with yours. I want answers. And I want them now."

As she said it, she realized it was true. For months, she'd followed their plans, their guidance. And she'd landed back in the human world, leaving behind an obliterated island, with no strategy to speak of. Only to find out that they hadn't been transparent with her after all.

"I may never have been in a car before, but I have seen accidents. And I know that you are in no state to drive right now," he said, his breathing fast and shallow as he unsuccessfully tried to track all the other vehicles around them. "Please stop the car, if we're going to talk this out."

Lyla provocatively turned her head toward him, as she pressed her foot on the gas. She knew there was no one ahead of her in the fast lane, she knew she'd likely be fine taking her eyes off the road for a few seconds. It wasn't wise to do so, but she couldn't help needling the angel. She'd trusted him. For months now, she'd put all her trust in him. But he'd attacked her, and apparently there had been more to her story than what he'd revealed to her. And for that, she was so angry, she wanted to hit him. Except that she wasn't strong enough to hurt him. That had been firmly established. But this car, this machine that was alien to him, was a weapon she could use to scare him back. She could use it to make him feel the insecurities and doubts she'd felt, while he'd been deciding what to tell her and what to keep from her, the terror she'd felt, when he'd slammed her against the wall and she'd thought she would die at his hands.

Azrael closed his eyes, and swallowed, sweat now beading on his temple.

"I understand. I'm sorry. I truly am sorry, Lyla. Every step of the way, I tried to protect you. I thought I was doing right by you. But I know that I also didn't always treat you well. And I kept things from you. And last night..."

He opened his eyes and turned his head to look into hers.

"I'll never forgive myself for last night. I'll tell you anything you want to know. I swear, I will. But please, stop the car first. Please."

Taking her foot off the gas, and turning her eyes back toward the road, Lyla moved over into the right lane and took the first available exit. Silently, she pulled up into the parking lot of a gloomily lit rest stop.

"Talk."

Looking around for danger, Azrael pulled out one of the knives hanging off his belt.

"Now!"

Finally, he turned toward her. The motion was so abrupt, it locked his seatbelt. Not understanding why he was trapped, he tried to pull at the top of the belt to no avail.

"Stop. That won't help."

Taking a deep breath, Lyla unbuckled him, then herself, and turned toward him.

"I'm tired of being in the dark," she told him, sincerely.

Azrael nodded and began.

"When your father first told me about you, he said it was of the utmost importance to keep you safe. He told me that he'd been scouring the planet for you for your entire life, and that Jeremy had finally figured out where they'd hidden you. He explained that you were stronger than regular angels, more powerful. He said, the Fallen wanted to use that power to their advantage, that that was why they'd taken you, that they'd probably tried to slowly break your spirit over the years, that they'd made your life difficult and painful so as to poison anything good in you. Their mistake with the lost was not to nurture evil in them, but to expect it to take root on its own. With you, they did the opposite: they tried to ruin your life so much, you'd naturally turn toward darkness. And then, they'd swoop in and make you their most powerful weapon."

"I know all that."

"Hermes said that he didn't think they'd succeeded. But he couldn't know for sure. He couldn't trust you. Not until he saw for himself. So, he made a plan. I watched you, out of sight, but I kept you safe while Jeremy slowly got to know you. He was supposed to introduce you to the concept of magic, gradually telling you the truth about who you were. It would take weeks, months perhaps, until he'd ask you to come train on the island. But Hermes knew there were traitors in the temple. He knew they'd plan an attack the moment they got wind of your presence on the island. So, he planned to hide you on the Sacred Mountain instead. You were going to live and train up there with me, and he'd visit and help teach you as well."

"I still don't understand why they're after me."

"Because you're different. I don't know what it is, but you're far more powerful than a regular angel. And they always knew you would be. I'm sorry, Lyla, I know it's frustrating, but I swear to you, Hermes never told me what it is that makes you special. All I knew was that I was to protect you at all costs. I was to keep you safe, and to take you to the island at the right time. And I failed."

"He wrote about that," she said. "He was furious."

"That he was. I'd never seen him like that. I was shadowing you for weeks. It never occurred to me that they might come for your friend first."

"Max," Lyla interrupted. "His name was Max."

Azrael eyed her, as if he'd rather dehumanize Max than call him by name, but he proceeded. "Max. You attacked the demon before I'd even stepped into the room. I'd never seen anything like it. I thought maybe Jeremy had been wrong. Maybe you were a fully trained angel. But then you collapsed, and I realized you'd wasted every last drop of your power without a thought. I killed the thing, and tried to wake you up, but you were barely breathing."

He stopped for a moment, lost in thought. He looked... pained by the memories he was reliving.

"I panicked. I should have brought you to the Sacred Mountain and then gotten Jeremy to heal you. It would have been a difference of twenty minutes. You would have been fine. You would have been safe. I should have followed the plan. You would have had plenty of time to train and learn. If it weren't for my stupid mistake, we'd still be there now. The island would be safe. Hermes would be safe. All those angels-"

He took a shuddering breath, and Lyla reached out to cover his hand, but he pulled away, recomposing himself, and continuing.

"Once I brought you to the hospital, it was too late to hide you. From that point on, we were on borrowed time. We couldn't know which of the other islands had been infiltrated, so there was nowhere safe to evacuate the villagers. All we could do was hope we'd be ready for the inevitable. I feared it would be bad," he said, looking down at his large hands. "But it turned out so much worse."

Azrael shook his head and continued. "The day after your arrival, Hermes said that what would come would come. He told me that my duty was no longer to the temple or to the village, but to you alone. He said, that if they got to you, it didn't matter how many islands full of angels we saved. So, I trained you as best as I could."

He paused, done with his part of the story.

"That still doesn't explain how Hermes treated me."

"He was trying to buy you time," Azrael replied, still staring at his hands. "He wanted to spread rumors about your incompetence, in the hopes it would slow down the Fallen, that maybe they'd let us do the hard work and wait until your true power manifested."

"That's why you forbade me from showing my magic?" she asked.

"Yes. I almost lost my mind when I saw you displaying it in the stairway. But it would seem they'd already planned on ambushing us anyhow. Either Michael caught wind of how your training was really going, or the Fallen ran out of patience. I don't know."

"He could have told me. You could have told me. Instead of letting me believe I was weak and alone," Lyla insisted, remembering how painful it had been to be humiliated by her father at the hospital, and then again at the party.

"Hermes didn't let me. He needed you to play the part, and he knew you'd best do so if you believed him yourself. He couldn't risk you knowing that he cared. That he was lying about your aptitude."

"That's not an explanation," she bit back, shaking her head. "I was in so much pain when I arrived on the island. How dare he hurt me more, just to make it believable?"

She was fighting it, but she could feel tears blurring up her vision. She didn't know if she was upset at remembering how much her father's rejection had hurt or outraged that he'd been so calculated and had used her like a pawn for her own good.

"You were in so much pain," Azrael said, looking her straight in the eyes. "The relief you would have felt at finding a loving parent would have shown. They would have come for you much sooner. And you wouldn't have been as ready as you are now."

She wanted to argue, but she'd gotten caught up on three word he'd said.

"A loving parent?"

As she said it, she pulled up her knees, trying to retreat into herself, arming herself against the things she was afraid to hear. She couldn't bear it if he retracted those words. But maybe it would be even worse if they were true.

"There's something few people know about the Gods," Azrael explained. "They retained more of their hive-mind nature than people realize. So much so, that each God has a constant connection to their entire bloodline. Hermes' connection is one of the most empathic ones. He can feel all his children at any moment. The way he has explained it to me, it's mostly background noise, but it is always there."

For two and a half decades, I couldn't feel my daughter. Which was an affliction like no other, not being able to feel where she was or what was happening to her.

But today, when I forced her wings out, I broke through the wall...
I can feel her now. And, by the Wheel, she is all pain.

"That's how he knew to train me," Azrael explained. "He hadn't just seen me fight as a young male; he'd been in my heart when he took over my training. The same way he's been in the hearts of most of his direct and indirect children. With you, he couldn't track you during all those years you were growing up. He told me it drove him half mad not to know if his child was safe. And when he finally established a connection with you, it nearly destroyed him to feel the pain you were in. I spoke to him that day. The day he forced your wings out. He hated himself for doing it. But he knew it would shake you up more to find out that he loved you than to think he was ashamed of you."

"How could he love me? He didn't know me! He doesn't know me!"

"I've heard it said that parents fall in love as soon as they meet their children... I don't know if that's true, but I know it's true of your father and you."

Lyla shook her head in disbelief, hugging her knees tightly.

"You know how I know?" he asked.

She looked up, not daring to believe it.

"I know because he had me report to him every single day. Not just on your progress, but on everything about you. He wouldn't let me go until I had told him every word that had come out of your mouth that day. He'd planned on taking over most of your education, but since you lived at the temple and he needed to keep up the appearance of being ashamed of you, he had to live vicariously through me, making me tell him every detail about what you'd done and said. Every. Single. Day. I've never seen someone as full of love and pride as he is for you."

Lyla let the words wash over her. They scared her. They terrified her. Love always had. That was the reason she hadn't recognized the nature of her feelings for Max until it had been too late. But parental love, that was something she'd believed to be long lost to her.

She'd often seen the pity in people's eyes when they found out she was an orphan, she graciously accepted their shock and their *Sorry*s, not understanding why they apologized for something that had nothing to do with them. But she'd always thought that they mistook absence for grief. They thought she missed her parents. But she could barely remember them. And she certainly didn't know what it would be like to have an adult relationship with them. How could she miss something she didn't know? No, she didn't miss them, and she'd long since stopped grieving them. They weren't a missing presence. They were an absence. They were a hole. That was the tragic truth about being an orphan: that you constantly felt that something unintelligible was missing; there was a constant emptiness inside of you, but you couldn't quite make out its shape. You simply knew that you'd never be complete because nothing quite fit the void death had left behind.

To think, that something might...

To think that someone truly wanted to. That someone loved her as his daughter. That he was proud of her. That he wanted to be in her life, to protect her just the way she had felt when he'd wrapped his wings around her...

She still had a father. A real father. Who loved her.

"We have to get him back," was all she managed to say around the knot in her throat.

"I know," the big angel nodded. "But we have to get you to safety first. You've barely slept for two days now. I think we should stay in this hamlet while you get some sleep."

She didn't attempt to explain what a rest stop was to him. She simply lowered her seat, curled up under her jacket and closed her eyes.

33

By the time she woke up from her dreamless sleep, the sun was rising and a second coat had been draped over her. Azrael, arms crossed and scowling, attentively scanned their surroundings.

She wore sunglasses and her hood low over her face to fill the car up with gas and grab food for the road, and Azrael insisted on standing right outside the bathroom door while she freshened up.

The next stretch of road was peaceful. The priest dozed off after she assured him she'd wake him up before stopping anywhere. She found a radio station that played classic rock and let it play in the background while driving, eating a breakfast of trail mix and energy drinks while slowly letting in the reality of the previous day's discoveries.

They were well into Virginia by the time they needed to fill up on gas again and Lyla had a chance to ask him her next pressing question.

"Why do you follow him?" she blurted out, turning the car over and getting back on the road.

"Excuse me?" he grumbled, suspiciously eyeing a blue M&M from his third pack of trail mix.

"Hermes. Why do you follow him? I remember how he treated you at the dinner. Every single priest had a seat at the table but you."

Azrael sighed, resignedly throwing the M&M back into the mix and picking out a peanut instead.

"You saw what you expected to see on that day. Admittedly, no one corrected you... Hermes was perfectly happy reinforcing your idea that he was a monster. The truth is that I have had a seat at that table every single time such events were hosted. In fact, I mostly sat at the center, right by his side. It was a way for him to make a statement to his less open-minded brothers and sisters, as well as to his entire bloodline, about how little he cares about the color of my wings. Your father has been nothing but supportive and inclusive of me. Even when it was damaging to his own hold on his blood line. But in that particular instance, he needed someone to watch his back. And, more importantly, yours. He wanted me to observe the room. He was hoping I'd find out useful information about who the traitors amongst us might be. And standing guard gave me the best vantage point for that job."

"I thought-"

"I know. Believe me, your father never starved or mistreated me. He's always made me feel just as welcome as Jeremy has."

So, her father didn't only love her. He was actually a good male. A progressive leader.

"The lost made it sound like..." she trailed off, not daring to finish the sentence.

"Like I was the angel's inferior servant? Their dog? Let them believe what they will. They will never understand why I chose the angel part of my bloodline. But I wouldn't have chosen one over the other if they hadn't made me."

"What do you mean?" she answered, gleeful to see a sign welcoming them into Tennessee.

"When I came of age, Hermes offered to make me his general. He'd gone without a second in command for a few years and everybody was expecting him to pick one of the older, more experienced priests. But he offered me the position... And I had the audacity to ask him for time to think about it. I'll never understand why he indulged me, but he did... I left the island for about a year, wandered the world in search of my father. I wanted to know where I'd come from. So, I spent time with every tribe of lost children I could find."

"Did you find him?" Lyla asked, enthralled.

"No. No one had ever heard of my mother. To this day, I have no idea where he is. But I found wisdom and knowledge. Particularly among the tribe we brought the fledglings to. I spent several months there. The lost are a secret treasure of historic and magical knowledge. And there is wisdom to their impartiality. I could have stayed with them, but ultimately, I wanted a purpose. And that was the one thing they didn't give me. Their Eldest and I got into a bad row the day I left. In my youthful arrogance, I said things I shouldn't have. And he told me I'd be a dead male if I ever showed my face again."

"He threatened your life? Remind me why we casually portaled into their territory and entrusted the fledglings to them?" she exclaimed, almost turning the car around on the spot.

"Because they'd never harm a feather on the wings of a fledgling. No matter the color. And they never would have hurt me in front of the little ones either. Well, Marcus would have. But I'd love to see him try it."

By the time she needed to sleep again, they'd almost reached Memphis. Lyla realized with a start that she'd been driving for close to fifteen hours in one day. She caught up by sleeping through most of the next morning, but her training and her magic had obviously made her more resistant to such things as fatigue and hunger.

They spent most of the following day listening to music while she found the most disgusting human gas station foods to make him try. He almost gagged on the pork rinds and wound up spitting them out the window. They tasted like death, not meat, was his explanation. Lyla advised him to try vegetarianism in the human world if he expected his meat to taste like anything other than death. And proceeded to stuff her mouth full of the greasy snack. At that, he grunted something insulting and proceeded to take his daily five-hour nap.

They made it to the border between Texas and New Mexico before she woke him so she could take her turn sleeping.

With every day, she slept in a little later. They didn't start driving again until the afternoon of the following day, at which point Azrael pointed out that it was time to strategize.

"The first thing we must do is contact Jeremy and take stock of the situation," he began.

"And how do you plan on doing that? He could be anywhere," she replied, defeated.

"I know exactly where he is. There is only one place he'd go. And he once made me learn a number for just this kind of emergency."

"A number? What kind of number?"

"A... tele-number?" he asked, uncertain.

"A telephone number? Jeremy made you memorize a phone number in case he was ever hiding in the human world and you needed to find him?" she asked, incredulous.

"A tele. Phone. Number. Yes."

Lyla couldn't help smiling. "That's handy."

"I don't exactly know what to do with the number though…"

"Leave that up to me," she assured him. "There's a burner phone in one of the packs. We'll call him as soon as we get to the cabin. And since he can make portals – way to bury the lead by the way – I'd think he'd be able to join us easily. What then?"

"Then, we figure out how to get Hermes back from Hell…"

"Hell?" she asked.

"I told you a long time ago that Hell is a very real place. The Gods live on islands scattered around the world. The Fallen live deep underground in a dangerous maze of caverns they've made their own. So much so, it's extremely perilous for one of us to set foot down there," he explained.

"How are we going to find him?"

"I'm not worried about finding him. I'm more worried about making it back out alive. They want us to find him. Hermes is just the bait. It's you they want," he mused. "Hopefully Jeremy has an idea, because mine just about stops where we make it to Hermes and all get killed."

She let that sit for a moment, looking around at the empty desert around them. She'd driven through New Mexico once before. There was an odd presence in this emptiness. Though her mind told her there was nothing around for miles, she could feel a constant ancient presence raising the hairs on her neck. It felt as if this part of the country was somehow older than the rest of it, as if it had existed before the beginning of time and would survive long after it.

Finally, she interrupted the silence. "Where is Jeremy, any-way?"

"Paris, France," Azrael replied without hesitation.

"Why Paris?"

"It's where he spent his year in the human world. And it's where his husband is."

"I wasn't sure if angels actually married," she answered. "I always thought it was such a human, transactional thing, wrapped up in the pretense of romance."

"I don't disagree," he replied. "But it's necessary for the survival of our species."

"What do you mean?"

"Angels mostly live in small, isolated communities. Monogamy is a really useful trait on an island where everyone knows everyone. Or else murder and chaos would ensue every time someone fucked their neighbor's partner. So, while angels are as sexually active and promiscuous as any other species, they tend to marry to reproduce. And once they do, they almost always stay monogamous. I've heard of the bond as a romanticized story about fate and destiny, but I think our programming just helps us find the most suitable partner and stick with them. And since it is a widely respected tradition, there is no place for adultery and jealousy in married angels, so they're free to safely propagate the species... I've heard marriage described as "coming home after a long journey at sea"... Which sounds wonderful enough. But I think it came about to safeguard our kind, in a way in which humanity has not needed to be protected for a long time."

"Does everyone wind up married?" she asked, unsure how she felt about the whole concept.

"Not everyone, no..." Azrael replied, slowly. "But most. Which is not to say that they are happy. Angels are still angels and relationships are flawed, so marriage bonds are just as strained as any other relationship."

"Are you... Have you..." She didn't know how to ask. She remembered, Jeremy telling her that Azrael was never in short supply of casual sex, but that angels wouldn't want to breed with him because of his wings.

Azrael looked out the window for a moment, before responding. "I doubt I'll ever marry. But I came to terms with that a long time ago."

She peeked in his direction and realized how hard he was clenching his jaw as he was saying it.

"If marriage is about breeding, how come Jeremy married a male?"

"The genetic reason for marriage might be about breeding, but in practice it happens as much in all-male or all-female couples as it does between males and females. And Jeremy happens to exclusively like males."

"Jeremy is gay?" she asked. She'd never really thought of Jeremy's private life, but now she realized that she wanted to know more about him. He'd become such a large part of her life, but she was painfully aware that she wasn't a part of his.

"What do you mean? He's jovial? You've met the male, haven't you? He's caring and loving, but he isn't exactly the most lighthearted angel there is..."

"No, I mean... gay... as in a male who only likes males," she replied, confused.

"Are you telling me that humans have a word for that?" he asked, clearly baffled.

"Yes of course. We have a word for all sexual orientations."

"Sexual, what?" he interrupted.

"Orientations. Concepts for who likes whom, basically..."

"Why would you have words for that?" he continued.

"Angels don't?"

"No, of course not. Some angels like females, some like males, some like everyone, some don't like sex... But it's their business. Why would we have words to distinguish them from one another? They're all angels, aren't they?"

"I... I'm not sure how I feel about that. But I have to admit that it does make sense."

On the one hand, humans fought for the recognition of their labels... On the other hand, they only needed to do so because their heteronormative world marginalized them. The way Azrael described it, angels didn't even have an expectation of heteronormativity...

"Jeremy told me he lived with a group of mixed children in the human world. Is one of them his husband?" she inquired, remembering Jeremy's tale of working at a human hospital.

"Yes... Jeremy has a bit of a fetish for grey wings..." Azrael replied, a mischievous smile on his lips.

It took her a second to realize what he was insinuating, but she got it and, just as they crossed into Arizona, she blurted out, "Wait, are you implying what I think you are?"

"Probably..." he chuckled.

"You and Jeremy?"

"A lifetime ago, but yes. He was actually the only long-term relationship I've ever had," he told her, wistfully. "Most angels don't want grey wings in their life for more than a few nights."

"Well, most angels are stupid," she said, trying to cheer him up, "Fuck 'em!"

"Oh, that I do!" he laughed.

"So, Jeremy, eh? Tell me more..."

"What's there to tell? We were friends. And then, one day, we became more. We were together for about a year before he left for Paris. I was deeply in love with him, and it was a wonderful time in my life. But then he met Julien. It broke my heart, but I knew he couldn't help it. Besides, he's Jeremy. He would have stayed away from Julien and smashed his own heart to pieces if I'd asked him to... So, I let him go..."

Lyla now remembered the longing in Jeremy's face as he'd told her about his time among humans. He'd seemed... homesick.

"He told me he'd considered staying in the human world. Julien is the reason he wanted to stay," she realized.

"He is. And Jeremy was going to stay. But then his mother – Aphrodite, as you now know – died and he inherited her power... He couldn't allow it to go to waste. And Julien would never be accepted amongst the angels. Jeremy visits him as much as he can, but the separation weighs on him greatly."

"Can I ask you something personal?"

"Ask away," he offered.

"Jeremy's power was more limited then, but... what's it like having sex with a priest of Aphrodite's?"

Azrael paused for so long, she didn't think he'd answer. When he finally replied, she realized how deeply affected he was by the memories. "It's the most wonderful feeling in the world. But it's almost too much. To be loved so completely, so unconditionally... it can be hard to accept. They see right through your flaws, and your insecurities, and your pain. And they just choose to embrace it all. Sex with Jeremy was... healing and overwhelming."

Wanting to snap him out of his nostalgic memories, she decided levity was called for and asked, "Speaking of sex, are we going to address the elephant in the room?"

"Excuse me?" Azrael responded and snapped his head in her direction.

Quickly covering up her embarrassment and slight panic at his confusion, she added, "The fact that you have handcuffs near your bed..."

"Oh," he replied and relaxed back into his seat. "Well... would you believe me if I tried to convince you that they weren't there for exactly the reason you're implying?"

Lyla giggled. "Nope! Kinky... So how do those uptight angels like being at big bad Azrael's mercy?"

"Who said I'm the one restraining them?" he chuckled. "My cuffs have been out of commission for a while though, considering I've been training your sorry ass for months!"

"Oh, I'm sorry. Am I getting in the way of your sex life?" she replied, feigning innocence.

"Yes, you wear me out, you smartass," he replied, fake slapping the back of her head. "By the time I make it through the day with you, sex is the last thing on my mind."

"So, now I'm killing your libido? That's charming."

"I didn't say-"

"Too bad, big guy. I haven't gotten laid in forever either. If I can make it, so can you."

"Really... I have trouble believing that, but pray, do tell, when exactly was the last time someone took you to bed?"

And just like that, their bantering was dead in the water.

Eyes glued to the road, she swallowed down the knot forming in her throat and replied, "The day before I met you. Max and I were just starting something when..."

She could sense the tension coil itself into Azrael's body. As much as they were trying to have a casual conversation, they kept mucking up the mood.

"I wasn't sure if the two of you were..." he began, discomfort in his voice.

But maybe it was about time they had an honest, open conversation about the fact that she had had a life before coming to the island. It hurt so much to admit, that she'd avoided talking about it at all costs. But they were driving toward Max's cabin. There would be no denying that she'd had a full life and that she'd lost it all.

"Max and I had been falling into each other's beds between relationships for years, but that last time was... different.

It should have been the beginning of something. But I didn't know... I didn't realize how I felt about him until it was too late."

There it was. The truth that had been twisting her heart every single day for months. Speaking it out felt like she was taking her first deep breaths since it had happened.

Azrael waited a moment, before asking, "How long?"

She shook her head, unsure what he was asking.

"How long had you been sleeping with him?"

It was an odd question, but she humored him. "On and off, since we were fourteen."

"Fourteen?" he exclaimed. "That's too young."

"I know," she replied, simply.

"Was he your first?" he probed further.

"No," she answered quietly, pausing, then adding, "but he was the first I chose."

The truth about just how much she'd been through, hung in the air between them.

"How old were you the first time?" Azrael finally asked between clenched teeth. She could see his balled-up fists out of the corner of her eyes, the white knuckles a stark contrast to his bronze skin. He was angrier than she'd ever seen him, but he was trying to keep it inside for her sake.

"Twelve," she replied, softly.

"When did it stop?"

"I was sixteen, the last time it happened," she told him.

She could feel the battle he was waging with himself. Every fiber of his being was trained to believe in redemption, to believe that everyone was worthy of a second chance. But in this very moment, she knew that he didn't believe in second chances.

"How many? How many people dared touch you against

your will?" he growled.

"Three. The Fallen did their work well," she told him, bit-terness dripping from her words. "They picked all the worst foster families they could find... Max went through the same ordeal... I didn't realize it then, but sex with him was a way to feel in control, I think. And to feel some sort of tenderness and care..."

Azrael looked out the window for a long time, taking con-trolled breaths.

"I'm sorry we didn't find you sooner, Lyla," he finally said, keeping his eyes on the passing trees. "I'm so sorry I wasn't there to protect you from those monsters."

"It's not your fault," she replied in a small voice.

"No, it's not. But I can still feel sorry for what you endured."

"Thank you."

They didn't speak for hours after that.

On a whim, Lyla detoured North with the setting of the sun. Azrael didn't realize, until she slowed down and finally stopped the car and stepped out.

Darkness had fallen, and she couldn't quite tell what she was looking into, but she could sense the ancient chasm, as well as the presence of wild animals surrounding them. Not that it bothered her. She had a knife clipped to her side, wings to fly away from danger, and whatever predator was nearby could probably sense that she was no regular human.

Finding a ledge, Lyla sat down, letting her feet dangle in the void, and pulled out the photograph that she'd been sitting on for days.

There he was. Max. Grinning maniacally on top of the Won-der Wheel. It had been the hardest year of Lyla's life. Her psy-che had almost broken. But she'd finally turned eighteen, and they'd celebrated at Coney Island. They'd ridden the cyclone, yet somehow it was the Wonder Wheel that had made her queasy. But Max had insisted on eternalizing the moment. They'd promised each other that everything would get better from there on out. And in some ways, it had. But now that she looked back at it, she could see how much fear they'd lived in. Right up to his death, their entire life had been constructed around protecting themselves from ever being hurt again. Between their emergency plans, their paranoid vigilance, and their inability to let anyone fully into their hearts, they hadn't really lived. They'd merely survived.

And, as much as she missed Max, she was tired of surviving. She was tired of being the strong female who'd make it through anything life threw at her.

For the first time, she wanted more.

She didn't know where that feeling had come from. Or when it had started. But she suspected it was linked to Jeremy's incessant insistence on healing her. Somehow, he'd put Humpty-Dumpty back together seamlessly. He'd repaired her broken heart to a point she'd never even known was possible. And though there was a God to rescue and possibly a war to wage, though she was still grieving, she wanted more out of life than she ever had. She wanted joy. She wanted happiness. She wanted to wake up in the morning and feel at peace.

Azrael carefully sat down next to her, a little further from the ledge, aware he'd be tracked if he fell and spread his wings. He didn't mention the photograph. He simply sat in silence with her for a moment, before asking, "Why here?"

Looking into the darkness, she told him, "The day he died, we were supposed to run away. Something had happened. Someone had beat him up a couple of days before. Something about the people he was working for... he didn't tell me the details..."

She sensed Azrael's intent eyes on her, but she didn't turn

around to look at him.

"We were going to drive to the cabin... I was supposed to be on this trip with him..."

Swallowing the knot forming in her throat, she took a moment to regain her composure, while Azrael waited, quietly.

"This was the one detour I was going to insist on taking. Neither one of us had ever seen it. Ironic that it's so dark, I still can't see it. Feels like some fucked up metaphor for my life."

"I hope you can see it someday," Azrael softly replied. "I hope you can fly through it. It's quite the experience..."

"You've flown through the Grand Canyon?" she asked, abruptly pulled out of her melancholy.

"I have. It's part of basic priest training. For a week every winter, we find a way to close the park off to humans and to planes, and priests in training practice flying through the Canyon. By the end of the week, there is a flight test. Only those who pass can go on to become priests of Hermes'."

And just like that, she was pulled back to her new reality, away from Max and her grief. But there was one more thing she needed to do.

"I want a piece of him to be here. Can you please go back to the car and give me a moment?"

Azrael gave her a quizzical look but didn't argue. When she heard the car door shut, she crouched up and stepped back from the ledge, carefully depositing the photograph on a flat rock.

In the human world, her rule had been to always carry a knife, a flashlight, and a lighter. She pulled out the latter and lit the bottom right corner of the photograph on fire. It curled up so fast, she barely saw it eating away at Max's smile, at his arm around her shoulders...

Blowing the ashes into the Canyon, she whispered, "Good-bye, Max. I love you. Always."

34

The next evening, they arrived at the cabin. They'd dropped off the rental car in the nearest town and hiked deep into the desert. It had taken them four hours to arrive at the remote cabin. Having just driven for four days, Lyla wanted to collapse into bed. But they needed to assess their situation first.

Checking food and water supplies, she showed Azrael around, and he made sure every lock and safety precaution was in place.

It was a tiny home, with an open kitchen and living space and a separate bedroom. The place was solar powered, and the outdoor shower ran off of recycled rainwater. Built by Max's old martial arts teacher, he'd inherited it, free of any paperwork. No one knew it existed, and the chances of anyone venturing this far into the desert were slim to none.

When he was satisfied with the number of weapons at both their disposal, Lyla helped prep the couch for Azrael and gave him some of Max's teacher's clothes. He'd been significantly larger than Max, and Max had never been able to get rid of the last few items that reminded him of the only father figure he'd ever had.

By the time she laid her head down, Lyla was so tired she barely registered that the sheets still smelled of him. But his scent, that sweet smell of baked bread and fresh laundry, followed her into her dreams. And from those, into her nightmares.

She'd had this dream before, though she couldn't remember when. The dream where all her abusers sported Max's face. She knew it was a nightmare because she knew Max. Max was loving. Max was kind. Max had always protected her. Max would never have done those things to her.

But she couldn't escape. She couldn't wake herself up.

It was torture, relieving every single physical assault. Every time she had been threatened, beaten, raped. And having to look into Max's eyes, as it happened.

But they weren't the eyes she remembered. They were the cold and calculating eyes of the boy she'd first met, the one who'd looked her up and down and assessed her, as if she were a liability.

He was holding both her shoulders down now, whispering to her, "Lyla... Lyla..."

She tried to shake him off, she tried to bite at his wrist, but her name got louder and louder, and as it did, the creepiness was replaced with an urgency.

"Lyla! Lyla! Wake up!"

Finally, she snapped to, finding herself back at the cabin, her legs trapped in the twisted sheets, tears drying on the sides of her face. It was Azrael's strong hands that had grabbed her shoulders, Azrael she'd tried to bite. He was bent over her, wearing nothing but his underwear and a worried scowl on his face. As soon as he saw that she was awake, he let go of her and backed up to the wall, crouching on the ground, making himself as small as possible.

Panting, Lyla sat up and pulled her knees and the sheets up to her chest. She took a few deep breaths, trying to control the trembling that was shaking her entire body.

"I'm sorry," she finally uttered through clenched teeth she was trying to stop from chattering.

"Don't apologize. Whatever you dreamt of, don't apologize."

"The things I told you about in the car yesterday... I hadn't talked about that in a long time..."

She couldn't meet his gaze; she was too scared to see pity in there. Or, worse, disgust.

But Azrael wouldn't have it. Keeping a safe distance, he knelt nearer to the mattress, putting himself in her eyeline. "I know what it's like to feel small and weak and ashamed for the things bad people did to you. But you are the strongest angel I have ever met."

"I'm not really feeling strong right now..." she replied, meekly.

"We all need a little help sometimes. Having those nightmares... needing someone else to remind you, you are safe... wanting others in your life... those aren't signs of weakness. They are signs that your heart is still whole, that you are still you."

Jeremy had said something to that same effect, what seemed like years ago.

Azrael let it sink in, then asked, "What can I do for you, Lyla?"

Taking a deep breath and taking his words to heart, she asked, "Would you... stay in here with me tonight?"

He raised an eyebrow and remained very still for a moment, but finally nodded. Getting up, he said, "Let me put on some clothes. I'll be right back."

A moment later, he returned, wearing a pair of sweatpants

and a t-shirt, both just a little too short and tight for his large frame. He stood in the doorframe, keeping that polite distance, and asked, "Where would you like me to be?"

The answer to that question was, *As close as possible.* Worried he'd balk at the idea, she looked at the opposite side of the bed. "Would you mind..."

Azrael hesitated for just a moment, then smiled and slowly walked over to the other side of the bed. He laid down on his side, on top of the sheets, keeping his distance but unknowingly replacing Max's scent with his own spicier one.

Lyla wrapped herself tightly under the covers, turned on her side, looking at him, and asked, "Can I... May I.... Would it be ok if I held your hand?"

Azrael extended his left hand to her with a chuckle and squeezed as soon as she put her much smaller one in it, soothingly rubbing his thumb from left to right.

Just like that, her exhaustion reared its head again, and she felt safe to close her eyes.

"Get some sleep, little fledgling."

For the first time, there was no animosity in that word. It wasn't an insult. It sounded... Tender. Sweet. Endearing.

"Good night, Azrael," she murmured.

35

Lyla woke up surprisingly refreshed the next morning. Opening her eyes to a sleeping Azrael, she realized that she'd gotten closer to him during the night and cradled her face into his hand. He, apparently, had not moved an inch all night.

Careful not to wake him, she got up and tiptoed out of the room, closing the door behind her.

Turning on some music on the old stereo, she began making coffee and pancakes with powdered milk. Within moments, she heard a voice behind her. "Turn off that music."

Whirling around, she looked at Azrael. He stood in the door, fully awake, repeating "Please, turn off the music," with more urgency.

"What's gotten into you this morning?" she mumbled, turning around and pushing the pause button on the old stereo that still played CDs.

"Nothing," came his grumpy answer. "If anything came to attack us, I wouldn't be able to hear it over the noise."

"You didn't mind in the car..." she replied, going back to flipping pancakes.

"We were in an armored vehicle moving at high speeds. This is very different. I need to be able to listen to my surroundings at all times."

Whenever Azrael became sweet or more personal, she forgot that she was dealing with a trained warrior, a creature that was constantly aware and ready to pounce. And these days in particular, he was on high alert.

"All right, it won't happen again," she told him, unplugging the stereo and serving breakfast at the little wooden table that passed for a dining table.

They sat on apple crates and ate breakfast in silence, took turns showering off five days of sweat and dirt in the outdoor shower, and met again in the living room where she pulled out the burner phone Max and her had purchased long ago for emergencies. Azrael rattled off an international number for her to dial.

Jeremy picked up on the third ring, his voice a ray of sunshine piercing through storm clouds she'd mostly gotten accustomed to.

"Jeremy," she sighed. "It's good to hear your voice."

"Lyla, where are you? Give me exact coordinates and I'll portal to you right now."

Five minutes later Jeremy appeared in the small living room, pulling them both into bone crushing hugs. Lyla prepared more coffee while Azrael caught him up on everything that had happened on their end, only leaving out the part where he'd attacked Lyla on the Sacred Mountain.

She poured them all cups of fresh coffee and joined Jeremy on the couch, opposite Azrael who was crouching on the ground.

"It's not your fault, Az," Jeremy was trying to comfort his friend.

But Azrael, refusing to meet his eyes, simply changed the subject. "How many did you save?"

"Thirty-six. Five priests and thirty-one civilians. Fourteen of them children. Three intact families. The rest are individual angels and orphaned fledglings."

The pain was visible on his face, and it hit Lyla like a million-ton weight. Thank god, thirty-six angels, Hermes, the three fledglings they'd found, and the three of them had made it out alive. But everyone else was gone. Hermes' bloodline was reduced to forty-three individuals, all of whom had suffered such excruciating losses.

"Artiya is among them," Jeremy informed them.

"And Jegudiel?" the priest asked. Jeremy shook his head, lowering his eyes. Only one of the tavern sisters had made it out alive.

Jeremy cleared his throat and continued. "Julien lives with four other mixed angels in a converted warehouse on the outskirts of Paris," he explained to Lyla. "They made room for the refugees. It isn't ideal, and the fledglings are a lot to keep track of, but there is just about enough room to squeeze everyone in and it's as safe a place as we'll find at the moment."

They proceeded to make plans for Hermes' rescue. Getting into Hell and being shown straight to Hermes wouldn't be the issue, Jeremy agreed. The difficulty would be getting out alive.

"Do you think Julien would agree to stay with Lyla while we go down?" Azrael asked. "I don't want to leave her unprotected."

"Are you kidding?" she interrupted. "I am coming with you."

"Absolutely not," Jeremy and Azrael responded in unison. "Your progress is incredible, Lyla," Azrael proceeded. "I don't mean to discount it. But this is as real as it gets, and we can't risk your safety."

"That's not the point. Believe me, I don't want to go," she

replied. "But you need me as bait. It's me they want. That's the only reason my father is alive. The only reason they'd have to not immediately kill you is if they think they can get me."

Instead of arguing, Azrael just smiled at her. "It's the first time you've called him your father..." he simply said.

It was true. She'd thought of him as such, but she'd never said the words out loud. But he was. He was her father, and she needed him back.

They ended up agreeing that they'd indeed need her as bait, as well as having a surprise attack plan. They had a few things playing to their advantage: the Fallen likely underestimated Lyla's power; five priests had survived; and they had no idea Julien and his four friends existed.

Apparently, Julien's mother had been one of the lost and his father had been a priest of Ares'. He'd grown up with one foot in each world, trained with both his warrior father's strength and the relentless discipline of the lost. Though he'd left both worlds for a third, he and his four roommates trained constantly and could contend with the best in a fight.

Lyla also found out that Jeremy had only recently come into his full power as the bearer of Aphrodite's mantle. The Fallen had no idea what he was, and they'd likely underestimate him too.

They would keep meeting and strategizing while they waited for the tracker in Azrael's blood to fade. That gave them just about until the New Year to tighten up their plan.

36

They spent the next couple of weeks training and preparing. Azrael tried to teach Lyla to use her magic under extreme duress, and Lyla in turn showed him how to work a firearm – which, predictably, there were a couple of at the cabin.

Julien joined Jeremy at their meetings, so she got to meet the beefy French angel, and he filled them in on every piece of information he knew about Hell and its demons. It turned out that he'd learned quite a bit growing up with a frontline soldier for a father.

They estimated that Hermes would be in bad shape and his magic incapacitated in one way or another, so they made plans for their ten fighters to be waiting, ready for Jeremy to open a portal as a distraction.

And they trained. And trained. And trained.

Though Lyla longed for the dreamless sleep she'd found the night Azrael had held her hand, they now slept with the door open between both rooms and it seemed to keep the nightmares away well enough.

She'd really wanted to take a day off for Christmas, so she

could introduce him to human holiday traditions, but when she'd described a regular Christmas to him, he'd flat out refused to have any part of it.

None of their canned and freeze-dried foods would have done a holiday feast justice. But Azrael also wouldn't drink any alcohol, not even to experience eggnog for the first time. He'd argued against any kind of music or singing, and he saw no point in cutting down a perfectly healthy tree for the sake of decorating it and letting it die a premature death in their living room.

Utterly disappointed by his complete inability to have fun, she warned him that he wouldn't get out of celebrating New Year's Eve, and still surprised him with a newspaper-wrapped gift on Christmas morning.

It was her old Mossberg 590a1, the pump-action shotgun she'd been teaching him to shoot. She'd bought it at a military surplus store a few years ago so she'd have something to defend the cabin with if she ever found herself there on her own. It wasn't the sleekest gun, but it had been cheap, and it had come complete with the original bayonet – which had always struck her as an immensely brutal safeguard for a gun that, admittedly, could take a second to reload...

But maybe it was the familiarity of the skewering implement at its tip that had spoken to Azrael. He had in fact taken to it so well, that she'd decided to gift it to him and keep Max's 1911 pistol for herself instead.

Azrael thanked her and basked in the moment for all of five minutes, before deciding it was time to train some more – which they continued doing non-stop until late on December thirty-first. At around ten at night, he finally admitted defeat: this was as much preparation as they'd be able to fit in before their suicidal Hell extraction mission.

"So," he said when they met back on the couch after their

respective lukewarm outdoor showers. "How do humans celebrate the turn of the year?"

"Well, they just get drunk, count down the seconds to midnight and find the nearest person to kiss, but I personally like to think back on how the last year went and to list my hopes for the new year... Not that we actually have to do any of that..."

He looked at her for a long moment before answering, "I like it. Let me go first. This past year started like any other. But it got a lot more interesting once Hermes told me he had a little fledgling for me to train. At first, I thought you were a massive pain in my ass," he jokingly continued. "But I'm really glad I met you, Lyla. My life has been... brighter since."

Turning towards her, he leaned his head onto the back of the couch and gazed at her for a moment before saying, "Your turn."

Crossing her legs on the couch to fully face him, Lyla sighed, and replied, "There are a lot of things I wish I could change about last year, but I wouldn't change meeting you. Or Jeremy. Or finding out who and what I am." She didn't want to go into another monologue about Max and her grief. Azrael knew what she meant, and this wasn't the time for more sadness. Not when they were about to breach the bowels of Hell. So instead, she added, "A year ago, my life was more stable, more normal. But I went into the New Year dreaming of nothing. Hoping for nothing. And dreading that it would simply be more of the same. As hard as it's been, there are new things I want for my life now..."

"Like what?" he cocked his head and asked.

"When all this is over... when we get Hermes and everyone safe again... I'd like to go into priest training. I don't know if I'll succeed, but I've never really had any ambitions, and... my wings, my magic... They feel right. Righter than anything else I've ever felt, you know?"

"I think you'd be great at it," Azrael smiled. "I don't know where we'll start on rebuilding the island, but we will need new priests and you'll make a fantastic one. I'll keep training you."

It didn't escape her that he used the future tense, that it was a done deal to him that she'd succeed. Nor did she miss the butterflies in her stomach at the thought of spending many more months under his tutelage. Before she could give that latter thought too much life, she asked, "How about you? What are your secret hopes and dreams?"

Azrael turned away and shrugged. "Nothing really. I know what my life is going to be. I will fight for the Ten – or what's left of them – until one day I fall in that fight. That's all there is to it."

"I don't believe you," she answered, leaning in. "So maybe that is what will happen. But there's got to be something else you sometimes wish you could do. If you made it to retirement age, what would you do?"

Azrael briefly peeked at her before looking away. "Nothing. You'll think it's stupid."

"Azrael," she admonished him, tugging at his wrist to turn him toward her. "I've spilled my guts to you several times on this trip. How dare you think I'd say your dreams were stupid?"

Shyly, he turned back around, crossed his legs on the couch, and held on to his ankles, avoiding eye contact as he spoke. "Sometimes, I think it would be nice to have a store in the village. In the back, I would teach lessons for fledglings. Training them. Not for priesthood or anything, but just so they could discover the full power of their magic and learn how to focus, and maybe also fight a little. But mostly so their magic could come into its own. Most angels just let their power develop as it will, so they never reach their full potential. The school in the village doesn't push them far beyond the basics. I'd like to teach the fledglings that they can reach their potential without having to become priests."

"I think that's beautiful. If you can teach a pain in the ass pseudo-fledgling like me, you'd be great with actual fledglings. I love that idea..."

"You do?" Azrael asked, looking at her with such vulnerability in his eyes. It was heart-breaking, but this male had never been taught he was worth anything beyond his service as a guardian and a warrior.

Lyla nodded, making Azrael blush, as he continued, "In the front, I'd like to have a store. I told you that I used to carve my own toys as a fledgling... I'd like to make and sell toys for all the young angels in the village... Like I said, it's dumb."

So, he wanted a kids' martial arts studio and a toy store... Lyla grabbed his wrist and leaned over to look him in the eyes. "It's not dumb," she told him. "I like it. And I hope it happens. We are going to rebuild that village, and toys are going to be more needed than ever."

"Thank you, Lyla," he replied, the shadow of a spark in his eyes.

Unsure how to carry on with this conversation of hypotheticals when they both well knew they might not even make it back from tomorrow's mission, Lyla got up and went to pour them two champagne flutes of non-alcoholic apple cider she'd found lying around, a substitute to toast with at midnight.

By the time she handed his glass to Azrael, the sweetness and vulnerability had left his face, making room for the deadly serious warrior she'd gotten to know all too well these last few weeks. So much for toasting and doing the silly countdown to midnight. Instead, he set his flute down and pensively looked out the window.

"Lyla, what we're doing tomorrow... it's suicidal. The only

reason I am letting you come is that I don't see another choice. But I don't feel good about it," he finally addressed her.

"Look, like you said, we don't have much of a choice-"

"I need you to promise me something," he interrupted without turning around. "I need you to promise me that you are going to make it out of there tomorrow, no matter what. None of the heroics I saw in Denning. You are there as the bait. As soon as Jeremy opens that portal and lets Julien and the other fighters through, you get out and let us handle the rest."

"No," she shook her head. "I'm not going to make a promise I can't keep. I'll fight until we can all make it to safety together."

"Lyla," Azrael thundered, turning to face her. "This isn't training and it's not an ambush in the human world. It is Hell. We'll likely face at least one of the Fallen. I need to know that you'll be safe. I need to know that you won't see one of us under attack and throw yourself at danger the way you did in Denning, or at your apartment the day we met."

She just shook her head. "You can't ask that of me, Azrael. It's not fair. Not after everything I've lost."

"Lyla, please," he begged her, as she looked around for any excuse to halt the conversation, her eyes stopping on the old clock over the fireplace.

"It's midnight," she whispered, reaching up behind his neck and pulling him down into a kiss.

Azrael froze as she crashed against his big soft lips, but he didn't push her away. Instead, he gradually relaxed and began to kiss her back, those full lips getting a hold of her lower lip, his tongue teasing the entrance of her mouth just so. Kissing him had been a desperate maneuver to distract him, but god, the male could kiss. She'd always complained to her girlfriends about men who underused their lips and overused their tongues, but Azrael? He could have written the book on how she wanted to be made out with. Her mind going blank, she melted into his chest as his arms snaked their way around her waist, pulling her in close.

An eternity later, she was running her fingers through the long hair at the back of his head and moaning into his mouth, as he pulled out of the kiss and rested his forehead against hers. Eyes still closed, he took a few shaky breaths before saying, "You need to get some rest. We both do." Opening his eyes and pulling out of their embrace he added, "Go to bed, Lyla. Good night."

She was tempted to bargain, to ask him to join her in bed, but there was something icy in his words. Maybe she'd misread their kiss. Maybe it hadn't been all that to him.

But at least it had done what she'd intended it to: it had stopped him from extracting promises she would most certainly break.

Lyla turned around and went to bed in a daze, hanging on to this moment for dear life so she wouldn't have to think about what was to come tomorrow. About Hell. About the Fallen. And about what they'd probably done to her father. Sleeping with Azrael would have been a mistake of colossal proportions, but that didn't stop her from allowing the fantasy of it to lull her into sleep.

37

All thoughts of hot, steamy sex with Azrael had dissipated by the time Lyla woke up, her heart beating a million miles an hour. She turned around to see that it was only five in the morning, but the thought of what they were about to do would not allow her to get any more rest. She sat up, trying to take a few controlled breaths, but quickly gave up and shuffled into the kitchen to get a glass of water instead.

Rather than Azrael, it was Jeremy she found sitting crossed legged on the couch, his wings folded around him like a cocoon.

"Did we wake you?" he asked. "We're not leaving for another few hours, you can go back to sleep if you want."

"I don't think I can," she replied, leaning against the counter and draining her glass.

Like every morning, Azrael had undone his makeshift bed, and neatly folded every item into a small pile in the corner of the room. But he himself was nowhere to be seen, or heard, which bothered her more than it should have. Catching her looking around for him, Jeremy stood up and came to stand across from her, explaining, "He's in Paris. I sent him through a portal, so he could prepare the fighters over there. He's the general after all, not me."

She knew the plan. Julien, his four friends, and the five priests of Hermes' would be ready for Jeremy to open a portal and let them into Hell. Jeremy would wait until they were close enough to Hermes to make an easy escape. Only then would he let the ten fighters through. They'd cause a substantial distraction with their shock and awe attack, and hopefully all fourteen of them – including Hermes – would step back out of Hell through the portal before the Fallen and demons knew what had hit them.

Jeremy was right. Azrael was a general, and it was his job to choreograph this maneuver to maximize its chances of success. Yet, she couldn't help the fact that she'd gotten so dependent on the safety of his presence, that something seemed to be missing in the room when he wasn't there. She would have laughed if someone had told her three months before that the day would come where she'd prefer to exchange Jeremy's presence for Azrael's.

"I'm glad to see you scared," Jeremy pulled her out of her thoughts. "I'm glad you're in a place where you have enough to lose to be scared. That's good, Lyla. It's very good."

"Are you scared?" she asked him.

"Of course I am. I'm scared for every single person who'll be there. But Julien most of all. It would kill me if anything happened to him. But if he didn't throw himself into the fray to save others, I wouldn't be with him. I've always known he was selfless; I've always known he was willing to sacrifice himself for a greater purpose... It's why I fell in love with him. So now, I have to live with it."

"How did you meet?" Lyla asked, pouring herself a second glass of water.

"I worked as an intern at a hospital during my year in the human world. He was an ER doctor there. I had no idea what he was, but he immediately caught my eye. There was something about how he spoke to his patients, about how much he cared. Most other doctors tried to put up walls, to protect themselves from their patients' suffering. I didn't blame them for it; faced with too much suffering, they tried to let all patients blend into one. But not Julien. He let it all in. Acknowledged each and every one of them for their individuality. Shared in their pain. It was the most beautiful thing I'd ever seen. He seemed like... a manifestation of my own world, if that makes any sense."

He paused, deeply absorbed by his memories, before continuing. "I assumed he was human. And he thought the same of me. The first time we slept with one another was torture for both of us, because we had to hold in our magic at any cost to avoid discovery," he chuckled. "But inevitably, I started healing patients in secret. I couldn't stand to let the suffering go on in that hospital when I knew I could so easily lessen it. I had to pick and choose who I would heal, how I could do as much good as possible without being discovered. But Julien figured out pretty quickly that there was an angel in the hospital. And ultimately, he caught me in the act."

His story distracted her enough that Lyla sat on the counter, finally able to eat a little breakfast.

"You have to understand, part of why priests of Aphrodite's are sent out into the human world is that we are supposed to witness human suffering without intervening. In that sense, I was utterly failing my mission. The patient he caught me healing was a child. She had such a high fever, anyone would have written off her claims about a winged angel as a hallucination. I couldn't do anything about her illness. A true intervention would have been a questionable miracle. But she had these nightmares and I just wanted to ease her suffering. So, I snuck into her room and used my magic to soothe her terror." He shook his head. "It was reckless. The rules against such interventions exist for a reason. When Julien caught me... Gods, I thought I'd just revealed a thousands-of-years-old secret to humanity..."

"It must have been such a relief though, to realize he was an angel too," Lyla interjected.

"It was. For me, at least. It took him a while to believe that I didn't care about the color of his wings. But once he did... Well, the rest is history, as they say."

"You must miss him," Lyla said, regretting it as soon as she did.

Jeremy had never cared to hide his emotions from her, and his pain at what she said was carved deeply into his face. "Every hour of every day," he replied, dropping his gaze to the ground. "But now you know, why I had to leave Paris. I couldn't let my mother's mantle go to waste."

And there it was. The secret he hadn't told her when he'd first spoken of his mother. The fact he'd lost everything the day the Fallen had attacked Aphrodite's island: his mother, his Goddess, his people, his home, and his future with the love of his life. And in exchange he'd been saddled with the burden of keeping his entire bloodline's legacy alive.

There were no words for how much she wished she could relieve him of his sorrow and ease his pain, that pain she now felt as her own, a black void in the middle of her chest threatening to eat her whole. And because there were no words, she jumped off the counter, spread her wings, tackled him in a hug, and wrapped her wings tightly around him the same way her father had done for her weeks ago.

For once, there was no need for words. Jeremy knew what she meant. And she knew that he did. She couldn't tell how, but she knew that they felt the same compassion for one another, and in that moment, their mutual pain was truly halved. They stood like that for a while, cocooned in their respective wings, sharing a fraternal moment, soothing each other's aches and fears.

"I'm glad I met you, Lyla," he said, finally breaking the silence but keeping a tight hold on her with his arms and wings. "It gets lonely being ... what I am. There are a few dozen of us left, all the priests of Aphrodite's in training who were in the human world at the time of the attack... But I'm her only direct descendant... I can't explain it, but I feel less alone when you're around."

He kissed the top of her head, gently untangling their feathers, and added, "Now, you need to catch those extra two hours of sleep. Knowing Azrael, he worked you to the point of exhaustion in a futile attempt to prepare you for every possible contingency. You need whatever rest you can get."

"I don't think I can. And even if I fell asleep, I doubt it would be restful," she replied, stepping back.

"Sweetheart, you've been away from me for too long," he chuckled. "Have you no faith in my gifts anymore?"

Five minutes later, she'd landed in a dreamless slumber induced by nothing more than one of Jeremy's warm hands on her forehead.

38

They waited until the last minute to wake her up, leaving just enough time to get ready but none to overthink things. Half an hour later, Azrael, Jeremy, and Lyla stepped through a portal that led them to the middle of an enormous cave system in Switzerland which was aptly named "Hölloch," "Hell Hole." Julien knew the location to a variety of entrances to Hell, but they'd chosen one that was widely known amongst angels so the Fallen wouldn't suspect anyone else's involvement.

They'd also agreed to walk in armed with their wings only and to skip any pretense that Lyla was a prisoner. The spies the Fallen had had in the compound must have reported that both Azrael and Jeremy cared deeply for her. No one would have believed it if they'd pretended to callously exchange her for Hermes. They might however buy it if they claimed to be desperate enough to have the God back that they saw no other recourse than to hand over Lyla. It would also be more credible to have her come willingly than playing scared captive.

And so, they strolled right into Hell through a gate a hundred miles past the cave's entrance.

It didn't take long for them to be intercepted by a pair of demons. Skeptical at first, they wound up patting them down for extra weapons, calling in reinforcements, and marching them deeper into Hell and into a large hall echoing a male's deep screams of pain.

They'd expected that part to be easy enough: they'd be arrested, claim to want to make an exchange, and wouldn't resist as they were brought to the demon's superiors.

What they hadn't expected was to be brought straight to Lucifer himself. Or that Hermes would be right there, chained up and tortured at his side.

In that moment, she knew Azrael and Jeremy were thinking the exact same thing she was: in some ways, this had been so much easier than they'd predicted, and in others it was, oh, so much worse.

The cavern they were in was so deep and dark, she couldn't quite make out its corners. To make it worse, it was lined with columns large enough to hide behind, making it difficult to gauge where the enemy was. And speaking of the enemy, the place was crowded. So far, she'd only met Princes of Hell, with their animal features and chitinous carapaces. But she'd seen drawings of all sorts of demons in the books she'd studied, and she knew that if you could picture it, Lucifer had probably attempted to bring it into existence.

What she hadn't realized was what it would do to her brain to witness them in person: hundreds of demons, all sporting a different number and shape of limbs and heads. She could feel the physical pain of her brain trying to assimilate what her eyes were recording, her mind's desperate attempts to make heads or tails of what it was seeing, to predict what a fight with any of those creatures would look like.

They'd known they would be outnumbered. They'd placed

their bets on surprise and luck. But these numbers far exceeded any intel they'd been able to gather. Lucifer had either greatly increased his numbers in the years since Julien had spoken to his father, or he'd been expecting them.

"Don't try to assess the overall danger," Azrael quietly whispered at her side. "Don't look at them. Just focus on one side of the room."

So, she did. She focused on the big bad in front of them. Standing on a dais just a few feet away from her was no other than Lucifer himself. She'd seen a picture of him too, but he was so much scarier than paper and pencil could convey.

Much like the Ten, he was seven feet tall and sported sharp claws and fangs. His wings, however, were of such a deep black that there wasn't any tinge of blue or brown in them. They were exactly what black was: the absence of light. In that moment, Lyla finally understood why wing color still carried so much weight with the angels. The Ten's white wings symbolized the light that fought the Fallen's void which would have gobbled up the world without them.

Lucifer's eyes weren't those of a raptor like Hermes'. They were the eyes of a goat: placed at the sides of his face and yellow with rectangular, panoramic pupils, giving him an almost 360-degree range of vision. And instead of the Ten's down, his head was covered with the same carapace as his princes' and crowned with two large goat horns, curling back.

But his features weren't the scariest part. She'd seen all sorts of strange, inhuman features on humanoid creatures recently. No, it was his smile that turned her veins to ice. His lips stretched over his large canines in a twitching grimace that no homicidal psychopath could dream of replicating.

And it was all meant for her.

"Lailah, Lailah..." he addressed her in a voice that echoed

longer than her father's, bouncing off the cave walls like razor blades flinging back at them. It made her irrationally angry to hear him use the name she'd first heard from her father's lips.

"I've waited a long time to meet you, my niece. You should have called ahead. I would have cleaned up the mess," he added, punctuating his statement with a turn of his head to the left. To what she'd avoided looking at until now. He'd chained both of Hermes' wrists to the ceiling straight above his head. His knees didn't reach the ground and his weight had long pulled his shoulders out of their sockets. But that wasn't the worst of it.

In the movies she'd seen, torture scenes always involved cuts and punches, pulled fingernails and waterboarding. None of that had been done to her father. Because Lucifer had exclusively focused on his wings. He'd meticulously ripped every last feather off her father's wings, leaving them a bare and bloody mess, every tendon, every bone, every square inch of membrane starkly visible, letting the light shine through the glistening, darker-than-human blood.

Unlike birds, none of them ever shed their feathers. Only once had she seen feathers come off an angel's wings. It had been when she'd unconsciously ripped out some of Azrael's in her fever dream. And she now suspected that it had been an infuriating and painful act that the priest had brushed off with his infinite patience.

Their wings stored their magic. But beyond that, they were sacred. Lucifer had not only incapacitated his brother. He'd humiliated him in the worst possible way, taken his greatest pride, his very essence from him. The ground was littered in his snow-white feathers, blood of several weeks of torture pooled under him, his clothes torn, his body shaking uncontrollably. His head hung so low, he looked asleep. But his eyes were wide open, staring at her. He was awake, he'd simply lost the strength to hold his neck up.

Before she realized that she was about to run to him, Azrael had an arm wrapped around her mid-section, holding her back. "You can't do anything for him right now. Stay close, keep your wings in and your wits about yourself," he whispered. "You trained for this, Lyla."

She wanted to scream at him, but instead she let his voice soothe her, nodding to him to let her go once she'd mastered her impulses.

"What a hold you have on her, Azrael..." Lucifer, who'd noted every detail of their interaction, purred, that name she loved poison on his lips. "Fascinating... Are you also the one who convinced her to come here? Or did the female sweet talk you?"

As Azrael, who'd dealt with plenty of taunting and humiliation in his life, stared daggers at the Fallen, Lyla couldn't help feeling like the two had met before. There was an intimacy in Lucifer's voice, a familiarity only used for people one knew closely. And Azrael looked like he hated it.

But that was a mystery for another day. Right now, they needed to get Hermes home.

"Neither of them wanted me here," she interrupted their staring contest and addressed the creature in front of them. "But I reminded them that you wouldn't give Hermes back for free."

"You're offering yourself up as payment?" he smirked. "Interesting. See, maybe you really did walk in here unsure whether you'd walk out, but I'm sure neither one of them would have let you come unless they believed they could get both of you out."

He paused, cocking his head to the side and pointing those goat eyes at her. Lyla's stomach sank. In that moment, she decided that they wouldn't have come in vain. She'd at least make sure that the other three made it out alive.

"I'm sure you wanted me to think you were all desperate enough to get my brother back that you'd sacrifice the girl. Oh, sweet things, did you really think I'd believe that? No, you have some sort of ace up your sleeve... And I'm going to have so much fun pulling it out," he told the two males at her side, snapping his fingers at the end.

As soon as he did, two demons approached Lyla, roughly grabbed her by the elbows, and pulled her up onto the dais. She could have easily gotten out of their grip, but they'd agreed not to use any magic or force until Jeremy opened the portal, and she could tell he was gauging how to get Hermes out of his cuffs and back on his feet. That did not, however, prevent Azrael from growling like a bear as she was dragged forward.

Once she stood a foot away from Lucifer, the demons let go of her, but she felt invisible shackles snake their way around her torso. Lucifer's eyes bored into her as his wings flared up ever so slightly. He was using his magic to hold her in place, she realized. He was getting ready to hurt her, but he was also keeping her wings from manifesting, which meant that he was in fact worried she'd retaliate magically. Storing that fact away, she ceased struggling against the invisible bonds and simply waited for him to slip up in one way or another.

Looking up into his face, she felt like she was gazing into madness incarnate, but she held those eyes, silently daring him to try his worst.

"So... Lailah... what's the ace up your sleeve?" his voice echoed in the air.

As brave as she tried to play, her bravado failed her a little bit more with every second she spent in the Fallen's proximity. Keeping her mouth shut, she wondered if it could even be called an ace up their sleeve.

"You know, this is a really fun game. If I hurt you, it'll hurt your friends and your father... oh, he will feel it in his deepest core. But if I hurt them, I can hurt you and keep you all new and shiny as you are. And your father will still feel your pain..." he continued, leaning in closely and tucking a loose lock of hair behind her ear, then casually trailing his claws down to her pulse point. She felt her breathing accelerate while her eyes closed against her will. As much as she wanted to play tough, she was in the hands of an almost all-powerful being, the only other one of his kind in the room currently fully crippled. Jeremy might wear the mantle, but his power could not compare.

"Am I going to have fun playing with you," he continued, and snapped his fingers toward the crowd without looking at them.

As he did, two things happened. Half the demons filed out of the hall, leaving maybe a hundred in the room with them. And Lucifer wrapped his clawed hand all the way around her throat, not squeezing, but asserting his power.

"Just sending a welcome committee for whatever friends you enlisted for your suicide mission..." he drawled, scraping her skin with his pointy claws.

And then she understood: he'd figured out the part where they had reinforcements coming, but he hadn't figured out where they would be coming from. Her heart leapt in joy as she realized he'd just sent half of his forces away, making their work that much easier.

"Your pulse just sped up, little bird," he remarked. "Am I scaring you? Don't worry, you'll come to love me some day. Once I break you, you and I will have a grand time together, I promise."

With those threatening words, her elation died, replaced with a deep dread. She knew that feeling. She'd grown up with it. It was that sinking feeling she'd gotten with every new family, every new house, every new setup. Hoping it would be better than the last but knowing it would only cut her deeper.

And this place had been meant as her final home. This was the place her entire childhood had been leading up to. This was where they'd wanted her to end up all along. Seized by a sudden panic, Lyla turned to the only source of comfort she could think of. She met Azrael's green-golden eyes just as hers started to tear up, and he gave her the slightest smile of encouragement.

They'd trained for this. They'd known that Lucifer would fixate on her, he reminded her with that smile. Lucifer's hand was still wrapped around her throat, but for a moment she forgot her fear as she looked at her trainer, her friend, the male who, just hours ago, she'd shared the most soul scorching kiss of her life with.

But just as her gaze dropped to those lush lips, just as her breathing evened out again, the Fallen caught on. "Shall we start with him? Is that what you're telling me, sweet bird?"

Gods, no, she wanted to scream, but that wasn't what Azrael had prepared her to do. Instead, she took a deep breath, turned back toward those rectangularly pupiled eyes, and said, "Do your worst. You spent years trying to break me, and you failed. What makes you think you'll succeed now?"

"I didn't have them to play with before," he nodded toward Azrael and Jeremy. "But don't fret, I wouldn't want to spoil the fun by starting with the crown jewel. No, no, little wing, we'll work up to that, shall we?"

With one last squeeze, he let go of her throat and theatrically put a hand to the ear hole at his temple. "Do you hear that? That irritating sound? Like scratching nails on rock? No?" he asked, that mad look in his eyes again. "It's the sound of feathers piercing through wing skin. It's the sound of my darling brother's magic growing back in. But we wouldn't want that now, would we?"

"No, we don't!" he answered his own question, stepping away from her, releasing the bounds that had held her in place, and snapping his fingers again. In response, one of the demons approached, offering a pair of tweezers on a platter to Lucifer, his head bowed as if he were presenting an immeasurable treasure.

Lucifer grabbed the tweezers with reverence, and sauntered over to Hermes, telling her "I could use my claws, but that just wouldn't be sanitary, would it?"

Dangling from the chains, there was nowhere to go for the God, but he tried to pull away nonetheless, twisting his large torso as far away from his psychotic brother as he could. Lyla hated seeing her father so powerless, so feeble. Whether from exhaustion or fear, his body shook, and she heard his raspy breathing accelerate with Lucifer's approach.

She wanted to throw herself at the Fallen, to attack him, to hurt him, or at least to try. But she had to follow the plan. And the plan was to goad him into a false sense of confidence, to look weaker than they really were, to let him believe they had no escape plan so they could get Hermes at the right moment and get out of Dodge.

But there was one thing she could do. While Lucifer carefully examined her father's wings, Hermes feebly trying to pull away from him, she stepped up to the God's other side. With a visible effort, he lifted his head to look at her. His knees hovering just above the ground, she was at the right height to look straight into his tortured face. There was dried blood on his chin, where his oversized canines must have bitten into his lower lip in his agony. Fresh sweat was beading on his bronze forehead. But it was his haunted eyes that knocked the breath out of her.

They were the same raptor eyes she'd been so horrified by when she'd first met him, but now she saw their depth, saw the pain in the lines around them. And in their deep, large, black pupils, all she saw, was herself.

"I... didn't want... you... to come..." his wretched voice echoed through the air.

"I know," she answered, her hands going up to his cheeks and wiping away his tears. "But I had to. I needed you to know something..." She paused, looking over his shoulder at the maniac who was tiptoeing back and forth in search of the perfect spot to continue his torture. Pulling her focus back to the God in front of her, she continued, "I needed to tell you, that I want to know you. I want to... I want to know what it's like being your daughter."

The smile that lit up his face at her words was interrupted by an anguished scream, as his brother tore out the first of his feathers. Before she knew what she was doing, her wings popped out of her back, and she was wrapping them tightly around her father's torso. She held him close, unable to make herself let go and step back, as his wings weakly drooped over her arms, his face close to hers.

Lucifer stepped back at the sight, eyeing her with interest. "Compelling turn of events, brother. She's coming into her own fast, isn't she? I can't wait to see what happens when I pull the next feather out."

Hermes ignored the taunts. "Let go, Lyla. I need you to let go right now," her father urged her. But she only gripped him tighter.

"I can't."

It wasn't her desire for a parent, or her fear of what could happen to him that made her hold on. It was his pain. She didn't know what it meant, or where that impulse had come from. But she knew she could not let go: for as long as the creature in her arms was suffering, she was meant to share in its ordeal, to alleviate it in whatever way she could.

Hermes' body went rigid as the Fallen stepped behind him, the tendons in his neck standing out against hers. He was readying himself for the pain, but Lucifer dragged out the moment, cocking his head to the side and silently staring at Lyla's wings.

She wasn't sure what happened when he finally brought those tweezers to a feather near her father's spine, his face getting creepily close to hers as he did. One moment, she was looking into his goat eyes. And the next, she was enveloped in darkness, long needles slowly piercing through her heart and lungs. That was as best as she could describe it.

An eternity later, the world reappeared in front of her eyes, but Hermes was no longer in her arms. Instead, she was retching, on all four, her head hanging over the edge of the dais. She hadn't eaten much for breakfast, but she vomited it all back up, alongside one too many cups of acid coffee.

Lyla was so disoriented, it took her a moment to realize that Lucifer had jumped over the edge of the dais and was now looking straight at her from the ground, a sick fascination in his eyes.

"Max never mentioned that you had a weak stomach."

The room stopped spinning, Lyla's world precariously hanging by a thread.

Slowly, she lifted her head to look at the Fallen in front of her through her teared-up eyes. He stood, more still than should be possible, movement only in the black feathers of his oversized wings.

"What did you say?"

She vaguely heard Hermes' powerless moans behind her. Out of the corner of her eyes she saw Jeremy move toward Azrael. But all her brain processed was the null void of those black wings, shifting around, slowly swallowing her into their emptiness.

"I said, Max never mentioned that you had a weak stomach. I hadn't expected you'd be on your knees quite so soon."

This was it. This was the torture. Her father had only been a vehicle, the threats to Azrael a tool. To get her to this moment. To get her to doubt the very axis her world spun on.

But some things you just don't touch. Lucifer hadn't cut off his brother's wings. Even he knew that there were things too sacred to defile. What he didn't know was that Max was one of those things.

He'd just made the biggest mistake he could have. He'd fucked with the wrong part of her soul.

All plans and all caution left Lyla's head, as she wiped her tears, jumped off the dais, and spread her wings to their full span. All she knew was the void in front of her, the void only her own magic could eradicate. It wasn't pain and despair she channeled as she screamed and hurled her magic at Lucifer. It was her memories of the island. The villagers' peaceful lives. Jegudiel's hospitality and kindness. Azrael's laughter as he pummeled her with magical snowballs. Her glee when he spat the pork rinds out of the car window. Jeremy's warm hands holding hers. Her father's soft wings enveloping her in his all-encompassing love. And the Wonder Wheel. That moment of youthful joy, that would forever be mixed in with the sands of the Grand Canyon, forever sleeping under the desert stars.

In that scintillating moment of clarity, Hell stopped moving. And as it did, several things happened. Demons cowered all along the walls of the hall, shielding themselves from her high-pitched scream's magical shrapnel, as some of them exploded into red mist. But her sonic attack wasn't directed at them. It was directed at the Fallen in front of her. The Fallen who was stopped in his tracks, immobile, individual feathers flying off his wings and littering the ground. Behind her, Lyla heard a crack, immediately followed by two hundred and fifty pounds of muscle dropping to the ground. And on her right, Jeremy sprang into action, jumping onto the dais and opening up the purple shimmering door that was the only part going according to plan.

She'd learned to pace herself in her training. She'd learned to focus less magic more efficiently. But today, her well was bottomless. She heard and registered the plan unfolding around her: Jeremy slowly dragging a moaning Hermes through the first portal after making another one appear in the center of the room, behind Lucifer, out of which ten warriors stepped out, immediately taking their places in a circle facing outward - the five priests of Hermes', in their full battle gear, facing the back of the room, white wings at the ready, and Jeremy's husband and friends on the other half of the circle, proud grey wings at the ready. All of them started firring the Benelli M4 semi-automatic shotguns Jeremy's friends had trained them to use. Julien himself threw her old Mossberg at Azrael. It wasn't as fast a weapon, seeing as he had to pump it after every round, but Azrael had refused the faster and significantly more expensive tactical firearm, and gone with Lyla's gift instead.

As the demons charged toward the sudden intruders in the center of the room, all eleven angels unloaded a hail of lead into the hoard. At nine shells fully loaded, spraying nine pellets per shell, the room filled with lead as over eight hundred pellets smashed into the horde in a matter of seconds, and halved their already depleted numbers.

While Azrael, calmly reloaded, eyeing the demons closest to Lucifer and Lyla, the rest of the angels simply dropped the eighteen-hundred-dollar weapons they'd bought on the black market, took to the air, and pulled out high-capacity semi-automatic pistols instead.

She saw all of that but didn't hear it. Rationally she knew that the boom of the firearms in such an echoey place, coupled with the wounded demons' screams should have created a sonic chaos beyond comprehension. But her world had gone fully silent with Lucifer's words.

Meanwhile, a few seconds had passed since Lyla had begun unleashing her magic, and the Fallen recovered from his shock at her power. Each of his wings threateningly unfolding to its full nine-foot length, he took a step toward her, slowly breaking the hold she had on him, and stopped its flow altogether with one sweeping gesture of his left arm.

As he kept getting nearer, Lyla realized how he'd done it: he hadn't cut off her magic, he'd cut off her breath. She could have tried to throw a different attack his way, but as her lungs fought for oxygen, her magic wouldn't obey, and instead of protecting herself, she simply slid to the ground, unceremoniously landing near the pool of her own vomit. *Appropriate*, she thought to herself, defeated.

Looking over her shoulder to the dais, she confirmed that Jeremy and Hermes were gone. The healer was stitching up her father back at the cabin. He'd feel it once they stepped back through the portals and would drop the doors behind them. *Once everyone else steps through.*

Lucifer was in no rush. Meanwhile, his foot soldiers were falling one by one, easily picked off the ground by the angels flying above them. Using fifteen round magazines with an extra round in the chamber, they barely needed to reload. Their guns barking at a steady rhythm, they occasionally threw a magical attack at the rare, winged demon who'd joined them in the air. Lyla had been told that the French angels were highly trained, but she'd greatly underestimated them. The ease with which they danced their way through this bloodbath made most priests of Hermes' look like young trainees.

They'd agreed on saving their magic for as long as possible, in case one or more Fallen were present. Lyla just hoped he'd be distracted enough by her to buy them time to leave.

Why weren't they leaving? They'd achieved the goal of their mission – to rescue Hermes. They should all be making their way back through the portal rather than fighting their way through the horde of demons.

They weren't leaving because they were waiting on Azrael's signal, she realized. They wouldn't leave until he deemed their mission completed. Turning her gaze away from Lucifer, she saw him, pumping the Mossberg and shooting at the Fallen. But nothing happened. It must have gotten jammed, leaving Azrael to desperately fiddle with the action, as Lucifer closed in on her.

Time had slowed down enough for her to observe all these details, but it snapped back into place as Lucifer crouched down inches from her face.

"You shouldn't have done that," he growled, snapping his fingers to restore her breath at the same time.

Lyla's gasp to fill her lungs only drew a sadistic smile from him. Sooner or later, he would break her, and he knew it. Sooner or later, she wouldn't be able to keep up with the hits life had dealt her. And when she fell, she'd turn into the monster she'd always known herself to be capable of being.

But that didn't matter now. What mattered was that he was about to turn around and hurt and kill the angels who'd stood by her side in this mission, who'd been willing to put themselves on the line for her. Jeremy would lose Julien. Azrael would-

Before she finished the thought, Azrael rammed his shot-gun bayonet straight into Lucifer's side, shoving him to the floor, away from her.

Getting back up on her feet, Lyla heard a heart-wrenching scream and looked up to see a flying Prince of Hell, his jaw firmly locked around the joint of Julien's left wing. His eyes wide with dread, the grey-winged angel's magic abandoned him, and he dropped to the ground. The demon who fell with him emitted a yowl of pain at whatever limbs it broke in the process and got ready to attack again. Lyla sent a targeted sonic attack at the opening in the plates around his neck and pulverized him, splattering Julien with demon blood.

Two angels immediately dropped down, grabbed Julien, and passed through the portal with him while the remaining seven rounded up the leftover demons. They'd be able to take them out and run through the portal in seconds.

Relief washed over her, realizing their band of outcast soldiers would make it out of Hell alive. Until she heard a crash to her left. Turning around, she gasped. Lucifer had twisted out from under Azrael and flung such a hard magical hit at him, he'd gotten pummeled into a wall ten feet behind him.

In two steps, the Fallen was towering over Azrael, keeping him magically locked in place.

Lyla tried to gather herself for one last outburst of magic, but she was running low. It took all her focus to calm the trembling in her body at the sight of Azrael's paralysis and to gather whatever dregs of power were left in her soul. Meanwhile, Lucifer started ripping feathers off the top edge of Azrael's wings.

"You really think the light in your wings makes you better, don't you? I should just make you one of my Hell hounds. You're no better than the rest of us. Your extra power comes from the black in your wings. You'd do well to remember that."

Incapable of moving or making a sound, Azrael's face contorted into a mask of anguish with each feather the Fallen

plucked. About to wail the last of her power at Lucifer, consequences be damned, she was interrupted by a shout behind her.

"Lyla!"

Turning, she saw one of Julien's grey-winged friends slide
something across the ground between them. It was her 1911 pistol. She'd forgotten it had been amongst the firearms. It was the
weapon they'd meant to pass her upon their arrival, but she'd
been too busy attacking a Fallen angel. Now she grabbed the
black gun and flicked down the safety, comforted by its familiar
weight and coarse grip.

"Get ready!" she responded, turning around into a relaxed
and well-practiced isosceles stance, gripping her pistol with
both hands, and shouting, "Hey, goat-face!"

Lucifer turned to face her, taking Azrael out of the danger
zone, as she started shooting at the large target that was the
Fallen's right wing. While she unloaded eight rounds into her
feathered target, Lucifer was momentarily too pained to react.
One of the grey-winged angels rushed in, and grabbed Azrael
under his arms, dragging him back through the portal.

In a practiced move, Lyla dropped the empty magazine,
replacing it with a spare she'd carried into Hell in her pocket,
unloading another seven shots into the Fallen's wing, while she,
herself, backed up through the portal.

EPILOGUE

Lyla stepped backward into the Paris warehouse that currently housed the refugees from Hermes' Island, her weapon still pointing out toward a target that was no longer there. The portal disappeared in front of her eyes, and her shoulders sagged.

Julien had told her that they'd converted the upper parts of the warehouse into bedrooms, but the lower floor was one large, connected space, currently housing makeshift beds for angels and homeless fledglings, all of whom were staring at her. She immediately replaced the safety on the handgun, and, lacking a holster, tucked it into the waistband of her pants. Looking around the room at the many silent faces, her eyes landed on Azrael. He was sitting on a mattress in the corner, propped up against the wall, his wings folded away. Artiya held a water glass up to his lips.

Lyla cautiously approached them and knelt on Azrael's other side. Looking at his hand wrap around the waitress' as he took the glass from her, she experienced an irrational pang of jealousy, quickly followed by remorse. Artiya had just lost her entire family, she'd been a friend to Lyla when almost no one else had been. She had a right to be the one tending to Azrael. But the younger female must have seen something in Lyla's eyes, because she immediately excused herself and walked away, telling the warrior he was now in good hands.

"Where's Jeremy? He should be healing you," she asked.

"He's upstairs, stitching Julien back together. Or at least getting him to a place where he can recover," he replied. "I will be fine. Lucifer ripped a few feathers out. The pain was excruciating, but now I just need to rest. I'll recover."

When she kept staring at him, scared he'd collapse at any moment, he added, "I assure you that I'm not badly injured. This has happened to me before. What I need is a half hour's worth of rest. Meanwhile, Jeremy is healing Julien upstairs, and your father is resting at the cabin, guarded by nine soldiers. Please, let me sleep Lyla."

Setting the empty glass down, the angel turned to lay on his side and closed his eyes. Lyla awkwardly stood up, realizing for the first time how dirty and torn her clothes were. Covered in splatters of dust and demon blood, she smelled of her own and Hermes' sweat, and she could still feel the lingering presence of Lucifer's magic, like a slimy sheen covering her skin.

Looking around the room, at the many pairs of eyes still pointed at her, in fear, intimidation, or anger – she couldn't tell – she headed toward Artiya and asked her to point her toward a bathroom. As they walked up a ladder and toward a room with a few shower stalls and sinks, she wanted to tell the young angel that she was sorry. Sorry that the Fallen had killed her father and her sister when it was her they'd wanted. Sorry, that she hadn't intervened. Sorry, that her very existence had killed so many innocent lives.

But she couldn't open that door. Not yet.

So, instead, she quietly thanked her, showered off the physical and spiritual grime stuck to her body, and graciously accepted a pile of new clothes and the small meal the female offered her. By the time she was done, Azrael had woken up from his nap, reinvigorated, and Julien was deeply asleep and recovering.

Jeremy went to check on Hermes and to relieve the nine angels of their duty. He stepped through a portal and left it up until white and grey winged soldiers alike were back in the warehouse. As soon as they all stepped through, the tension in the room disappeared as the refugee angels sprang up and ran to the center of the room to hug and hold their heroes. They hadn't thrown Julien or Azrael a parade because both of them had returned injured, adding to the anxiety these angels must have felt, waiting around while they'd stepped into Hell. But now that Julien and Azrael were both safe and healing and the other nine fighters had returned intact, they could finally let their guard down.

Shouts of relief echoed through the warehouse, as they all got high on the notion of just how narrowly they'd escaped death. Within minutes tables were carried in and set up into one long banquet, and, while the fighters went to shower and change, the civilians prepared a celebratory feast and brought out drinks and music. As the soldiers trickled back into the room, they encouraged Azrael to join them, offering him the seat of honor at the table. Lyla sitting between two of Julien's roommates, would rather have skipped the celebrations altogether, but they forced her to the table, telling her that this was as much her victory as theirs.

It didn't feel like it though. They were celebrating now but these people had mourned for weeks. And she was the cause of their grief. She'd been hiding out on the mountain while their brothers and sisters, their spouses and children had been slaughtered. And she knew that they thought it too. After all, no one had cheered at her return from Hell.

After the meal, as the fledglings left the table to play and the adults got drunker and drunker, Lyla finally slipped away, finding a dark bedroom upstairs to nap in and wait out the celebrations.

Finally, Azrael found her and told her that Jeremy was awaiting them at the cabin. The pair of them stepped through his portal back to the familiar little house, where Jeremy still tended to Hermes behind the closed bedroom door.

Looking at Azrael, who stood with arms crossed behind the couch, she realized there was tension in the air. Maybe it was the after effect of such a dicey mission. She decided to ignore it, pouring two glasses of water at the sink.

When she turned around to offer one to Azrael, he shook his head, refusing the glass.

"What was that, Lyla?" he confronted her, in a quietly menacing tone.

"What was what?"

"You knew the plan. You knew we needed to free Hermes. You knew your role. You knew what not to do, for the Ten's sake! You risked all our lives by going rogue!"

"I know, okay?" she replied, slamming both glasses on the counter and turning around to look him in the eyes. "I know. And I'm sorry. We made it out in the end, so can you please just take my apology."

"I'm afraid that's not good enough, Lyla," he shouted angrily. "I need to know I can rely on you. I need to know you won't go off at a Fallen saying a few words that rub you the wrong way."

"Rub me the wrong way? Are you serious? You know very well what he was doing!" she replied, her own voice rising. "Bringing Max into things, that was the real torture. Trying to make me doubt the one person in my life I trust the most? That was more painful than anything else he could have done, and you know it!"

"The one person you trust the most? Please tell me you don't mean that," Azrael replied quietly, a look of disgust on his face.

"Yes, I do! I know he's gone, but he'll always be my home. He was the only person I could count on during all those horrible years. He was the only person who protected me and kept me safe. He was -"

"Lyla, stop!" Azrael bellowed. "Stop fooling yourself! You know Lucifer wasn't lying. You know the truth! I heard the things you mumble in your nightmares. I know it's him hurting you in your dreams!"

Lyla's head started spinning again. Grabbing the counter behind her with both hands, she shook her head. "Those are just dreams."

"They're not, and you know it! Stop lying to yourself!"

As thoughts she didn't want to have snuck up on her, like dominos falling one after another to reveal a picture she didn't want to be true, she simply shook her head.

"Max was the one reporting to the Fallen. He was the one who betrayed you your entire life. He was the one feeding information to them, so they could tailor your torture to your personality."

Max's calculating eyes the day she'd first met him flashed in front of hers. Those same eyes that popped up in her nightmares. "No. No. No, no, no, no..." She tried to replace them with the eyes that would smile at her, and hold her, and tell her everything would be ok. Her breathing rising in her chest, she avoided Azrael's gaze.

"You don't know anything. I don't know why you'd think this, but it's not true, it can't be."

"I know it, because the piece of shit told me himself!" Azrael roared.

"What?" Lyla's head snapped up to him.

"Who do you think beat him up that day? I figured it out and confronted him. He confessed to me, Lyla! He told me he'd been betraying you your whole life... Look," he added in a more soothing tone, approaching her and attempting to touch her shoulder, a gesture she shied away from. "I'm not saying he didn't love you."

Backing up to the couch again, he continued, "He was scared to death of them, so he did their bidding. But he ruined your life in doing so. He was a coward, and he would never have stopped. So, when I found out, I showed him that there was someone he should be even more afraid of than Lucifer. I beat the living shit out of him and told him to leave town. I can't believe he tried to take you with him. He had no right to breathe the same air as you, let alone pull you deeper into his mess!" he shouted. "I fucking hate that you--"

"Get out," she interrupted him.

Taken aback, Azrael froze.

"Get out," she repeated, more confidently. Looking straight into his green-golden eyes, she continued, "Get. Out. And don't come back. You're not welcome here. Or anywhere near me for that matter."

"Lyla, please, don't do this..." Azrael begged, backing up to the door.

"I said, GET OUT!" she shouted, stepping in his direction, her wings manifesting and flaring vehemently behind her.

Opening the door and stepping through, he turned back to her one last time. "Lyla-"

Flapping her wings in his direction, she ignored his plea, starting a low hum in the back of her throat, readying herself to attack. Azrael's eyes went wide at the sound, and, with one last look into her face, he took to the skies.

A moment later, Jeremy cleared his throat behind her. She turned around, letting her wings drop, and saw him lean against the bedroom door, his face a mask of diplomacy. "Your father is resting. I've done what I could for him. He'll need time, but he will make a full recovery."

"Did you know?" she asked, ignoring his words.

"Lyla..." he started, stepping toward her.

"Don't avoid the question. Did you or did you not know about Max?"

"I did," he admitted, continuing to walk toward her. "I'm so sorry Lyla. I couldn't tell you. I couldn't break your heart any more than it already was."

She stepped to the side, as he arrived at the door, indirectly showing him the way out. "I want you to leave as well," she told him.

After a long pause, he asked, "Are you sure?"

"Azrael had no right to throw it in my face the way he did. But you had no right to keep it from me either. Please, leave."

Sadness and concern on his face, Jeremy nodded, and took to the skies after Azrael.

Lyla looked up and saw the two shapes in the far away winter sky, one light, one dark. She loved them both. And their loss was another crack in her broken heart.

But this time, she wouldn't shatter. Because this time, she knew there was someone who cared, someone who'd always cared for her. And right now, that someone needed her.

Turning her back on the two shapes above her, she went to check on her father.

Ophelia Wolf firmly believes that all stories float in the ether waiting to be told in whatever medium captures them best. She's a novelist who also writes for the screen and has worked as a director for theater, opera, and film. Originally from France, Austria, and Germany, she kept on moving west: she received a philosophy degree in London, went to The Juilliard School, became a New Yorker for almost a decade, and finally landed in Los Angeles where she is happily setting down roots and currently working on the final installment of the *Gods & Angels* series.

For more information and updates on upcoming merch as well as the release of the final installment of the *Gods & Angels* trilogy, visit:

https://opheliawolfdirector.com/

Or follow **@gods_and_angels_book** on Instagram

www.ingramcontent.com/pod-product-compliance
Lightning Source LLC
Chambersburg PA
CBHW031333020726
47499CB00005B/1240